LETHAL TARGET

A Jack Kane Thriller

Dan Stone

For Fiona, Sean, Rian and Liadh

LETHAL TARGET

By Dan Stone

ONE

Kane had always dreamt of a quiet life. But dreams and reality are often very different things. The factory was heavy with the stink of soap and chemicals, but it provided simple, honest work. Kane lowered the lever on his pallet truck and drove the forks into a timber pallet, its contents wrapped in cellophane shrink-wrap. A gap-toothed man in a Metallica t-shirt laughed across the conveyer belt of the machine he tended. He wore jeans hung so low around his heavy gut that the crack of his arse showed. A lantern-jawed twenty-something colleague sniggered along. Kane ignored them, taking the pallet of chemicals from the machine to the warehouse, where it would wait to be loaded on a delivery truck.

The factory was nestled in the middle of an industrial estate in Warrington, a town once famous for wire production but now better known for its Rugby League team and reputation as a tough town that filled the gap between Liverpool and Manchester in England's northwest. The pallet truck rumbled on the black, shiny factory floor, and Kane checked his watch for the fifth time in twenty minutes. Break time at last. He left his pallet truck parked on the wall beside the warehouse shutters, where it would wait until after his break.

Kane had worked in the chemical factory for eight months. Before that, he had worked on a motorway maintenance crew for four months. Kane was thirty-eight years old, of average height and build, and found work wherever he could get it. He had to pay his wife maintenance for the children he loved and missed all day, every day. Unfortunately, the skills Kane had spent a lifetime honing were of little use in the real world, so he worked in the factory to pay his way.

"Alright, mate?" said a chirpy voice as Kane entered the factory break room through the white plastic door. Kane smiled at Vik, an Asian man who worked on the machine lines and was always happy, always wanting to chat. Vik spent his working life loading empty plastic cartons into a machine so it could fill them with industrial-strength cleaning liquid. There were five machines in the factory, long, complicated things which required four operators to keep each one going, and Vik handled number two.

"Good, thanks, Vik. Didn't realise you were on tonight?" said Kane.

"Overtime, mate. My eldest turns ten next month, so I need a few extra quid. You see the game last night?"

"No, I didn't, sorry. How did it go?"

"Two nil to united." Vik shrugged, and Kane smiled, rolling his eyes to sympathise with the team's loss. The mention of football brought back memories of Kane's childhood bedroom. He used to plaster his walls with posters of Liverpool Football Club players like Steven Gerrard. Over the years, Kane had gradually lost touch with the game as life became more complicated. Vik moved to exit the break room, and Kane went the same way. They tried to get past each other, but both men went the same way again, and Kane laughed. Vik grinned and clapped Kane on the shoulder. He stood aside to let the smaller man slip through the door. Once Vik left the room, the smile vanished from Kane's face. It hadn't been a proper smile. He never smiled anymore.

Kane swerved around metal chairs left askew next to the chipboard dining tables and took his plastic tub of leftover pasta from the staff fridge that was filled with pots of yoghurt, lunch boxes, drink bottles of various colours, microwaveable pies and other meals. He stuck his pasta in the microwave and waited whilst it turned, whirring hypnotically on the glass plate. Kane stared at a yellow stain on the ceiling, and he thought about his family. They would have been at their swimming lessons that day. A memory of too-small changing rooms, chlorine and laughter came to him but escaped before he could remember the details.

The door to the break room opened again, and a woman crept in, keeping her eyes down and skirting around the sides of the room. She was small and thin, hair scraped back from her face in a ponytail and wearing a plain t-shirt above tight leggings. She didn't make eye contact with Kane, and nervousness emanated from her in a wave, so he stepped away from the fridge to give her space. Gap-tooth and Lantern-jaw bustled in after her before the door even had time to close.

The microwave pinged, so Kane took his food out and sat alone at a table. The woman sat at the table beside him and drank from a water bottle.

"You see the match then, Bill?" asked Lantern-jaw.

"Yeah, pile of shit," Gap-tooth answered, and the two men giggled. "I wish I had a little Ruski to cuddle up to last night instead of watching that drivel."

The two men broke down into peals of

laughter, and Bill pointed at the seated woman and made a lewd gesture with his hand. Thankfully, the woman was spared the humiliation of witnessing his indecency as he was standing behind her. He winked at Kane, but Kane turned away to focus on his food. Bill and his friend continued with their banter, and Kane tuned them out. There were fifty people in the factory, and Kane worked hard to talk to as few of them as possible. He just wanted to work, get paid, send money to his ex, and forget.

Kane's night shift ended at seven o'clock in the morning. He exited the factory through the employee side door, waiting until most people had already left. Kane walked to his bike, which was locked to an iron post set into the concrete car park like an upside-down U. Kane yawned, eyes heavy and sore as though sandpaper had rubbed across them. The ride to his flat took twenty-five minutes along the carriageway, which linked the industrial estate to Warrington's suburbs.

Kane lived in a one-bedroomed flat as close as possible to his family without being too close to annoy Sally, his ex. He unlocked his bike and threw his rucksack containing his lunchbox and empty coffee flask over one shoulder. Kane mounted the bike, clicked through the gears as he peddled, and rode around the car park towards a line of hedges. People had trampled a gap in the waist-high hedge to create a shortcut to the closest bus stop. He went through the gap and around a corner, heading towards the main road. His brakes squeaked as he turned, and then he abruptly slammed them on as a blacked-out Range Rover Evoque SUV came screaming around the bend in front of him. Shining rims sparkled on its wheels, and dance music thumped from the sound system even though it was early in the morning. Kane skidded to a halt, cursing as his groin smashed into the handlebars. He watched the car come to a jarring halt ten metres away, and three men hopped out. Big men with suntans, shaved heads and muscles bulging from too-tight t-shirts.

The woman from the factory canteen stood against a wall, her head turned away from the big men and her arms folded tight across her chest. She waited at a bus stop, marked by a weather-worn yellow sign fixed to a lamppost by a rusted iron bracket. The men strode from their car with arms held wide at their sides as though they carried invisible rolls of carpet. They huddled around her, barking in a European accent Kane could place somewhere between Polish and Scandinavian. Another man sidled around from the driver's side. He was shorter and less pumped up than the others, with a brush of stiff, blonde hair sticking up from the top of an otherwise shaved skull.

The smaller man marched up to the woman, and without breaking stride, he slapped her across the face so hard that she fell to her knees. Kane's knuckles whitened on his brakes as he was shocked by the noise and suddenness of the slap. The short man hauled the girl by her arm, pulling her savagely towards the SUV. She cried out and tried to resist by leaning away from her attacker, her unbranded white trainers dragging on the pavement. Then her eyes locked with Kane's. His heart rate increased, heat churning in his stomach. He had spent so long trying to keep his head down, to live a normal, boring life. That was the arrangement, and he was supposed to stick to it. To Kane, boring meant safety; he knew more than most that safety was a gift, a precious thing most people took for granted. Her eyes pleaded with him.

Shit. I can't. She'll be alright. Maybe he's her husband.

She broke away from her attacker and ran towards Kane, crying hysterically. Kane was still sitting on his bike, staring at her, wanting to ride away and keep out of trouble, needing to keep out of trouble. One muscle man with a tattoo on his neck lunged after the woman and grabbed her arm, swinging her around like a rag doll. He slammed her into the window of an office building, and that was it. Kane cocked his leg over the frame of his bike and let it fall to the road. He slipped off his rucksack and shook his head.

Another job gone. What am I doing? I can't let them treat her like that.

Kane ran at the man with the neck tattoo, and the sun-tanned men all turned and stared at him, the muscles in their necks and shoulders bulging. An enormous man with bright blue eyes came at Kane with a snarl, wagging a thick finger.

Without breaking stride, Kane grabbed the finger and twisted it brutally, the bones cracking and crunching like dry kindling. Kane kicked the instep of the hulking man's leg and tossed him over his hip. Blue Eyes hit the floor, and Kane broke his arm with a savage yank. Another giant came at him with a gleaming, bald head, slowed by his bulk. He threw a wild haymaker punch which Kane swayed away from. Kane grabbed the brawny arm. He tripped the bald brute, using his own momentum to bring the man down. Kane stamped hard on his face with the heel of his right shoe, crushing the bald man's cheekbone into the pavement. Kane should have asked them to leave her alone before resorting to violence. Better still, he should have minded his own business and cycled away, but Kane's true profession was violence, and a deep, dark part of him still enjoyed it. The part men don't want to admit to. He felt the exhilaration of combat. An old feeling, primal, vicious and familiar.

TWO

Four men lay still or writhing on a pavement spotted with old chewing gum and dog shit stains. They groaned, blood bright on white muscle-fit t-shirts, clutching at broken bones and bruised flesh. The woman held a small smartphone in a pink case to her ear. She was half crying, sucking in gasps of air, half babbling to the person on the other end.

"Is that the police?" Kane asked, and she nodded. Shit. Kane looked up and around. Security cameras were everywhere. Gut-wrenching regret replaced the thrill of combat, along with the realisation that he had been a fool. Even if he hopped on his bike and scarpered, the police would find him easily. They would have questions about his fight with the men and their attack on the woman. She knew him from the factory. The camera footage would show him leaving the factory, and Sandra from Human Resources had his flat address and mobile phone number.

"You should not have done that," she said in heavily accented English. "They will now hurt both me and you."

"I couldn't just let them treat you like that. You ran towards me, looking for help. What did they want?"

"They are from my home country, from Estonia. They want me to work for them like other girls they bring here to England."

"Estonia?" Kane had always considered that country a place of wealth and prosperity.

"Yes, there are bad guys there, just like everywhere. Russian mobsters, poor people trying to live off the scraps of the rich."

The man with the brush-stiff hair rolled from his back to his front and coughed up a gobbet of thick blood.

"That one works for evil men. You should go; I won't tell the police it was you."

Kane shrugged. "They'll know anyway, so I might as well wait for them here. I've seen you at the factory."

"My name is Yelena," she said. She had an oval elfin face and dark eyes.

Sirens blared in the distance, and Kane retrieved his bike and rested it against the glass-fronted office building next to the bus stop. Yelena stood away from the injured gangsters, one of whom sat upright, cradling a broken arm and staring at Kane with malevolent fury. Three police incident response vehicles came hurtling around the corner, their flashing blue lights shimmering from office windows. The noise of the sirens was deafening, echoing off corrugated roofs and thick windows. Kane waited with his hands by his sides, wondering wearily what would happen when they took his details and ran him through their systems. What would it mean for his wife and kids, who had finally settled in the town? It wasn't fair for them to have to move again. He should have ignored the girl and the gangsters. It wasn't his problem.

The three Škoda Octavia police vehicles, marked in bright yellow and blue squares, screeched to a halt around the parked Range Rover. Police officers burst from cars dressed in their black uniforms, stab vests and caps. A female officer ran to Yelena, and she sobbed again, crossing her arms across her stomach. She babbled at the policewoman, pointing first at the beaten-up gangsters and then at Kane. A burly officer with a closely trimmed beard slipped his telescopic baton from his belt and flicked the weapon out to its full size. Kane raised his arms with his palms open, facing the officer to show he was no threat.

"Stand back, sir," said the officer in a broad Liverpudlian accent. Kane shifted back towards the office building. Other officers raced to the injured men and helped them to their feet. One called for an ambulance on the radio clipped to the shoulder of his vest.

"Can I take your name, please, sir?" said another officer.

"David Langley," Kane replied.

THREE

Craven marched along the station corridor. His shoes squeaked on the navy blue, ancient plastic flooring, and his phone rumbled in his jacket pocket. It was his wife, no doubt. Craven's shift was almost over. He was on the early shift, and she would have an errand for him to run on the journey home. Buy milk, or collect dog food. He ignored the phone because a uniform constable came through the swinging double doors ahead of him. He glanced at Craven, attempted to turn back and hold the door, decided against it, and darted towards the wall to get out of the way, knocking a mental health awareness poster from a cork noticeboard. The constable's clean-shaven face reddened, and Craven glowered down at him.

"Sir," said the constable, his voice breaking like a teenage schoolboy.

Craven ignored him and burst through the double doors, his frame filling half the width. He was a head taller than most men, broad-shouldered and heavy with a gut he wished was half the size.

"What the fuck is going on?" he barked, emerging into another corridor where interview rooms spanned off in both directions.

"Sorry, sir," said a lanky sergeant in a Mancunian accent. "Funny one here for you."

"Funny? My shift's over in half an hour, dick head. Is that why you asked me to come out here, for a joke? Just get on with it."

The sergeant straightened his shoulders, considered pulling Craven up on his inappropriate belligerence and thought better of it. Everyone on the force knew Craven would never change, including himself.

"Heavies from a gang you've got an eye on were beat up by a guy in an industrial estate in Warrington."

"So uniform brought them here to Warrington station?"

"Yes, sir."

"Which gang?"

"Eastern Europeans, sir. Not sure which gang, though."

Craven sighed, looked at his watch, and resigned himself to another late shift. Barb, his wife, would not be happy, and his dinner would more than likely end up in the dog. He would text her once he found out what all this was about. The uniformed officers had done well to bring the men to Warrington Police Station for questioning. Warrington's suburbs had various smaller stations dotted around, and they could have taken the gang members to Great Sankey, Westbrook, or any of half a dozen stations.

Craven was a Detective Inspector in the Serious and Organised Crime Squad based in Manchester. He also moved around satellite towns like Warrington, Oldham Widnes, Wigan and St Helens to work with the local forces and follow breadcrumb trails of drugs, prostitution, and violence left by the major gangs operating in the UK's northwest.

"Lucky for me, I'm in sunny Warrington, then," said Craven. "Let's get the bastards interviewed as soon as we can. Who's this bloke who worked them over?"

The sergeant shrugged. "Just a fella from a factory on the estate, but he's the main reason we wanted you to get involved, sir."

"Rival gang member? Armed? Who is he?"

"The gang members were apparently

attacking a young woman, also Eastern European, when this fella steps in and sorts them all out."

"Pimps, more than likely."

"Yes, sir. The Deli Boys, we think. Trying to get her roped into prostitution. So we took this bloke's name and brought him in to give a statement. Only when we've run him through the system, the thing has lit up like Blackpool Pleasure Beach."

"Deli Boys. Those shitheads have been on our radar for too long. They hang around a deli they own in the arse end of Manchester, and the bastards have a reputation for bringing young girls into the country, getting them hooked on smack and putting them to work. A young girl died last year. I worked on the case. Has he got any previous, this bloke?" Craven's mind was briefly haunted by the harrowing image of that dead girl. No name, no identity. The gang had beaten her to a pulp, crushed her skull and left her in a ditch. She was somebody's daughter or sister, and those bastards had treated her like an animal.

"No, sir, an alert. Code number 765X."

"What the fuck does that mean?"

"We didn't know either, but when we looked it up, it means he's part of some protection programme, living under a new identity."

"Did he grass on someone?"

"No, he's not in witness protection. The code means we are supposed to contact a specific government agency."

"Not fucking spooks?" Craven sighed, a vision of nightmarish paperwork and meetings with public school MI6 toffs flashing before his eyes.

"I'm afraid so, sir. They're on their way."

"Well, let's have a talk with this lad before they get here, see if we can't get some info before they get hold of him. Where is he?"

"In the cells, we're supposed to keep him here but not talk to him."

"That's a load of bollocks. Get him in interview room two. You and I can talk to him together. Just an informal chat, no recordings, nothing official."

The sergeant fussed with his belt, unsure whether a Code 765X was serious enough for him to go up against Craven. He swallowed his concern with a bounce of his Adam's apple and strode away to bring the mysterious man to the interview room. At that same moment, the secure doorway leading into the corridor from the cells burst open, and two uniformed officers bundled a monstrous, blonde-haired bodybuilder through the doorway. The big man's muscled arms ripped through his tight t-shirt as he struggled with hands cuffed behind his back. He cursed at them in his own language, then barged a young officer into the wall, all but crushing him with his brawny shoulder. Craven darted forward and stamped on the prisoner's instep. The big man roared and turned on Craven; his eyes widened to see he faced a man of similar height.

"Be good, big lad. This can happen the easy way or the hard way," Craven warned.

"What is the hard way?" said the man in a heavily accented, strangely high-pitched voice.

"Trust me, son. You don't want to know."

The two constables dragged the detainee off for questioning, and Craven made his way to interview room number two to await the mystery man.

FOUR

"Brush your teeth," said Sally for the third time that morning, which was usually the tipping point where her gentle voice became stern. Sally's daughter, Kim, giggled and ran from her bedroom into the upstairs bathroom. Kim took out her battery-powered pink toothbrush with a picture of Peppa Pig bright on the handle and brushed.

"Mum, do I have to read this?" complained Kim's brother Danny. He leaned out of his bedroom, holding a book his teacher had assigned for homework. On the cover was a picture of a girl injured during the war in Afghanistan, and Sally pushed her memories of that war out of her mind before they dragged down her mood.

"Yes, you do," said Sally. She moved across the upstairs landing, ruffled his chestnut brown hair, and cupped her hand around his face. "You'll finish it soon if you read five pages every day. We can do some more tonight."

Danny sighed and shuffled back into his room, past the Pokémon wall posters, which were gradually being phased out by posters of Ronaldo, Lionel Messi, Mohamed Salah and other famous soccer players. He was nine years old and every bar of his father – funny and surly in equal measure. Danny cast a longing look at the pile of short story books on his bedside table. The books had colourful pictures of his favourite players and summarised the footballers' life stories. Sally smiled to herself as Danny stuffed the school book back into his bag. He was changing so much, growing up fast. When Danny was younger, he would play with toys all day. He would play with Lego or his action figures at every opportunity, but now, all he was interested in was kicking a ball.

Kim announced she was done, standing in the bathroom doorway, smiling widely to show her missing teeth. Sally helped Kim clean the toothbrush, then set about ensuring the kids had all they needed for the day ahead. Kim was six years old and had started school that September. She remembered very little of their old life; her school and friends in Warrington were the only ones she had ever known. Sally and the children made the short journey to their school, the early morning air turning their noses a soft pink. As they reached the school gate, Danny caught up with a friend, and Sally stopped to kiss Kim on the head.

"Have a good day, sweetheart," said Sally warmly, brushing some stray hairs away from Kim's face with her fingers. She had Sally's blue eyes but her father's dark hair.

"Mummy," said Kim, and Sally smiled at her. "When will we see Daddy again?"

Always the same question at least twice a day. Sally sighed. "Next weekend. Your Dad will come and pick you up and take you to his place for the night. Will that be fun?"

"Yes. But why can't he just come back and live with us?"

"He just can't, ok, princess? Now, hurry, you'll be late!"

Sally waved to the children as the bell rang and made her way back home under a cloud of guilt. Danny and Kim missed Jack so much. Before they had moved up north, they had hardly seen him. Jack was always away. They rarely allowed Sally to know Jack's whereabouts or what he was doing. She would worry for days on end, waiting for a text message or a call from a number she didn't recognise. Secure lines, satellite phones, and messages without information. Yet in Warrington, Jack had been home a lot. He worked shifts at the factory, but if he was on lates, he would take the kids to school, and if he was on earlies, he could pick them up. Jack had really bonded with the kids since the move, which was a good thing. But part of him, the part Sally had loved, slipped away on the day they had entered the programme.

When she got back, Sally took out a wash from the machine and put a load in the dryer. The kitchen, much smaller than the one in her previous home, was quiet. Sally whiled away some time by making the kids' dinner for later that day and turned on the dishwasher. Cautiously, she glanced at the clock but decided to ignore the time. She went over to the fridge, took out a half-empty bottle of Sauvignon Blanc, and poured a glass. As she placed the bottle back in the fridge, Sally caught her reflection in the window, made visible by the overcast sky. Her hair was untidy, and she fiddled with it. She wore a baggy t-shirt and leggings, a far cry from her old clothes. Sally had been stylish back when she had had a career of her own and a life of her own with friends and a job she could be proud of.

Sally sat down on the living room couch, took a sip of her wine, and used the remote control to click on the TV. She flicked through the channels, chat shows, news, and a programme about renovating properties. Sally turned the TV off. She bent and rummaged around in the coffee table drawer before pulling out an envelope of photographs. Sally sipped her wine again and went through the pictures; some of her on her wedding day and a few of the kids when they were babies. She came across a picture of Jack in his army dress uniform, looking young and handsome with his pressed SAS trousers and a fierce look in his eye. The following photo was of Sally in a business suit. It was part of a professional photoshoot for her LinkedIn profile after being promoted to Marketing Director. A job she had loved. Sally threw the envelope onto the coffee table and sighed. She had another long sip of wine, its sharpness soothing as it cooled her throat. In the late afternoon, she'd collect the kids from school, feed them and put them to bed, and then the same monotonous day would repeat tomorrow, save for her working for three hours in a coffee shop, waiting tables and washing dishes.

After everything Jack had been through, it had been Sally who'd persuaded him to go into the programme, to tell all to Jacobs and his government agents. He had promised her and Jack a better life, a safe future together, living in a quiet town where their kids could grow up. It had all seemed so perfect until it actually happened. Jack was changed, bored without his old life of action and danger. She was miserable without her career and had nothing but a takeaway on a Friday night to look forward to. They had struggled on for a year, and then the arguments had become too much, too loud for the kids not to hear. Now she was alone, with no career and no hand to hold in the darkness. Just a mother without a personality of her own. Glancing toward the kitchen, she remembered there was another bottle in the fridge, knowing full well how she'd spend her evening that night. Sally sighed and picked up the photographs again.

FIVE

Kane sat down on the hard metallic chair inside the interview room. A boxy tape recorder was on the desk, and the bitter smell of citric floor cleaner clung to the grey walls. Kane ran his tongue around his mouth to remove the claggy taste left behind by the bad, acidic coffee the duty sergeant had brought him half an hour earlier. The big man sat opposite and glowered at him, thick neck and broad shoulders with a stomach bulging at the buttons of his white shirt. A navy high street suit jacket hung from the back of the big man's chair, and he leant forward on the table with chunky fingers clasped together. He was bald, with a centimetre of salt and pepper hair around the lower half of his skull. His hooked nose sat beneath dark eyes and a wide slash of a mouth surrounded by stubble.

"So, you're the reason I'm missing steak night?" the big man began, his voice deep and cracked like a sports coach after a weekend of shouting at his team.

"I just helped the young lady, that's all," said Kane. Kane felt a throb of pain in his shoulder as if a piece of shrapnel was still embedded there. An old wound which ached in the cold or when he was worried.

"Very noble of you."

"Why are you detaining me? Am I under arrest for something?"

"No, nothing like that. I'm DI Craven, and I just need to ask you a few questions about the scum you brutalised today."

Kane stared into Craven's hazel eyes, and a smile played at the corner of the detective's mouth. Kane sighed. The interview was not a surprise. He had given the name David Langley, but they would have run him through their systems by now. The programme he was in would raise a flag against his identity. A warning of danger and some instructions on whom to call if the police came across him – things that would attract interest and curiosity too mouthwatering to ignore. Kane had worried about that whilst waiting in his cell. The duty sergeant hadn't officially booked him. He had just explained that Kane wasn't under arrest but that they wanted to question him further about the incident. Yet a witness would wait in the station reception area, not in a cell.

"I already went through the details with the other officers at length. What else do you need to know?" Kane had given a statement about the fight, but that was before they had decided to hold him.

Craven sat back in his chair and raised his hands to show he did not mean any aggravation. "Look, the men you tuned in were pimps and in need of a good hiding. They don't let us push the boundaries as much as we did in the old days. So, you won't get any complaints from me. Thing is, though, we put your name through our systems…" he trailed off with a shrug.

"And?"

"Well, I'm not recording you because I'm not supposed to talk to you. Your name came up with a flag. There are government bods on the way down here to see you. What sort of programme are you in?"

Kane's stomach turned over, the heat of fear kindling in his gut. "How long ago did the system trigger a flag?"

"About half an hour, maybe an hour."

"Arrest me or let me go. You can't hold me like this."

"Fair enough. I'll charge you with ABH or GBH. Take your pick, smart arse."

Craven smiled at him, stood and left the interview room. Kane cursed his impetuousness for getting involved with Yelena and the gangsters. It had been naïve. He should have left the girl to her fate and rode away. He had his own family to think of. His wife and kids were settled in the North West. It had not been easy, and the relocation had cost Kane his marriage. If the trigger flagged what he thought it did, they would move him again. Interested, vengeful eyes were waiting for that trigger and would never stop searching for it. What Kane knew and what he had done could cost his family everything. If the police systems flagged his name, they would also have his address. Shit.

Two uniformed police officers entered the interview room door and led Kane to the main booking desk. It was a semi-circular white structure, rising to chest height and surrounded by a clear, heavy plastic window with square holes for the desk sergeant to speak through. A black camera mounted on a jointed arm stared at Kane, and the fear which had kindled in his belly was now a raging fire. He had to get out of the situation. The government people coming for him could either be his programme handlers or his enemies. If his enemies had spotted the red flag in the police database, they would have him taken away and shot before the day was over. A bullet in a forest, or some abandoned building, to remove the risk of him ever talking about his old life again. Ministers, generals, and many powerful people would be relieved to see Kane dead.

"So, do you know why you are here?" asked the desk sergeant, a woman in her forties wearing black glasses. The glasses sat low on her nose with a tan string looping around each arm and draping around her neck.

Kane scanned the space around the booking desk, two doors locked and only accessible by a coded keypad or swipe card. Cameras recorded him from multiple directions, and behind him, an internal release system secured the front door. Scanning a room for exits and threats was second nature. He did it in every room and every situation.

"ABH or GBH," said one uniformed officer. "Craven hasn't decided yet, so type both in."

"Name?" the desk sergeant prompted.

Kane shifted, licking his lips. The police officers hadn't handcuffed him yet, and they hadn't booked him. He couldn't let them hold him. To wait was to die. It was a flip of a coin. Someone would come for him soon, friendly or hostile.

"Your name?" the desk sergeant said more forcefully, removing her glasses and pressing long-nailed fingers to the bridge of her nose.

"David Langley," he replied. They had taken his phone, his keys, and his wallet. So all he had were the clothes on his back.

The front door to the police station opened with a buzz and a click. A uniformed officer bustled through, dragging a thin man in baggy clothes with the sunken cheekbones and gummy lips of a drug addict. Kane pushed off his right foot and made the two long strides to the door before any of the police officers could react. He hooked the fingers of his right hand around the door frame and slipped himself through it, bursting out into the open like a caged lion escaping its captors. The heavy door slammed and cut off the shouts of the officers inside the station. Kane leapt down three concrete steps, sprinted across a car park, and hurtled over a set of railings. He emerged, heart racing, onto a road busy with cars. It was two o'clock in the afternoon, and the remnants of lunchtime traffic were backed up at a set of traffic lights at a crossroads.

Kane raced along the line of cars until he reached the first in the queue. The man inside was tapping his fingers on the steering wheel in time to music. Police officers poured from the station like a kicked wasp's nest, shouting and roaring across the car park and street. He opened the door to the iron-grey Mazda and dragged the man out of the driving seat. He was in his fifties and yelped like a frightened dog as Kane extricated him from his seat belt and threw him into the waiting car behind him. Kane jumped into the driving seat, took the hand break off, and slammed his foot down. Tyres screeched, and the engine roared as he burst through the red light. Vehicles from the opposite direction honked their horns and slammed on brakes to avoid colliding with him.

Kane had to run from the police, and there was no going back now. He had to warn his wife, for the past would find him now; he was sure of it. The hunters would come looking for blood, seeking to destroy him and the man he had been. But Kane wasn't ready to die yet.

SIX

"Are you sure it's him?" asked Fowler. He sat cross-legged on a tufted brown leather sofa punched and creased by buttons. The office was decorated with thick, tasteful wallpaper, oil paintings hung from the walls, and a vast mahogany desk dominated the room in front of a north-facing window.

"It's him. Police pulled him for an assault. We sent two men to pick him up, but they were too late," replied the woman behind the desk. She was a tall, slim, good-looking woman in her mid-fifties. Her hair hung about her angled face in a short, severe bob.

"Only two?" said Fowler, chuckling and shaking his head.

"They were dispatched before I was made aware," she retorted, rewarding his laughter with a frown like a thunderstorm. "I want you to go today. He's in the northwest. Warrington, of all places. Take a team and clean it up."

"I don't know why you just don't leave him alone. He won't talk again. He isn't the type. If you leave him alone, he will disappear, and no one will hear from him again."

"When I want your opinion, Fowler, I will ask for it." McGovern rose from her desk with a start, lips pursed, and pointed a long finger at him. "You are a blunt instrument, a remnant of a bygone age, made redundant by technology. But you still have one use, so find Jack Kane and kill him."

"Yes, ma'am." Fowler stood, towering over her. He smiled, ignoring her scathing comments because she was a bureaucrat and had no experience in the field. She could never understand the value of his line of work. He shot the cuffs of his shirt in his jacket sleeves and adjusted the gun holster strap around his shoulders.

"No mistakes. You know what it means if he talks. There's a file waiting for you. Read it on the plane north. If he opens his mouth, it means a tsunami of shit for the PM, the army, foreign governments, and everyone. The war might be long over, but the retribution for what we did will be unflinching. Things are worse now with wokeness and moral outrage. There's simply too much at stake. So do it. Clean up the mess."

Three hours later, the agency jet landed

at Liverpool Airport, and Fowler found eight operatives waiting for him in a cavernous aircraft hangar. They wore suits and long coats, like businessmen on a sales trip. Beyond them, a short man in combat trousers and a wool jumper arranged weapons on a trestle table. He clicked triggers and checked magazines amongst an array of shining pistols and automatic weapons laid out in perfect order.

"Fowler," said a stocky man Fowler knew as Barnes. He had a scar-twisted lip and pale blue eyes. "Word is it's Kane?"

"Jack Kane," nodded Fowler, standing with arms clasped behind his back, searching each of the seven faces lined up opposite him. Each one bore the dead, shark-like eyes of a killer. He knew five of them; Barnes, McCann, Hendry, Cole, and Krasinski, all excellent operators. SAS and SBS soldiers moved into special ops, just like Fowler himself. The other three came recommended as top-level operatives. Assassins. "Kane used to be one of us, multiple tours in the desert. Black ops all over the world. Worked on cross-jurisdictional crews with MI6, Seal, Delta, and CIA Black Ops teams – a dangerous man with too much in his head. If you find him, kill him clean."

"I hate these jobs on home turf," said Hendry, a rangy man with a Scottish accent. Fowler understood. They were soldiers, or at least had been once, so fighting at home went against the grain.

"He worked the job, then?" asked Cole, a tall black man with a shaved head.

"He worked the job when the world was on fire, more kills than a fake US Ranger sniper's Facebook profile," quipped Barnes, and the group chuckled.

"He's dangerous," said Fowler, fixing them with his blue eyes. "We will receive any intel directly." He is in the northwest somewhere and on the run. He has a wife and kids under protection, but their new identities are all in the file. Each of you has everything we know about him, his job and his address. He isn't stupid, so there won't be a phone to track or a trail of breadcrumbs to follow. When you find him, kill him. No mess."

This time, Jack Kane was the target. He had to die, and Fowler always followed orders. If McGovern was right, and Kane talked, it would bring down the UK Government, and most likely the US Government with it. Too many secrets, too much blood.

SEVEN

Kane abandoned the Mazda in a supermarket car park and jogged the half mile to Sycamore Lane Primary School. He still wore the clothes from his last shift at the factory – jeans, trainers and a blue hoodie. Kane reached the corner of a street of red-brick houses opposite the school and watched the entrance. He wasn't in the shape his old profession had demanded, and he cursed himself for giving up on his old regimen of running, swimming, and weightlifting. Even the quick jog from the car to the school left him sucking in gulps of air and a film of sweat upon his brow.

Across the street, a dozen women loitered at the school gates, gossiping and waiting for their children. Behind the gaggle of women stood a clutch of old men and women, grandparents on child-minding duty. And further beyond them loitered the parents who kept away from the talk of kids' football clubs, teacher issues and arranging playdates. It was ten past three in the afternoon, and at any moment, children would come streaming out of the gate wearing bright trainers and puffer coats, backpacks jangling and emblazoned with Liverpool FC, Manchester United, or unicorns. Kane scanned the crowd but couldn't see Sally amongst them. He looked left and right along the road. Cars, arriving late, crept past, looking for a spot to park, but the spots close to the school gates were already taken. No sign of police sirens yet, but they would find the discarded Mazda soon enough. Kane didn't have long, and he hated to come to his kids' school and risk Danny and Kim witnessing him being arrested like a criminal, but he had to warn Sally.

A woman with red hair and black leggings marched down the road towards him. She powered along the pavement with long strides, two hands stuffed into the pockets of a green gilet. Sally looked good, as pretty as ever, with her long face and freckled cheeks. Kane pushed himself off the wall and strode towards her, stepping onto the road to cut off her approach to the gates.

"Sal," he called, and she turned to him. Her mouth opened in surprise, and then her green eyes narrowed.

"Jack, you can't be here. You know that. You have them next weekend," she said, weary rather angry at his continued breach of their separation agreement. A separation Kane had neither wanted nor understood.

"Sal, listen. Something's happened. I just need to talk to—"

"No, Jack, I'm sick of this. The kids will be upset if they see you. Go, now. Before they come out." She started walking again, and he ran after her.

"Sal, wait. They've found me."

She stopped in the middle of the road, a woman in a red Mini Cooper swearing and gesticulating behind her. "How? Are you sure? Are we in danger?"

"I can't explain now, but you need to call Jacobs. Tell him they have dispatched agents to pick me up. He might know already, but call him now."

"Alright, alright. I'll call him when I've got Danny and Kim."

"Don't go home until you have spoken to Jacobs. Promise me."

She glanced at the school gates where smiling-faced kids had emerged from the building, still young enough to run and hug their parents at the end of their school day. The woman in the Mini beeped her horn, and Sally raised a shaking hand to brush a stray strand of her hair behind her ear. "I promise. Are you OK?"

"I'm fine, but you must take care of the kids. Do only what Jacobs says, no matter who contacts you." She nodded and made to move towards the school. Kane reached out and grabbed her hand. A fizz of potent energy travelled between the touch of their skin, making Kane's heart leap with the love he still held for her. "Is my emergency bag still in the house?"

Sally looked at their hands and then dragged hers away, her bottom lip trembling. "It's in the attic. I haven't touched it. I thought all of this was over."

Kane let her go, jogging back to the red brick street corner, but he couldn't resist a look back. Danny came running from the school in his uniform and grabbed Sally's leg. He held a large, brightly coloured drawing and grinned as he showed it to her. Moments later, Kim came hurtling from a group of other kids and started talking effusively with her hands about some exciting news. Sally knelt and hugged them both. Kane swallowed the lump in his throat. He wanted to dash across the street and sweep them all up into his arms, to just take them and drive away to freedom and safety. But life wasn't that simple. Sally didn't love him anymore, and he was a danger to Danny and Kim. Kane turned and ran, leaving them there, the distant howl of police sirens hauntingly echoing across the rooftops as his feet pounded the pavement.

EIGHT

"You actually had him in custody?" intoned the man in the black suit. He spoke with a crisp, well-educated accent. He was of average height, broad-shouldered, with a sharp part in his sandy hair and a red tie in a perfectly thick Windsor knot.

"We had him," said Craven, casting a withering look at the Chief Inspector across the table. "And he got away." Chief Inspector Kirkby had made the short drive from Manchester to Warrington once the news of Langley's escape had broken. Kirkby was responsible for the Serious and Organised Crimes Unit and was Craven's boss.

"How, precisely, did he get away?"

"Look, Mr Jacobs," said the Chief Inspector, leaning forward with a wide grin and removing his clear spectacles with long fingers. "We hadn't arrested Mr Langley. We held him in a cell based on the flag against his name. He was becoming agitated and wanted to leave, so we decided to book him."

When Chief Inspector Kirkby spoke, it made Craven shift in his seat as though the man gave him an actual pain in the arse rather than just the metaphorical irritation. He had known Kirkby for years and had watched him climb the greasy pole of promotion despite doing very little to earn it. Kirkby had the uncanny ability to make minor accomplishments appear significant, and with that eloquence, Kirkby convinced others he was a man worthy of respect rather than an absolute shithouse, which Craven had always perceived him to be.

"Listen," Craven enounced, folding his arms. "We had him. He broke out of the front door when someone else came in. We didn't have him in handcuffs because he wasn't booked or charged yet. He worked over a handful of bad lads outside a factory, and we brought him in for questioning. We put his name into the system, it flagged up a code we've never heard of, and now you're down here talking to us like we're complete fuckwits."

"DI Craven," Jacobs responded, "I assure you I am not here to insult you. I am here to locate a man who received the Government's protection for his services to the Crown in a matter of utmost national security. Any information you have on this man is of vital importance."

"DI Craven gets carried away sometimes, Mr Jacobs. We will, of course, do all we can to assist you in this matter. Did anyone offer you a coffee?" said Kirkby.

"Who are you anyway?" Craven blustered. He handed Jacobs his card, a standard police-issue business card with his mobile number, name and rank printed upon it. Jacobs smiled wryly and handed Craven his own card.

"Ministry of Defence." Craven read the words slowly and nodded with his mouth turned in an upside-down smile. "Serious stuff then? What can you tell us about Langley and the trouble he's mixed up in?"

"Can't tell you very much, I'm afraid. Very serious business of national security, as I said. There will be others searching for David Langley now that you have telegraphed his whereabouts, so please be vigilant and contact me if he resurfaces. I'm going to need everything you have about the gang members he roughed up." Jacobs paused, reaching into his suit jacket and pulling out a silently vibrating smartphone. "Excuse me," he said and then left the room.

"Don't interrupt me like that," snapped Kirkby. "I am the senior officer here."

"Piss off, Peter. Why don't you grab the man a coffee and get your nose out of his arse." Craven laughed at the look of horror on Kirkby's face and groaned, hefting his bulk out of the chair and towards the door.

"Craven, don't turn your back on me. We tolerate your behaviour here because you got some results in the dim and distant past. But what have you done recently? I won't put up with your bullshit any longer. You don't deliver any arrests and have no respect for authority. You are skating on thin ice, Craven. If I had my way, you would be out of Serious Crimes and put on training duty, or better still, why don't you just retire?"

Craven stared at Kirkby, and for once, a quick comeback didn't materialise. The truth hurt like a kick in the nuts because Craven needed a result badly. Craven's refusal to fawn to the top brass resulted in him being stepped over for promotion many times. But he was a true copper, and his place was on the street. Not training new recruits, or worse still, retired prematurely to sit at home watching reruns of fucking Bonanza all day. He checked his pocket for the post-it note on which he had scrawled Langley's address and fingered its corner reassuringly. Most of the force was out searching for Langley and the car he had stolen under the very nose of the police station. Craven, however, was going to pay the man's wife a visit and see if he could find out more about him there.

NINE

Kane waited for an hour, more time than he could afford, watching his house for a sign of the enemy. Only it wasn't his house anymore; it was Sally's. He hadn't wanted to steal another car and draw more attention to himself, so Kane had walked the two miles from the school to Sally's home. It was spring, and a red sun descended beyond jagged suburban rooftops, leaving a darkening sky the colour of old gunmetal. Then, after crouching, hidden beside a hedgerow, he realised he wasn't even sure he knew who the enemy was.

The only people he knew were chasing him at that moment were the police. No government agents or military personnel had yet shown themselves. If the police were in the house, they would not care about discretion, so lights would be on, and there would be a commotion outside. Kane dragged himself from the undergrowth and walked across what had once been his own lawn. He lifted a ceramic plant pot on the patio and found the spare back door key. He opened the back door, pushed the cat litter out of the way with his foot, and crept through the house.

The semi-detached house smelled of Sally's cooking. *Mexican food,* Kane thought. There were breakfast dishes still in the sink, and Kane felt a pang in his gut when he noticed the small plastic cutlery and plates. He longed for his family. Kane saw a vision of himself moving around the kitchen island, making porridge or bowls of cereal and laughing with his children as he prepared breakfast. He left the lights off, so he saw everything through the evening gloom and the neon light of the fridge clock. Kane moved along the hallway and up the stairs, the fourth of which creaked as loudly as it always had. Kane reached the top of the stairs, which turned right into the landing and bedroom doors. He was about to reach up for the toggle from which he could pull down the attic stairs when a clicking sound came from the front door. He ducked behind the bannister.

The sound came again, followed by the clunk-click of the lock turning. The door opened, and a dark shadow crept in carefully and slowly closed the door behind it. A torch lit up the downstairs hall. Footsteps and controlled breathing followed, moving with precise caution. So there was an enemy, after all. And they were in Sally's house. His house. As far as the person entering the door knew, the children could be asleep upstairs. Kane ground his teeth, the muscles beneath his jaw working. Giving his name at the police station had triggered hell, and he'd been a fool for stepping in to help Yelena at the factory. His emergency bag was in the attic, and he had to get it. Enemies had come to the safe place where his family lived, but instead of finding children, they would find him, and anger flooded his senses like a drug.

Footsteps inched carefully up the stairs. The fourth step creaked, and Kane braced himself. He crept along the upstairs landing so that he stood with his back against the airing cupboard, away from the bannister balustrades, which would have given him away as soon as the torchlight shone up the stairway. The shadowy figure led with a silenced pistol, the torch held extended in the same two-handed grip. It was a man, large and bulky, in a black sweater and combat trousers. The gun would terrify an ordinary person, but the weapon was as familiar to Kane as a chisel to a carpenter or a trowel to a bricklayer. The torch swept the landing, and the man gingerly opened the leftmost bedroom door to what used to be Kane and Sally's room.

The man peered inside, sweeping the space with his torch and gun. He crept in after noticing the en-suite and wanting to go over that room before he continued on. Kane moved carefully, two long steps along the landing, and then shoved his back against the wall above the stairs so that his left shoulder was close to the master bedroom door and his right shoulder faced down the stairs. His feet were off balance, one foot above the other on the steps, so the emerging torchlight wouldn't catch them. His heart hammered in his chest like a heavy metal band, anger mixing with fear, making his muscles tense.

They sent this man to my family's home, an armed man. Bastards.

The torchlight beamed out onto the landing, growing in brightness as the man approached. Kane held his breath, muscles bunched. The pistol's silencer poked around the corner like the nose of a curious animal, and Kane's hands snapped up to grab it. Cold gun metal filled his grip as he turned, yanking the weapon over his shoulder, twisting and sticking his hip out. The man grunted and lost his balance before dropping the torch and using that hand to grab Kane's neck from behind.

The torch clattered down the stairs, bouncing on the carpet and sending a spinning light around the stairway like a fairground ride. Kane swiftly ducked under the arm around his neck so that the assailant's limb turned on itself, and Kane kicked the rear of his leg with force. The man fell to his knees but kept a tight hold of his weapon. Kane tried to push his body on top of his attacker, but the man rolled his hips and positioned his knee beneath Kane's stomach. He was skilled and strong. A trained killer.

The man in black punched Kane in the face and then steadied his weapon in two hands. Kane still gripped the barrel, but the enemy jerked it towards Kane's head and fired. Even with the silencer, the sound rattled Kane's ears, and he twisted away. However, Kane kept hold of the gun and slipped into the instinctive movements of his old self, training and repetition taking over. Kane pulled the release clip so that the mag dropped from the gun. He squeezed the trigger himself so that the bullet in the chamber shot into the ceiling, sending a cascade of plaster spilling into the hallway. Kane let go of the gun and then fell with a heavy elbow into the man's face, diving over his body and pivoting so that he could kick his enemy down the stairs.

The man rolled down the staircase, grunting and gasping as he tried to regain his balance. The gun slipped from his hand, and he came to a crumpled stop at the foot of the stairs. Kane jumped after him, and they fought for dominance, trading blows and trying to gain the upper hand. The man surged to his feet and stamped on Kane's ribs, the pain rocking him. Kane rolled away and got to his feet, gasping for breath, ribs burning. The man reached behind his back and pulled out a flick knife, the handle a dark shape in his fist. There was a click, and the blade flicked out, the attacker holding it before him in a reverse grip.

"Who sent you?" Kane demanded, keeping his eyes on the steel blade.

"Who do you think?" the man retorted in a broad Scottish accent.

"Are you Mjolnir?"

The man's teeth showed dull white in a smile, and then he sprang at Kane, knife arcing in a wicked slash towards his throat. Kane raised his forearm and grunted in a flash of searing pain as the blade cut through his hoodie to slice the flesh of his shoulder. He deflected the blow and punched the attacker in the stomach, hooking his arm around the enemy's knife arm to gain control of him. Kane shifted his leg between the attacker's feet, drove him off balance, down the hallway, and threw him at the front door. The attacker's head smashed through one of the two oblong glass plates situated on either side of the door's white cross piece. The blood-splattered glass tumbled onto the hallway tiles to shatter into tiny pieces, and Kane hauled the man back from the door. He twisted the knife free of his enemy's grip and let him slump against the wall.

The attacker's face was a ruin of torn flesh and

pulsing dark blood.

"Did Mjolnir send you?" said Kane.

"An old friend of yours sent me," replied the injured man, the words garbled by his glass-mangled lips.

Kane sighed. "An old friend?"

"A friend of yours from Mjolnir. From before this mundane suburban nightmare of yours. Back when you were a killer. Fowler sent me."

Kane rocked back on his heels. Fowler. They had served in the Regiment together as young men, then risen through combat missions to be drafted into the Mjolnir agency. Kane knew too much, and they had sent his friend to kill him. Kane shot his arm forward with incredible speed, and the knife blade punched into the assassin's gullet. He twisted it and pulled the blade free. A long hiss whistled from the wound as the Scotsman slipped into darkness, and Kane felt nothing. The man had come for his wife and children, so he had to die. There was no pity or remorse. And death was as much of an old friend to Kane as Fowler. Kane pushed the killer to the floor tiles and searched him, finding a wallet, a magazine of bullets for the handgun, and a phone. He held the phone in front of the dead man's face to unlock it.

"Well, well," came a deep voice over Kane's

shoulder. "You've been busy."

Kane looked up to see the broad face of DI Craven staring at him through the smashed door window.

TEN

Craven slowly pushed his hand through the shattered window, keeping his eye on Langley. He reached around, found the door lock, turned the cold metal, and retracted his hand. The door swung open, and Craven raised his hands to show he came in peace. In any other circumstance, he would have crashed through the door the moment he saw the suspect kneeling over the lifeless body. Yet Craven felt an unexplainable urge not to, just like when your neck prickles when danger is near or sensing somebody watching you.

"I haven't called this in yet," Craven said, lowering his hands slowly. "You won't attack me, will you, Langley?"

Kane clutched a bloody knife. Dark crimson spattered his hoodie and face, and a pistol topped with a silencer lay on the hallway floor. Langley rose slowly, poised and lithe, like a panther.

"I don't want any trouble," uttered Langley.

"And stop calling me Langley. My name's Kane."

Craven blew out his cheeks and shook his head. "For a man who doesn't want any trouble, you have a knack for finding it. He's dead." Craven nodded at the lifeless man. "So Langley wasn't your real name? Should have guessed that." People in any sort of programme, like witness protection, always used new names to go with their new lives.

"They sent him here, to my wife and kids' house, thinking I would be here. To kill me, maybe to kill them as well. You don't have to get involved. Just let me go."

"I can't just let you go. You've killed this poor bugger; prior to that, you stole a car and escaped from police custody. The lads back at the station want you bad, mate."

"So why are we talking, then?"

"Is he a spook?" Craven edged into the hallway, stepping around the increasing pool of blood seeping from the dead man. He moved slowly, his heart racing, hands held out with palms open to be clear that he was approaching peacefully. Kane was clearly a dangerous man. Any normal person who had just killed someone would be in shock.

"A government agent, yes. They sent him. More were coming for me at the police station.

That's why I ran."

"I can see that. I came here to see your wife…or ex-wife. Thought she might know where to find you."

"I don't have time for small talk." Kane peered through the broken door for any sign of blue lights or officers.

"I came alone. I thought that there might be something we could do for each other." The words came out before Craven had processed them in his head. His mouth was dry, and beads of sweat dotted his forehead.

What am I doing?

He remembered Kirkby and the sneer on his pompous face, calling Craven a washed-up has-been. Craven hadn't had a result for a while. It had been too long if he was honest. He needed a break, needed to crush one of the major gangs, a win.

Kane sighed, turned and strode down the hall, picking up the pistol as he went. He headed to the sink, turned on the tap, and washed the blood from his hands. Craven followed him, wondering if he was making a terrible mistake. Craven always trusted his gut, and it told him that Kane wasn't an out-of-control threat to the public. If you disregarded the dead man in the hallway, that is. There was some sort of government shit show at play, and Kane was only trying to protect himself and his family, but he was clearly a man who knew how to get things done.

"Go on then, spit it out," said Kane, finding a tea towel and drying his hands. "I need to go. I need to find Sally and the kids. More men like him will look for them."

"Why do they want you so bad? What did you do?"

"You said we could help each other?" Kane pulled a chair back from a small, round wood effect dining table in the kitchen's corner. The chair scraped on the tiles, and Kane placed the pistol on the table. He pushed a magazine into its grip before examining its barrel. Kane clicked a lever and slid out the magazine. He tilted his head to look down the gun's length and clicked the trigger, examining other parts of the gun Craven didn't have a clue about. Kane, however, knew his way around the weapon. Kane clicked the magazine back into place and snagged on the safety.

"Well, if you do something for me, I can help you with the spooks."

"Help how?"

"I met one of them today, Jacobs from the Ministry of Defence."

"He's one of the good guys, my handler in the

programme. He can help Sally and the kids."

"But others will come to talk to us if you say an agency is trying to hurt you. If they do, I'll let you know."

"In exchange for what?"

"Remember the lads you roughed up on the industrial estate? They are part of a ruthless gang of high-level criminals – prostitution, human trafficking, drugs, you name it. Scum, in other words. Estonians, Latvians, and Russians all united together into one band of merry men. I've been working on them for a while but can't get enough evidence to bring them down. We have to be precise and careful of how we gather evidence. The gangs know how we operate. They are clever with phones and messaging, leaving barely a trace of their activities. I've seen so many evil men walk free from court on technicalities. You, however, can work around the rules and hurt them… force them into making mistakes. If you help me with them, I'll help you with your government problem."

"I'm no policeman. Gathering evidence isn't my forte. I just need to get my family safe."

"I can see that, but what if I don't want them arrested?"

ELEVEN

Kane flagged a taxi from the dual carriageway five streets away from Sally's house. He asked the driver to take him to a bed-and-breakfast in Warrington town centre. It was risky, given that every policeman in the town was looking for him, and, more worryingly, so was Fowler and whatever crew was with him. But Kane couldn't leave Warrington yet. As the driver went around a traffic island, Kane checked the contents of his emergency pack. The rucksack held a change of clothes, a survival tin, two thousand pounds cash, a burner phone, contacts for Sally and Jacobs, and a fake driving license.

Kane still had the phone he'd taken from the dead assassin, whose name he now knew to be Hendry, from the details in his wallet. He had unlocked the phone using Hendry's face in the hallway and changed the settings so that he could access it without the facial recognition software. It was dangerous because Fowler's team would track the phone once they knew Hendry was dead. So, Kane turned on his burner phone, extracted some useful numbers from Hendry's and entered them into his burner. Kane threw Hendry's smartphone out of the taxi's window.

The driver, an Asian man in his early forties, glanced at Kane from the rearview mirror as the phone spun off to smash on the road beneath the yellow streetlights. But he looked away once Kane caught his eye. Fowler's number wasn't in the phone, yet Kane hadn't expected it to be. The Mjolnir agency used codenames: Frey, Thor, Tyr, Heimdall and other names related to Norse mythology. That told Kane that Odin was still involved. The operation was called Mjolnir, named after Thor's hammer, because his old commanding officer, whom Kane had never met, was a fan of mythology. Each agent had a codename derived from mythology, and Kane's had been Lothbrok.

Kane took the burner phone, typed in Sally's mobile number and sent her a text asking if she was alright and if she had contacted Jacobs yet. The taxi stopped outside a Victorian building two roads away from Warrington town centre. A white painted sign outside the building, cracked with age, had the words *Guest House* painted in black.

Kane paid the taxi driver in cash, left the

car, and walked to the front door. The door was enormous, aged timber showing through fragments of old paint, and Kane rang the bell. After a minute, an old lady in thick glasses, wearing a purple cardigan, answered the door with a broad smile. He asked her for a room, paid in cash for one night, and she showed him to a second-floor room with one bed, a sink, and a wardrobe. The room was heavy with the musty smell of old curtains and a faded paisley carpet on the floor. Nevertheless, it provided a place to stay and would be difficult to trace. Kane removed his gun from the rucksack and placed it on the bedside table before laying down to stare at the burner phone, waiting for Sally to reply.

When she hadn't replied for what seemed like an eternity, though in actuality was only ten minutes, Kane went to the window and pulled aside the net curtain, which had once been white and fashionable in the eighties but was now yellow and decidedly not. He checked for any sign of the police or other enemies. A Citroen Saxo drove past with dance music blaring, but other than that, the street was clear. He rechecked the phone. Still nothing. Kane sat on the edge of the bed and checked the gun again. It was a Glock 17 pistol, the semi-automatic weapon of choice for UK special forces, and one Kane was more than familiar with. It was a light pistol with a comfortable grip and used a double-stack magazine with seventeen rounds of parabellum ammunition. Two shots had been fired in Sally's house, so there were fifteen left.

Kane clicked the safety back on and put the weapon on the table. He rolled his shoulder to ease the dull ache from his old wound, recalling the sensation of the bullet entering his flesh like a horse had kicked him. Even though he had taken the bullet years ago, Kane remembered the pain like it was yesterday. It had healed badly, and fragments of the bullet were still in there somewhere. It was a battlefield wound, and the damage had already been done by the time he got a proper surgeon to look at it. Kane removed his hoodie and t-shirt and cleaned the knife cut on his opposite shoulder over the sink. He took his survival tin, a remnant from Kane's days in the Regiment, and used an alcohol wipe to disinfect the area. Kane grimaced as he tightly closed the wound using medical sutures, feeling the blood pulsing as he forced the edges together. He then used an adhesive bandage to keep the wound closed before sinking into an old armchair and clenching his teeth, waiting for the pain to relent.

The burner phone's face glowed yellow with a text message notification as it rumbled on the bed. Kane leapt out of the chair and picked it up.

Jacobs helped us. We are in a safe house. Kids are scared. What's going on? What did you do?

Kane sat on the bed, ran his fingers through his hair, and blew out his cheeks with a long sigh. They were safe. Jacobs was a good man. He was the contact assigned to Kane and Sally after their lives were turned upside down by entering the programme. Jacobs had protected them, set up their new identities and moved them north. He would help Sally, but only with the resources he could leverage from his agency. Kane replied to Sally's text, saying he was glad she and the kids were alright but didn't acknowledge her questions. Kane dialled Jacobs' number, and after three rings, a familiar voice answered.

"Jacobs," came the chirpy, upper-class English voice.

"It's Kane."

"Bloody hell, Jack. You were supposed to stay quiet and hidden. Never to be heard of again," said Jacobs, and then he sighed deeply. "Sally and the kids are safe. You need to come in."

"It's Fowler, Jacobs. They sent Fowler after me."

"What? Are you sure?"

"I'm sure. I just killed one of his crew at Sally's house. He was a sweeper. They've sent a Mjolnir team after me."

"Come in, Jack. Let me sort it out. We need to get you and your family out of here. You should have stayed disappeared."

"When is it ever going to end, Jacobs?" Kane stood and stared out his window at the street below, a realisation dawning on him.

"What do you mean?"

"They'll never stop hunting me, not after what happened. I know too much. I should never have talked in the first place. They are too powerful."

"We can help you, Jack. Just come in. New lives for you and your family, same as last time. The information you gave us helped save lives. We won't forget that."

"It cost me my marriage, Jacobs, and my old life. I used to be at the cutting edge, running ops all over the world, handling millions of pounds worth of equipment. Now I can't even hold down a job digging up roads. I'm out in the open now anyway, so I might as well finish it."

"Now, calm down, Jack," Jacobs spoke slowly, his voice deepened. "Don't do anything rash. Finish what?"

"Mjolnir. I need to cut the head off the snake once and for all."

"You are talking about a black ops government agency with complete protection and deniability. Who are you going to target? They are invisible. Just come in, do the sensible thing."

"What's the safe house address?"

"Not there. I'll meet you somewhere else in case they follow you."

"I'll meet you, Jacobs," Kane lied, "but first, I want to check that Sal and the kids are protected."

"They are..."

"Just give me the address, and then I'll come in."

Jacobs sighed again and then gave Kane the address. It was a farmhouse on the outskirts of Warrington, a place on its own surrounded by fields. It was close to a village named Great Sankey. Kane ended the call.

Familiar thoughts raced through his mind of how he'd ended up in this situation, his fractured family, his false identity, and the ever-present danger. After a failed operation that resulted in brutality, a terrible fight in dark tunnels, Kane had agreed to give evidence against Mjolnir's activities, knowing full well that the agency operated far beyond the confines of conventional warfare and international law. He shook his head and thought of Fowler.

So many memories.

They had fought together, lost friends together, and killed together. The bond between men forged in the crucible of combat was unparalleled, the camaraderie of fighting for survival alongside a trusted friend. However, now even Kane's closest ally had turned against him. Kane had lived in fear for too long. It was time to go on the offensive, and he would need money and weapons. Decidedly, he sent a text message to Craven's number.

You're on.

TWELVE

"Have you found the target yet?" asked McGovern, her voice terse, like a school headmistress.

"Target has not been located," said Fowler. "Agent Njorth made contact but was eliminated." He used Hendry's codename, derived from the Norse god of the sea.

"Kane killed him, you mean?"

"Yes, ma'am."

"Speak plainly, for Christ's sake, man. Find Kane and take him out quickly. Any more mistakes from you and I will have to notify Odin. We haven't hunted Kane because he was simply untraceable. But now he's popped his head up. He must be silenced."

McGovern hung up. Fowler placed his phone on the desk next to the encrypted, secure laptop. He punched in a search for David Langley. Fowler was not tech-savvy and had no desire to understand the program's inner workings. A little wheel spun around slowly on the screen.

McGovern used Odin's codename as a threat – which it was these days. If she told Odin that the op wasn't going well, the Commander of Mjolnir would get nervous, and all hell would descend on Kane, and Fowler himself, for that matter. McGovern wasn't Mjolnir. She was a civil servant, a top brass decision maker, but not a soldier or even a spook. Odin had recruited Fowler and Kane back when they were in the Regiment. Although they had never met the commander, he had sent them to the Mjolnir training headquarters to acquire advanced skills and learn the dark arts of undercover and espionage operations. The training transformed them from SAS soldiers into assassins, able to move through cities and borders undetected. They were grey men, like ghosts, elite operatives carrying out jobs for the protection of the British people. Or so they thought. Fowler just followed orders. That was his job. It wasn't for him to question the morality of those orders or who gave them and for what reason. That was what had caused the Kane shitstorm in the first place, questioning orders.

The laptop screen changed from a black background with a whirring circle to a white screen with a list of search hits. The National Insurance database had Langley's place of employment as a chemical factory. Fowler checked his weapon and radioed for one of his crew to meet him there. He decided to personally lead the operation and chose Tyr, the most skilled member of his team, codenamed after the Norse god of war, to accompany him.

THIRTEEN

Kane slept fitfully, fighting the urge to immediately get to Sally's safe house. It made more sense to get some sleep and give things the night to calm down. Even if Craven had not called it in, the police would have found Hendry's body by now unless Fowler's team had moved it, which was also possible. He woke up early, walked into Warrington's town centre, and bought a coffee and a bacon sandwich at a cafe just off the main street. Kane walked as he ate, coming to a rest at the ornate, golden gates that ringed Warrington town hall. He scanned the area for somewhere to steal a vehicle before deciding on a Lidl supermarket across the road.

A man in his early twenties, wearing Snickers work pants flecked with paint, jumped out of a red Vauxhall Corsa. Kane waited for a few minutes and then stole the car – another skill he had picked up during his Mjolnir training, which had come in handy many times over the years. He drove out of the car park and fiddled with the radio, looking for a news station. Kane followed the signs for Great Sankey along a dual carriageway and listened as a woman with a Liverpudlian accent read the news. The headline was about two men caught on a motorway with a car full of heroin, but there was no mention of the dead man at Sally's house. Either the police kept it quiet themselves, or someone ordered them to do so. He took a right turn at a large roundabout and then again at a set of traffic lights. The road took him out beyond a dense suburban sprawl of red brick houses, pubs, and newsagents before it narrowed and led him into farmers' fields thick with bright yellow rapeseed flowers.

Kane found the safe house using a map he had bought from a newsstand next to the café in Warrington. He parked two kilometres away and walked the rest of the distance to the farm. Despite the prevalent civilian usage of miles, Kane had retained his preference for kilometres. During his days in the army, when distance and topography were of vital importance, they had taught Kane to operate and think in kilometres.

Rather than walk down the heavily potholed country road, Kane moved along the hedged borders of furrowed fields. As he came cautiously within a kilometre of the farmhouse, the blackened tiles of its roof poked over the branches of a sprawling willow tree. Kane jogged across a field, his trainers picking up clods of heavy earth as he followed a furrow to a north-facing strip of dense bramble. He waited.

A man strolled across the space between the tree and the driveway entrance to the farmhouse. He wore a bulletproof vest and held an automatic weapon high upon his chest. It was a two-story building, and ivy crept up the walls around a black door. The windows were timber-framed and not UPVC, easy to break into unless Jacobs' team had fitted motion sensors to the safe house. Parked in the muddy courtyard were two black SUVs with blacked-out windows. Kane waited and saw a woman in a cap also armed with an automatic weapon. He squinted and thought it was a Heckler & Koch carbine. So, two armed guards, at least. Based on the presence of the two SUVs, there would likely be two more operators patrolling the southern perimeter and then a couple more inside. Jacobs had done his job. Getting to Sally and the kids in the farmhouse would take a heavily armed team.

He watched for a while longer as the spring sun rose to its zenith in a pale blue sky. Kane hoped to catch a glance of Danny or Kim or Sally. Even the sound of their laughter would give him a lift, provide certainty that they were well. But there was no sound other than the lowing of cattle to the east and the hum of traffic in the distance. Kane made sure the guard patrol did not spot him and backed away. He was glad his family was safe, but the weight of the trouble he had caused was like a millstone around his neck. They would move the kids to new schools and change their names. Danny and Kim would need to make new friends. They had done it once before, and the process was confusing and traumatic for young children. Kane reached the potholed road again and returned to his stolen car. He drove twenty minutes to the chemical factory, stopping at ASDA to get another burner phone and new clothes. His mind twisted over and over at the warp of his problems. How would he get to Mjolnir? And should he really help Craven bring down the gang in return for his help?

FOURTEEN

Sally stepped out of the open car door and winced as her white Nike shoe squelched in the mud. She looked at the agent who had opened the door for her, but his bearded face was impassive. He didn't even make eye contact with her. She put her other foot down and hopped onto the filthy driveway to open the SUV's rear door. It was a black BMW, all shiny bodywork and blacked-out windows. Danny jumped from the backseat, clutching his backpack like it contained treasure, which to him, it did. His PlayStation and iPad were in the bag, along with his football boots and a football.

Kim poked her pigtailed head out of the door and frowned at the mud.

"I am not standing in that," she said, pointing at her new birthday Converse shoes. Sally reached out and grabbed her. She carried Kim towards the two-storey red brick farmhouse, picking her way through the mud until it turned into a flagstone pathway. Stables surrounded the house, and the faint smell of animal shit caught in Sally's nose.

A tall agent in a tactical vest and black trousers opened the front door and gestured down the hallway. Sally smiled at him, but he ignored her. They were surly, but it was their job. The agents were there to protect her and the kids until Jack turned himself in and was reunited with them. Then, Sally assumed, it was off to another place and another new life. Jacobs hadn't told her what Jack had done or why he was on the run. She worried for Jack, even though he was more than capable of looking after himself. She still loved him, despite their break up. Sally thought the split would solve her melancholy, but it didn't. Life was the problem, or her new life, to be exact. She missed Jack now more than ever, his arms around her, his calm and strength.

The hallway was chilly with its terracotta tiled floor and nineties-style magnolia wallpaper. There were three closed doors along the hallway, but it led to an open door that revealed a bright room. Sally followed Danny inside, and they found themselves in a farm kitchen with a deep, white Belfast sink and pine-stained worktops. The cupboards were also pine, as was the island at the centre of the room. A woman stood beside the sink holding a mug, which she placed on the worktop and smiled at the children.

"My name is Sarah," said the woman. She had striking red hair and a complexion that resembled pure milk. But whilst her mouth smiled, her pale blue eyes possessed a flinty coldness.

"I'm Sally, and this is Danny and Kim."

"Right, kids, go on through there, and we'll see if we can get you set up with the Wi-Fi password and the TV." Sarah pointed towards a large sunroom off to the right-hand side of the kitchen, and the kids ran in, jostling each other to get there first and take the prime spot in front of the television.

"Is Jacobs here?" asked Sally. She had spoken to their handler earlier that day, the same man who had looked after them the first time, and she trusted him. Jack trusted him.

"No. But he's on his way. I work with Jacobs; we are part of the same agency. He's asked me to look after you and your family and make sure you are comfortable and have everything you need."

"How long will we be here?"

Sarah shrugged. "Just until we can set you up with new identities and a new location. And until Kane comes in, obviously."

"Have you spoken to Jack? Is he OK?"

"No, I haven't spoken to him, but Jacobs will

bring him in."

"Will they come for us, the agency?"

"No, they won't target you. They will, however, probably come after your husband now that his location is out there. His evidence laid their activities bare, and they can't risk that happening again."

"Will they kill him?"

"Hopefully not. Now, I've done some shopping, so shall I make us all some dinner?"

Sally smiled wanly and pressed her hand to her mouth to hide the wobble on her lower lip. Why had she and Jack entered the programme in the first place? They should have just left things as they were. Yes, Jack had a dangerous job and was away a lot. But Sally had her own career, an au pair, and the kids were happy. Now neither she nor Jack were happy. Things between them were strained, and their world was about to be turned upside down again. She hoped Jack was OK and that he would return to her soon. She needed him, and so did his children.

FIFTEEN

Kane dumped the stolen car in a cul-de-sac of bungalow houses and walked ten minutes to his old place of work. His bike was still at the bus stop, but the front forks were bent, and the wheels were buckled. Kane suspected local kids had smashed it up. He bought a coffee and sandwich from a snack van near the chemical factory and stood near a shuttered loading dock.

The sandwich was soggy, but the coffee was nice and strong. He rolled his shoulder, and the old wound caused no pain, but the cut on his opposite shoulder was stiff and tender. Kane took out his burner phone and read over the most recent message from Craven.

The girl will lead you to the gang. I will let you know if we get any more visitors today.

Kane didn't want to help the police, and he didn't really know or trust Craven. But Yelena could give him some idea of where the gang operated from, and he could pull on that thread to get cash and weapons. Fighting Hendry had come as a shock. Kane was out of shape and out of practice, and he needed to sharpen up if he was going to stand any chance of defending himself against his old friend Fowler, never mind taking down Mjolnir. He viewed his involvement with the gang as a workout, a means to an end. Plus, if Craven tipped him off about government agents poking around, then he would be one step ahead.

The chemical factory had two entrances: the official trade entrance at the front and the staff entrance on the west side. As Kane finished the dregs of his coffee, the heavy metal door that served as the staff entrance swung open, and a throng of people strode from the factory's gloom into the daylight. They squinted and smiled up at the clear sky, chatter ringing out across the shared units' car parks. Vik was amongst them, walking along with a smile on his face as he talked effusively to Bill, their words lost amidst the surrounding voices and the noise of machinery and vehicles on the estate. Kane wondered if he had missed his opportunity for a simpler life. Ordinary work, spending time with his kids, watching football, holidays in Spain every summer, car loans and date nights with Sally. That was all laid out for him, but neither he nor Sally had really settled down and enjoyed the simplicity of a regular life.

Yelena came out of the staff door alone, head down and feet shuffling across the concrete. Kane's thoughts cleared, and he reached for the small of his back to check that his gun was secured in the waistband of his jeans.

Yelena bustled forward wearing a navy hoodie, black leggings and white trainers. Her gait spoke of nervousness and fear – her arms folded tight across her chest as she took rapid, tiny steps. Kane waited until the crowd of people finishing their shifts subsided and followed Yelena to the bus stop. A white minibus rattled around the corner and stopped just in front of the rusted yellow sign, hissing as it came to a halt, and Yelena stepped on through the open doors. Kane jogged to close the distance and hopped on just behind her. He tossed a £2 coin into the black tray beside the driver's protective glass and sat opposite Yelena's seat. They were the only passengers, and she stared at him open-mouthed.

"Hello, Yelena," said Kane, doing his best to smile in a friendly manner.

"What are you doing here?" Yelena replied. She leant to her right to look towards the driver and then around her at the empty bus.

"Don't worry. I just want to ask you a few questions, that's all."

"You weren't at work today."

"No, I won't be coming back to work. Those men who attacked you yesterday…"

"Thank you for helping. I am sorry if I made trouble for you." She spoke in halting English, heavily accented by her native Estonian.

"It's fine. But I need to find them, the men who attacked you. What can you tell me about them?"

She licked her lips and fussed with the sleeves of her hoodie. "Why do you need to find them? They are evil men. Just forget about them."

The bus turned a sharp corner and pulled into a layby. The engine ticked over as the driver waited for a moment. Yelena wouldn't meet Kane's eye, and he couldn't give her a convincing reason why he needed to find the gang.

"Why did they attack you?" he said eventually, wanting to keep the conversation going but running out of ideas.

"They want to put me to work. Bad work. My brother owes them, so they punish me for his debt."

"Your brother?"

Yelena looked up at him then, her big eyes wide. She bit her bottom lip as though she worried about divulging her private business. She checked the time on her phone and sighed.

"My brother Oskar owes them money. He can't pay, so they will make me work off the money instead."

"What does he owe them money for?"

"You don't want to know. Please, why are you asking me these questions? I have never seen you on this bus before."

"Maybe I can help you and your brother. If you can trust me."

The bus moved again and picked up speed onto the main road into Warrington town centre.

"They are from Manchester. Estonians like me. They call themselves the Deli Boys. It's a stupid name, but they are very dangerous. They are from the city centre. Look for the deli close to Piccadilly train station. There is a Polish food market next door."

"Thank you, Yelena."

"My brother has three days to pay what he owes, or they will come for me again. Take me with them, make me into…"

"I'll try to help you, so it won't come to that. I'll need to take your phone number, though."

Yelena looked at Kane as though he were a fool. She read out her number, and he keyed it into his burner phone. She smiled wanly at him and then buried her head in her phone, scrolling through her social media apps. Kane rose from his seat, and the bus driver stopped outside the golden gates of Warrington's town hall. He got off the bus and walked straight to Bank Quay train station, which was only five minutes from the bus stop. Kane paid cash at the desk and caught the next train to Manchester Piccadilly Station.

SIXTEEN

"Someone to see you, guv," Jess chimed. She poked her head around Craven's office door, her chestnut hair tied up in a bun and a wide smile splitting her face. She was a bright, friendly uniformed constable and would go far in Craven's opinion.

"Who is it?" the DI asked. He closed his laptop and stood up, returning her smile.

"A guy named Fowler. He asked for Chief Inspector Kirkby first. Kirkby met him. Now he wants to meet you."

"Did he show any credentials?"

"I haven't spoken to him, sir. I was just asked to come and find you."

"You drew the short straw, then?"

She laughed. "No, sir. It's just that I'm the only one who isn't afraid of you."

Jess led the way through the twists and turns

of Warrington Police Station's corridors and stairwells.

"Do you want a coffee or anything before you go in?" Jess asked as they marched past the break room.

"No thanks. Although I could do with a stiff drink if bloody Kirkby is there."

Jess laughed again and led him through to the Chief Inspector's office. Craven caught sight of Kirkby through the office window. He was seated behind his desk, engaged in a conversation with a man facing away from the door. With a smile, Jess settled at her desk a couple of rows ahead of Kirkby's office. Except for Kirkby's enclosed space, the rest of the office layout consisted of an open-plan area. Each desk had a computer terminal, while movable whiteboards were parked around the floor, each one scrawled with updates on different cases or investigations. Craven knocked on Kirkby's door, and the Chief Inspector waved him in.

"Ah, Detective Inspector Craven," Kirkby intoned. He wore his white uniform shirt, ironed with crisp creases on both sleeves and his black tie held in check by a silver pin. Fowler rose from the chair facing Kirkby's desk. He was as tall as Craven, which few men were. He wore an expensively tailored suit, navy with a light check running through it, and a white shirt. His shoes gleamed and were as expensive-looking as his suit.

"Fowler," said the tall man to introduce himself, and he extended his hand.

"Craven," the DI replied, even though Kirkby had already introduced him. The handshake was firm, and Fowler's hand was calloused. As they both nodded at each other in a respectful yet not friendly manner, Fowler's hand fell to his side, and Craven thought he saw the bulge of a shoulder holster beneath his suit jacket.

"Sit down, Frank," said Kirkby, gesturing to an empty chair next to Fowler. Both men took a seat.

"The Chief Inspector here tells me you spoke to David Langley yesterday?" Fowler spoke with a southern accent, possibly from Essex or London; Craven wasn't sure. There was a hint of a common drawl beneath the posher tones. The man's accent had been softened and polished, just like his shoes.

"Yes, I spoke to him for a minute or two here in the station," said Craven.

"You weren't supposed to engage with him. He is a dangerous man. What exactly did he tell you?"

Craven stared into Fowler's eyes. They were piercing blue with a cliff of a frown above them. Fowler held his gaze, unflinching.

"I am the Detective Inspector with the Serious and Organised Crime Squad. Who are you with?"

Fowler sighed and sank back in his chair. He crossed his legs languidly and looked at Kirkby. Kirkby set his elbows down heavily on his desk.

"Craven," Kirkby spoke with a stern tone, reminiscent of the way you might caution a dog to stop barking before losing your patience and raising your voice at the animal. "Just tell the man what he wants to know."

"MI6?" said Craven.

Fowler raised his eyebrows, shrugged his shoulders, and looked at Kirkby again.

"Craven, you don't need to know where Mr Fowler is from. As your superior officer, I order you to tell him what Langley said to you." Kirkby's face had turned the red of a Pink Lady apple.

"Nothing, really. He told me that men would come asking questions about him. He said he was in a programme, living under a new identity. That was it."

"He said nothing else?" asked Fowler. "About his address or where his family was?"

"Nothing."

"And you were first on the scene at the house where the murder took place?"

"Murder? I was there after Langley killed an armed man in the house where his kids sleep. Do you know that man? Was he one of your lot?"

"Craven!" Kirkby shouted, and for a moment, Craven thought the Chief Inspector would lunge across the table at him out of pure embarrassment.

"Look," Fowler interjected, raising his left hand to allay the situation. A silver Omega watch glistened on his wrist. "We want the same thing here, to catch a man who is a danger to the public. In the spirit of trust, I'll give you some information on this man, and then I want you to tell me what you know and keep me in the loop about your pursuit of him."

"That's kind of you," said Kirkby, struggling to offer a pretence of calm.

"Langley's real name is Jack Kane. He is a government operative and former special forces soldier. Kane is a killer, and he's wanted by several agencies with reach and influence far beyond Britain's police force. He is a highly trained soldier, agent, and assassin. You and your officers should not try to apprehend Kane without my support. He turned on his colleagues a few years back, becoming an informant in a highly charged political situation. As a result, he was moved here with a new identity. To ensure Kane and his family's safety, I have to find him because his new identity has been exposed, and harm might come to them. So, DI Craven, what can you tell me about Jack Kane?"

"Nothing other than what I already have," Craven answered. He hated MI6 spooks. He had run into a few of them over the years whenever he got close to one of the big criminal firms, especially the ones with ties overseas. Compromised international drug dealers often made good informants or could be useful in destabilising governments and the like, or so he had been led to believe. "He was already gone when I arrived at his wife's house and called in the… murder. I gave the same information to a man like you named Jacobs. You remember him, sir, Jacobs?"

Kirkby nodded, and Fowler fixed Craven with a level gaze. There was something strange about Fowler's eyes. They were cold and hard, the pale blue of fresh water beneath a film of ice. He didn't comment on Jacobs, and Craven assumed the two men didn't know each other.

"If you give me your card, I'll call you if Kane turns up or if we get any further leads on him," said Craven.

Fowler slipped his hand into his right jacket pocket and fished out a blank card with a mobile number on it. There was no official agency insignia, no email address, or even his name. Just his number. He handed it to Craven.

"Are we done?" piped Craven.

Kirkby ground his teeth and gestured towards the door. With a wink at Fowler, Craven rose from his seat and left the office.

SEVENTEEN

Kane left Piccadilly station and emerged into a vast square in Manchester city centre. It was five in the afternoon, and people strode purposefully along the pathways and across the square made brighter by a pluming water fountain and triangles of deep green grass. Walkways and park benches sliced through the square, but few people took time to relax during rush hour. Most wore headphones of some description, listening to podcasts, audiobooks, or music and trying desperately not to make eye contact with anybody else.

Kane strolled around the large square to get his bearings. He had been here before, years earlier, but the place had changed significantly. Back then, it was drab and grey but had undergone significant refurbishment. Kane had spent the forty minutes on the train to study his road map. North of Piccadilly was the Northern Quarter, with bars and shops. Towards the west were hotels and art galleries, and to the south was Ancoats, a residential area. To the east of the station and square, there was a snarl of backstreets and alleyways, so Kane headed in that direction to search for the Deli Boys.

Piccadilly Gardens gleamed with its newness, bustling with a mix of busy office types and students, resembling a scene straight out of a promotional video for Manchester. The streets behind it, beyond Dale Street, were a jumble of older buildings. Gutters and corners were heavy with old litter and leaves, faded crisp packets and discarded plastic drinks bottles rustling and rattling in the breeze. Kane turned down Mangle Street into a wall of iron-barred filthy windows, their thick, spiked bars well-crafted as though forged in Victorian times. On either side of a narrow road, red brick buildings towered above him, graffiti daubing the walls with tags Kane couldn't understand.

At the end of the street, an iron staircase with standing platforms crawled up the wall of a corner building, reminiscent of those seen in New York or other American cities. Opposite that was the deli next to a Polish grocery store with the words *Polski Sklep* lit up in neon. Similarly, the deli had its own sign, glowing in green with the name *Rambo's*. Outside the deli, a black Range Rover idled with rap music thrumming from behind closed windows. A collection of mopeds and electric scooters waited for their riders on the pavement like a mechanical herd.

Kane considered watching the place for a while to assess the threat. That would be the correct thing to do, what he had been trained to do. But Kane didn't have time to mess around. Every day that he delayed crushing Mjolnir was another day his family was in danger, plus Craven wanted this crew taken down, although he hadn't said how. His first and preferred option was to march in and attack the gang head-on. He was tired of running and skulking. He had been hiding from his past ever since he had agreed with Sally that going into the protection programme was the best thing to do for their family. Kane wasn't a mouse to cower from those who wished him harm. He was a wolf. He liked Yelena and wanted to help both her and her brother. It took guts to leave her home country and move to a place where she didn't know the language. She was trying to better herself and had been targeted by these lowlifes. Kane hadn't met her brother, and of course, he could be a bum, but if Kane could help Yelena, then he would. The gang would also have cash and weapons, which Kane needed to equip him for the fight against Mjolnir.

Kane strode towards the deli. He wore jeans and the navy hoodie he had bought from ASDA, but he would need to pick up some new clothes.

What he wore was fine in an emergency, but if he was to feel like his old self again, he needed to up his game. The Glock sat snug in the rear waistband of his jeans, and the knife he had used to kill Hendry was in his pocket. The Polish food store's window was full of delicious-looking pastries and tins of vegetables, all listed in the Polish language.

Kane reached the deli and didn't pause as he stepped through the doorway. It was brightly lit, with a high counter at one end and a board behind it with pictures of the available sandwiches, rolls, and other foods. It was larger than Kane had expected. To his right, the deli stretched away into an eating area with six plastic tables and benches, all full of young men wearing tracksuits and talking loudly. Many wore their hoods up or had headphones snug around their skulls. It was like a photo shoot for a JD Sports catalogue.

All the chatter in the deli stopped. Youthful faces turned towards Kane with vacant looks. Uncaring and challenging at the same time. Kane strolled up to the counter and scratched his chin as he looked over the menu board behind the counter. A large, big-bellied man with sallow skin and hooded eyes shuffled out from the back and fixed Kane with an open-mouthed stare.

"I'll get a ham and salami, please, mate," said Kane with a big smile. "On a white roll, toasted.

And a coke."

Big-belly grunted and set about preparing the order. Kane peered over the large man's shoulder and noticed four burly men playing cards around a table. One of them sported a black eye and a white sling around his right arm. Kane recognised him as one of the thugs he had dealt with on the industrial estate. He faced the gang of young men and leaned against the counter. Music pumped out of a phone somewhere, and the gang kept their flat stares in his direction. Kane reached into his pocket and pulled out a handful of cash, two hundred pounds, from his emergency pack. Kane's wallet was still at Warrington Police Station, so the notes were loose, and he fumbled with the money as he tried to count it. A bunch of twenties floated down to the deli's tiled floor, and Kane knelt clumsily to pick them up. He stood and looked nervously at the gang, their eyes so hungry for his money that he almost laughed.

"Fiver," barked Big-belly as he handed Kane his roll and drink. Kane paid the man and took his change. He hustled out of the deli, but not before shooting a furtive glance at the men inside. The street outside was empty, and Kane walked slowly away from the deli, heading deeper into the back streets and away from Piccadilly Gardens. A peal of laughter rumbled out of the deli, and the pitter-patter of trainer shoes padded along the pavement behind him. Kane quickened his pace and turned down an alley, thick with the stink of piss and piled high with rubbish bags. He risked a glance over his shoulder, and three of the Deli Boys had followed him.

"Slow down, chief," one of them shouted. "You forgot your ketchup, mate."

Kane stopped and turned around. He carefully placed his roll and drink on the clean-ish corner of a green dumpster and held his palms out.

"Please don't hurt me," said Kane in his best impression of a man afraid for his life.

The three tracksuited Deli Boys swaggered towards him, lips curled with arrogance. They were all in their early twenties and walked with a predator's confidence. Kane was surprised to see men of all ages dressed like kids since he had moved to the North West. Tracksuits, hoodies, chains and the like. The irony, of course, was that as that particular thought crossed his mind, Kane himself wore a hoodie.

"Give us your money, boomer. Then you can jog on," said a man with a scraggly black moustache like Mickey Pearce from the Only Fools and Horses television show. He had a sparkling earring stud in his right ear.

"OK, you can have it." Kane put his hands up

like a caught bank robber in a cowboy movie. All three men came within Kane's reach, and he laughed. He couldn't help it. He felt joy at the prospect of violence, thinking of all the innocent people the three Deli Boys must have inflicted misery upon.

Kane punched the one with the moustache hard in the solar plexus. In the same instant, Kane whipped his left hand out with the first finger's knuckle extended and smashed it into the throat of the left-most Deli Boy. Both thugs crumpled, gasping for air, clutching at their injured selves. Kane smiled at the third man.

"Alright then, my leisure suit-wearing friend," said Kane. "We can do this the easy or the hard way. I think you can guess what the hard way is. So, I want you to take both of their possessions, phones, cash, and jewellery and add them to your own. Then you're going to take off your hoodie and put the items inside it like a good lad." The third Deli Boy looked at his mates writhing in the stains of old piss in the alleyway, licked his lips and did as he was told. "If I wanted to buy a weight of drugs from the Deli Boys to sell outside of Manchester, who would I need to talk to?"

EIGHTEEN

"So, what have we got?" said Fowler. He sat in an armchair in the apartment he had rented in Lymm, one of the nicer parts of Warrington. It had three bedrooms, an open plan living room/kitchen diner and a balcony overlooking Lymm village. The team had been called together for a progress report, each finding a seat on the couches and armchairs. Barnes stood at the sliding window which led out to the balcony, staring into the distance.

"No sign of him at the factory," said Cole. He was a tall, rangy black man with a shaved head. "I spoke to an Asian guy at the coffee place on the industrial estate, and he seemed to think Kane might come back, so I'll stay on it for a while."

"Why would he go back there?"

"The guy says Kane had a locker there with some clothes in it, and his bike is still there. Also said something about the girl he helped, that he might come back to see her."

"A girlfriend?"

Cole shrugged. "No idea. I've left a camera to watch the factory while we are here." Cole held up his smartphone to show how he could watch the footage whenever necessary via the feed from the small camera he had attached to the office building opposite the factory.

"What about the copper who found Hendry's body?" asked McCann. She was short, with raven black hair styled in a bob, and wore a trouser suit.

"Cranky bastard," tutted Fowler, brushing a speck of dust from his knee. "Jacobs had already been in there. He's the man who whisked Kane and his family away before."

"We need to get a line on that prick Jacobs," said Barnes, without turning away from the view out of the large window. "He fucked us up last time. Can't you make a call? Get some info on him so we can get to the bastard?"

"Already done. I've sent the request up the chain. If he works for MI6 or MI5, we'll know soon enough. I've got the detective's number. His name is Craven. McCann, get a tap on his phone, will you?"

"Sir," she affirmed, reaching forward to take Craven's card from Fowler.

"Hendry's dead." Barnes shook his head. "He was a good agent, a veteran. We were in Sudan together last year and in Kyiv before that. Now he's gone, killed in this shithole town by a fucking grass."

"Calm down, Barnes. We need clear heads here."

"Don't tell me to calm down," barked Barnes, pivoting to face Fowler, hands curled into tight fists at his side, his scarred face twisted into a frown. "Hendry is dead, so we can add his corpse to the poor bastards Kane dusted the last time we were after him. I want that arsehole dead. Working in a fucking factory like Joe Soap for two years, like butter wouldn't melt. He's done things just as dark as we have. Why should he get a new life just because he squealed?"

"That's enough." Fowler rose slowly from his chair, and Barnes looked him up and down, blew out his cheeks and stared out of the window again. "We'll keep on the factory. Krasinski, you follow the copper, Craven. He's up to something; I can feel it. McCann, you monitor Kane's house, get inside and see what you can dig up. I'll follow up on Jacobs. We need to close this one out in the next forty-eight hours. Otherwise, McGovern will notify Odin, and you all know what that means."

The team exchanged furtive glances, and Fowler went to the kitchen to pour himself a whiskey. He had picked up a bottle of Jameson in the village, along with a local newspaper and some protein snacks. Amongst themselves, the team used their own surnames rather than their mythological codenames. It was a bit much to sit around calling each other Freya or Heimdall when they all knew each other's real names. But if Odin descended on Warrington, that would all change. He would come heavy, and with a governmental mandate, he would turn the town upside down in the interests of national security. Fowler sipped his whiskey, enjoying the bite at the back of his throat and the warmth in his chest.

Barnes ambled across the room and took a glass from the overhead kitchen cabinet. Fowler smiled and poured him a drink.

"I just want this to be over," Barnes uttered, softly this time. "Working on home soil, against our own people, gets my back up."

"We all hate it," said Fowler. "So let's get the job done and get out of this place."

"You ever think about getting out? Not like Kane, not as a squealer. But retiring with honour. I heard a bloke got out last year, took his parachute payment and rode off into the sunset."

"Yes, sure," Fowler lied. "Why not? Another year, maybe two."

"I want to go after this job. Would you talk to

Odin about it for me? Rumour has it that he has a soft spot for you and Kane."

"No problem, mate." Many had heard that retirement story too. Of how the agent had taken his last payment, the one promised to all Mjolnir operatives after their service to Crown and country was over and retired into a life of sun and relaxation. But in the version Fowler had heard, they'd found the agent floating in the Caribbean with his throat cut. Too many secrets to have out in the open. Too much risk for the top brass. Fowler poured himself another drink and wondered about his own endgame. What was he doing all of this for, anyway? The money was good, and the thrill was just like the Regiment, yet he couldn't help but question whether he, too, could end up lying face down in the water with crabs feasting on the gash in his neck when it came time for his pipe and slippers.

NINETEEN

Kane ate the last bite of his steak, using the forkful of meat to mop up the remaining pepper sauce on his plate. The three phones taken from the Deli Boys lay face up on the glass table next to his dinner. Kane had unlocked them in the alleyway before leaving the thugs to lick their wounds. He'd obtained some valuable numbers and had used their banking apps to pay for his food and a trip to a clothes store in Manchester. He also had seven hundred Deli Boy pounds in a leather wallet inside the jacket of his freshly purchased Hugo Boss suit. Kane finished his sparkling water and paid the bill. It was seven o'clock, the time Kane assumed that the gang members he needed to talk to would emerge from their nocturnal activities.

He left a tip for the waitress and exited the restaurant. Kane wore a navy roll-neck jumper beneath his black suit and had bought some Italian leather shoes. As he marched along King

Street and headed towards Piccadilly again, he felt more like the old Kane. No more jeans and hoodies, and the cloak of David Langley fell away with every step. Whilst eating his steak, Kane had taken the numbers from his burner phone and wrote them down on a piece of paper which sat in a new rucksack slung over his shoulder. Kane had visited an army surplus store and bought the bag, some khaki cargo trousers, an army-style shirt, a black field jacket and some black tactical boots. The change of clothes sat folded neatly inside the rucksack, along with other useful bits and pieces he had picked up in the store.

Kane disposed of the stolen phones in a bin as he walked, aware the Deli Boys might use a find-my-phone app. He took out his burner and dialled the number for a man named Rasmus, a name given to him by the frightened Deli Boy in the alley.

"Kes see on?" said the voice on the phone in a language Kane didn't understand.

"I'm looking into paying a debt for a friend of mine," said Kane.

"Where did you get this number?" The voice had a heavy accent that sounded like a mix of Russian and Scandinavian.

"A mutual friend. Listen, I want to pay you a debt that's owed and maybe take some more goods off you at a similar price."

"I don't know what you are talking about," said Rasmus after a few heartbeats of silence.

"I want to pay what Oskar owes."

"Who the fuck is Oskar?"

"If you want his debt settled, plus a new order paid up front in cash, meet me outside the Malmaison Hotel in Piccadilly at eight o'clock."

Rasmus coughed, grumbled something which Kane couldn't make out, and hung up the phone. Kane stepped into a tech repair shop and bought three new burner phones, putting two in his pack and one in his jacket pocket. He bought the cheapest Android smartphone he could find and four mini-GPS tracking devices. Each one was smaller than the palm of his hand. The trackers were the type that can be attached to a keyring to track individuals with dementia. He threw the old burner into another bin fifty metres along the road.

The pristine Malmaison stood proudly on a corner of Piccadilly. A wash of iron clouds filled the spring evening sky, making the city darker than it should be at a quarter to eight during that time of year. The hotel was a large luxury venue in the city centre. The decorative stone window surrounds and elaborate architecture of the hotel's façade framed its red brick walls, which rose high into the Manchester skyline. Kane waited outside the entrance. He wore a new pair of sunglasses and stood beneath a black canopy which reached out from the hotel's restaurant windows. Kane had time before the potential meeting with Rasmus, so he called DI Craven.

"Craven," the DI answered in his gruff, hassled voice.

"I contacted the Del Boys today," said Kane.

"Good. And?"

"Any news on your end?"

"Yes, I was about to call you, as it happens. A man named Fowler came to visit my Chief Inspector and me today. He was asking questions about you. Says you're a dangerous man."

"Fowler came to see you? Why didn't you tell me straight away?"

"You know him then?"

"Don't tell him anything. He isn't what he appears to be. He's Mjolnir, be careful."

"What the fuck is Mjolnir when it's at home?"

"Never mind. What else did he say?"

"He told us that your name is Jack Kane. We've opened a murder investigation into the man killed at your house. I didn't tell Fowler anything, but he got in to see my Chief Inspector at the drop of a hat, and the CI was fawning all over him like a twenty-year-old at a lap dancing bar. So he must have some clout."

"Keep him close, Craven. Find out what he knows. I need to know immediately if he gets close to my family."

"I will. Keep your hair on. So, tell me about the Deli Boys?"

"I went to their deli. Took a few of their phones and will hopefully meet one of their higher-ups in a few minutes. A guy named Rasmus."

"OK, great," said Craven, a genuine tone of pleasant surprise in his voice.

"I'll keep feeding you info and help you bring this crew down, but you have to help me too, Craven. This isn't a one-way street."

"Will do, don't worry. Let me know how you get on with this Rasmus character. I'll punch his details into our system and see what it throws up."

Kane ended the call because a white BMW 3 Series came around the corner and pulled to a stop in front of him. A tall, wiry man in a bright blue puffer jacket stepped out, his skinny wrist heavy with a thick gold chain.

"You the guy about the cash?" asked the man in accented English.

"I'm the guy," said Kane.

"Get in."

TWENTY

Craven opened the door to his house and kicked off his shoes. The smell of roasting meat wafted into the hallway from the kitchen, filling his mouth with saliva. He took off his coat and hung it on the hook by the door next to his wife's raincoat. He put on his slippers and made his way along the hall and into the kitchen. Their Alexa was playing an upbeat love song, and Craven's wife sang along loudly, blissfully unaware that he had arrived home. It had been one of her favourites back when they had been high school sweethearts.

Barb jumped and screamed like a woman in a horror film as Craven sneaked up behind her and shook her shoulders. She turned and laughed, playfully hitting Craven in the chest as he pulled her in for a bear hug.

"I hope the food's better than your singing, love," he said.

"I thought I'd make a roast tonight. Your favourite, in case you didn't make it home, and you could warm it up if you were hungry." She smiled, creasing the crow's feet at her eyes and the lines on her forehead. Barb was the same age as Craven, fifty-one years old and still as beautiful as she had been on the day they were married twenty-five years ago. She coughed, but the sound was more like a rattling wheeze from deep inside her. Barb winced at the pain and coughed again. She tapped her hand to her chest, and Craven helped her to sit on one of the high stools at the kitchen breakfast bar.

"Thanks. How was your day?" he said, refraining from asking her if she was alright because he knew she was not.

"Good. The kids are all getting ready for mid-term exams, so the place is a bit tense." Barb worked as a receptionist at the local high school and had done so for the last ten years. It was a part-time job that she enjoyed, and it contributed to the bills. Barb loved being around children, and it was Craven's life's regret that he could not give Barb any of her own. They had tried many times, and tests had shown that the problem lay with Craven. His sperm count was low, and although he was initially devastated by the emasculating knowledge that he was infertile, they both learned to accept it. Since falling ill two years ago and having to leave work to undergo ravaging chemotherapy treatment, Barb had returned to work at the school part-time. Craven was glad because the goings-on of both pupils and teachers took her mind away from the disease.

"How long until dinner's ready?"

"Half an hour."

"I'll take Lucky for a quick walk then. When I come back, I'll finish the dinner off. You have a rest. Maybe see what's on the telly later."

The dog seemed to telepathically understand Craven's intentions because the Labrador came bounding into the kitchen with his tail wagging furiously as Craven knelt to stroke, scratch and fuss after the dog. Lucky was their joy, and both Craven and Barb doted on him like he was a child. Craven grabbed the lead, put his shoes back on, and headed out of the front door. He took Lucky on his usual route around the block, hoping that the dog wouldn't shit. He loved the animal, but any dog owner who says they don't mind picking up soft, warm turds with only a plastic bag between hand and shit is a liar.

The house next door still had the 'For Sale' sign in the front garden, but it was now covered with a white and red 'Sold' poster. The house had sold for less than Craven and Barb had assumed their own house was worth, which put a dent in their desire for a retirement home abroad.

Barb needed better air to help with her chest, and a place in Spain's warm, clean air was their dream. To get there, however, Craven needed a promotion to bump up his pension pot, and they needed to achieve a good price for their house when it came time to sell.

If Barb stayed in the UK, she would die. Craven could feel it. The air was damp, and he suspected the factory and power plant chimneys of Warrington and Widnes were hurting her chances of beating cancer for good. Spain would save her, and as he walked, he thought about the gangs and the scum and how he had to bring one big gang down to secure his promotion. If the collar was big enough, then there was nothing Kirkby could do to hold him back, even if the two men hated each other. Then Craven would retire in a few years and get Barb away to a nice little cottage or apartment by the sea. They would spend their days breathing in the sea air, walking the dog and taking lunch in sun-drenched courtyards, sipping red wine and reading. But to do so, Craven needed results, and he needed a promotion.

Craven hurriedly crossed the road to avoid a yapping Jack Russell just as his phone rang.

"Craven," he answered, taking the phone out of his pocket.

"DI Craven, it's Jacobs here," said Jacobs in his

crisp, well-to-do accent.

"Ah, Jacobs. I was wondering when I would hear from you again."

"Really? I thought I would check in and see if you had got any leads on Jack Kane?"

"Hasn't he contacted you yet?"

"Not since our little meeting, no."

"No new leads, I'm afraid. But I did get a visit from a man named Fowler. I thought he was MI6 or something like that. A bit like you, actually. But rougher around the edges. Asked similar questions, though."

The phone went silent for ten seconds. "They're here already, then."

"Who?"

"Never mind. If you get any leads on Kane, let me know, Craven. Do you understand? There is more at stake here than you know."

"Funny thing is, Fowler said the same thing."

Craven hung up and walked the four roads of his block in the suburbs of Wigan, Manchester. Lucky scrabbled in a thick bush on the pavement's edge, and Craven yanked the lead to pull him along. The dog growled under its breath, and a sudden veil of worry descended over Craven. What was he doing? Kane was obviously some sort of government spook or agent, something Craven had no desire to be a part of. Since meeting him, Kane had already killed one man, albeit a man who had tried to hurt his family, and three of the Deli Boys had needed a trip to A&E after the assault at the industrial estate. Craven had thought himself clever, thought he had found a way to give himself a jump up the greasy pole of promotion. If Kane could help him bring down the Deli Boys, where was the harm in that? At least, that was what he'd initially thought. Kane was a killer. What if he was using Craven for his own ends? How could he hope to control a man like that?

Lucky jumped up Craven's leg and licked his hand. At that moment, the thought occurred to Craven that Kane was like a hunting dog, kept on a leash and at bay for a time, but now loose in the wild. Men hunted him, dangerous figures from a world of government secrets and international conflict. Craven didn't have a clue who Fowler or Jacobs were, who they worked for, or what they were capable of. But he knew what Kane was capable of, he had witnessed that first-hand, and he knew Kane was a man to fear. Craven swallowed his doubts and told himself to take what he could from the opportunity. He only needed Kane to help him with this one thing, and there was no harm in helping the man keep his family safe from spook bastards. He'd be OK. Once he brought the Deli Boys down, he could shoot for a promotion and increase his take-home pay. Then, he and Barb could think about early retirement. He just had to keep Kane onside and hope it didn't all blow up in his face.

TWENTY-ONE

The smell of woody aftershave was so overpowering that Kane had to slide open the passenger side window of the BMW before his eyes watered. The man in the blue puffer jacket stayed silent after Kane entered his car. It could be a problem if he drove to the deli and the guys Kane had roughed up recognised him. Puffer-jacket parked two streets away from the Malmaison Hotel and switched off the engine.

"So, you have money now?" said Puffer-jacket, fixing Kane with a flat stare.

"What money?" Kane replied.

"You say you want to pay off Oskar's debt, no?"

"Are you Rasmus?"

Puffer-jacket chuckled to himself. "No, he doesn't waste his time meeting pieces of shit like you. You have money or not?"

"Yes, I have the money, but not here. I have

some on me, but I can get more. I want to pay what Oskar owes and also buy some more."

"Pay first."

"How much does Oskar owe?"

Puffer jacket smiled at one corner of his mouth. "Oh, he owes twenty grand, big man. You going to pay that?"

Kane kept his cold face on, the face they had taught him to maintain even under enemy interrogation during Regimental training in Brunei. Keeping it still and flat in front of some jumped-up thug was easy compared to some of the questioning Kane had endured in his time.

"How much for the same order again?"

"Another twenty large for more coke. Up front this time."

"OK then, take me to Rasmus, and I'll pay him."

"You pay me. Nobody meets Rasmus. Are you mad, fam?"

Kane stared at Puffer-jacket and saw no indication of deceit on his face. There was no chance of a peaceful meeting with Rasmus. So Kane smiled and reached down into his rucksack, which rested between his legs in the passenger footwell. He unzipped the bag as though he would dig into it and pull out some of the money. Instead, he pulled out the Glock. Kane kept it low and pointed the muzzle towards the young thug's face.

"What the fuck, man?" Puffer-jacket cried out, trying to push himself back further into the corner of his driver's seat. "Easy, man."

"Do you know where Rasmus is?"

"No, I don't, I swear it. I was told to come and meet you and see if you were the real deal and get money, that's all. I never even spoke with Rasmus, or Aivar or any of those guys."

"Aivar?"

"Any of the top boys, I swear it. I deal with my boss but not the top guys. We all have Rasmus' number in case of an emergency, but it's only to be used if things kick off."

"Do Rasmus or Aivar ever come to the deli?"

"Yes, a couple of times per week. They also have a bar across town. It's called Diego's."

"Get out," said Kane, waving his left hand in a dismissive gesture.

"What?"

"Get out. Get your boss to tell Rasmus I'll call him and not to send one of his muppets next time."

Puffer-jacket appeared confused until he realised Kane was taking his car and dismissing him. He swallowed, the Adam's apple in his throat bouncing like a tennis ball, and then he opened the driver's door.

"Wait," said Kane. "Is this petrol or diesel?"

"Er, petrol hybrid."

"What the hell does that mean?"

"Well, you charge it up, and it drives on electric…"

"Doesn't matter. Go on." Puffer-jacket got out and ran down the street, almost tripping over as he glanced back over his shoulder towards Kane. Kane hopped into the driver's seat and started the car. He drove out of the city towards the M62 and back to Warrington, still wondering what a petrol hybrid was and how much the world had changed. His world had changed with it, but as he sat back in the new BMW in his new clothes, Kane had to admit he felt alive again.

TWENTY-TWO

Kane spent another night in the B&B and paid the landlady for two more nights in cash. The arrangement suited him. Cash was untraceable as far as Kane could tell; he was only a patron. He slept fitfully, worrying that Fowler had found Sally and the kids or that his old friend would come swinging in through the window on a fast rope, MP5 blaring. Kane's family was safe for the time being, and Kane had to trust that Jacobs would do his job. He made a mental note to call Jacobs that day, got dressed, hopped in his new BMW and drove out towards the industrial estate.

On the way, he sent a message to Yelena to meet him before her shift started because he had news about Oskar. He told her he would wait in the office car park on the next block of units over from the chemical factory. She replied with a thumbs-up emoji. Kane had left his rucksack and tactical clothing in the B&B bedroom and wore his new suit and jumper. He had also purchased spare shirts and underclothes, all of which he had put into a bedside drawer beside an ancient, yellowed bible.

Upon his arrival at the industrial estate, Kane tried to be discreet by parking in a dark corner. He would have to ditch it soon. The car was too conspicuous for a man who had spent a lifetime trying to blend in, to be the grey man in any room or environment. Just then, Yelena appeared around the corner. It was a warm day, and she was dressed in a simple blue T-shirt and jeans. She greeted him with a wave and a smile. Kane couldn't help but think Yelena was pretty, and he felt guilty. Even though he and Sally had separated, Kane had never been interested in other women and held out hope they could one day get back together. Kane opened the door and stepped out, smiling in greeting.

"I found the men Oskar owes money to," he said.

"Will it all be OK?" Yelena asked. She swept her hair away from her face with thin fingers.

"I need to meet with Oskar. Can you arrange it for this evening?"

"I can ask him," she said.

"Does he live in Warrington?"

"Yes, over in Orford. I'll call him."

"Good. I'll text you later to confirm the time."

"Thank you, David," she said. She had never used his name before, his alias.

"We haven't sorted it out yet. I just need to ask Oskar a couple of questions, then I can get all of this put to bed, and you can get on with your life. Have the gang come for you since the incident here?"

"No, there's been nothing. But the clock is ticking for Oskar, and he is afraid."

"How did he get mixed up in all of this? He approached notorious gangsters for a large quantity of cocaine and planned to sell it. That makes your brother a drug dealer."

"He has always been in trouble, even when we were kids back home. We came to England to look for new lives, better lives. But we found only hard jobs and bad wages. He wants money. He wants to live like the people he sees on Instagram and YouTube. He is young." Yelena sniffed back a tear and cuffed at her eye.

Kane waited for her to compose herself. "Set up the meeting for tonight. I bought you this." He handed her a small GPS tracking device he had picked up in Manchester. "Keep this on your keys, with your phone, or in your bag. When you have it, I can find you anywhere."

She took the small square device, shot him a

worried look, and then shoved it in her pocket.

"I have one for your brother as well. Don't worry, I'm not following you. It's just in case."

"In case of what?"

"Never mind. I'll be in touch later."

She nodded and stepped out of the car. He watched her go and started his engine. Time to grab some food and try to contact Jacobs for an update on Sally and the kids. The BMW was an automatic. He pushed it into drive, and the car moved off. The radio clicked on, playing a Bryan Adams song Kane couldn't remember the name of.

Just as he was about to dial the number, Kane's windscreen exploded suddenly with a piercing burst of smashing glass. He ducked instinctively, and his seat thrummed under a massive impact. A dull thud rocked the chair again. Kane's stomach flipped violently, and his heart thundered in his chest. Someone was shooting at him. He cursed himself for not scouting the area properly before his meeting. The lapse in his vigilance reminded him of how he had become somewhat complacent – too much time away from danger. Kane slammed his foot down on the accelerator, and the car roared into life, lurching forwards with its tyres screeching on the tarmac. Kane kept low, pressing himself deep into the seat, head and torso below the steering wheel. He couldn't see where he was going, but he had to get away from the shooter. Another bullet impact on his chair. He glanced up and around. It looked like a bear had savaged the seat's headrest, tearing it to bits and turning it into a tangle of white leather, fluff, and yellow filling.

The car sped forward until its driver's side tyre exploded. Kane cursed as the car pulled violently to the right, twisting his hand on the steering wheel. The thud of a bullet banged into the driver's side door like a hammer ringing in a blacksmith's forge. The car slammed into something hard and stopped it dead, catapulting Kane forward into the cushion of an exploded airbag. Blood rushed in his ears, panic swamping his senses, and he fumbled for the seatbelt button. The car had struck the car park wall, leaving him trapped. Kane swiftly managed to undo the seatbelt, opened the door, and scrambled out of the car. To stay still was to die. The shooter would approach cautiously and pump him full of bullets, so he had to move.

Kane's palm touched the cold car park tarmac as he launched himself into a run. Another bullet slapped into the car behind him with a metallic bang. He leapt over the contoured back of the vehicle and crouched behind the rear passenger side wheel. Screaming and shouting echoed around the industrial estate. Kane hadn't heard gunfire, so he knew his attacker used a silenced weapon. It could be long-range, but he doubted it. The bullets seemed too low calibre for that. He pressed his stomach to the ground and peered beneath the car. Black boots approached slowly, side over side. Ten paces away. The gait of a person holding a submachine gun in two hands and peering along its sight. All Kane could make out were the boots.

Kane returned to a crouched position and reached behind his back for the Glock pistol in his waistband. The weapon had no safety, and so was ready to fire. He had removed the silencer as it was too long for the gun to fit comfortably in the small of his back, so it stayed in his room with the rest of his gear. Kane took a deep breath and surged into a standing position. He squeezed off a shot, and the sound of the weapon tore through the air like thunder. Kane's shot missed, going over the gunman's shoulder, but he had been close enough to make the attacker lower his weapon and dive towards the car.

His attacker was a tall man with a scarf pulled up around his face. Without hesitation, Kane jumped around the car, his arse sliding over the back end's polished, curved surface. He brought his pistol around to fire on the gunman but was met by the muzzle of a silenced MP5 pointing at his chest within arm's reach. Kane whipped his right hand out and pushed the weapon aside just as it spat a bullet over his right shoulder. He pulled the trigger of his own weapon, but the gunman jerked aside so that the shot ricocheted off the tarmac. Kane rapidly grabbed the MP5 with his left hand, and his attacker grabbed Kane's Glock. Engaged in a fierce struggle, both grunted as they forced one another's weapons wide. Kane tried to bring his knee up into the gunman's groin, but the attacker's thigh blocked it. Kane threw himself to the right, rolling the man with him, then he jostled the attacker back the other way, feet scrambling to gain a dominant position in the grapple.

Their eyes locked, and Kane saw a momentary reflection of his own self in those wide, dark eyes. A warrior. Trained for combat and familiar with death. The gunman let go of his own weapon and punched Kane in the face. The blow cannoned off Kane's eyebrow, and he saw stars for a heartbeat. Kane surged his head forward in a savage headbutt, which crunched his enemy's nose beneath the hard bone of Kane's forehead. So he did it again, thrusting his head forward with snarling savagery. Resistance lessened, and Kane exploded upwards from the ground, letting go of his attacker in favour of a standing position. The man sprang up with him, and with eye-watering speed, he kicked Kane's gun out of his hand. Kane chopped his left hand at the gunman's throat, but he blocked the blow, so

Kane slipped his right hand under the attacker's armpit, stuck his hip into the man's midriff and threw him to the ground. He tried to stamp on the man's face, but the assailant twisted away, launching a savage kick at Kane's thigh. Kane fell to one knee, his leg burning with pain. It was a desperate fight, both men using maximum force in defence of their lives.

Sirens blared in the distance, nearing closer by the minute. The gunman pulled down his scarf and spat out a gobbet of blood. His nose streamed dark crimson. He was a tall black man, and he fixed Kane with a hard stare.

"Times up for you, Kane. You can't betray the agency and live," the man sneered.

"You're Mjolnir then?" said Kane.

The sirens grew closer, and his attacker nodded his head. Frightened faces appeared around the edges of buildings and behind windows, peering at the unthinkable violence unfolding around them. Gunfire in a bleak, mundane industrial estate on a regular Wednesday in Warrington. The gunman whipped a knife from his belt and lunged at Kane, but Kane caught the assailant's knife hand and stepped into the attack. Kane was fighting on instinct. Years of training and fighting for his life in the field burned into his memory. He viciously kicked the gunman's shin, and the man barked in pain as his leg went from under him. He fell to the ground, and Kane twisted the knife hand savagely, ripping the weapon free. Kane dropped his left knee onto the fallen man's elbow, and in one fluid movement, he stabbed the knife, full force, into the gunman's shoulder. He cried out in pain, and Kane twisted the blade to rend and tear at the man who'd tried to kill him.

Blue lights flashed in Kane's peripheral vision. Time was short. The police would descend on the scene of chaos in no time, all units speeding to respond to what must surely be multiple reports of gunfire and fighting.

"Say hello to Fowler for me, or rather Thor, I should say. Where are you holed up?" said Kane, even though he doubted the gunman would respond. He curled his lip and stayed silent, his face sheeted with sweat from the fight and the agony of the knife wound.

Kane searched the wounded gunman quickly, twisting the knife to keep him at bay. The gunman's pockets were empty, as Kane knew they would be. He carried only spare ammo for his MP5. Kane stepped off the man and picked up his Glock from beside the ruined car. He pointed the weapon at the gunman's face to warn him, to show that he could have killed him but did not pull the trigger. Kane could hear the roar of police cars hurtling towards the industrial estate, and he smiled at his fallen adversary.

It would cause both him and Fowler more problems if the police arrested the gunman. The questioning and red tape would slow them down and give Kane a chance to hunt them.

Kane turned on his heel and ran. Just as he launched into an all-out sprint, he caught a familiar face gawking at him from behind the white coffee van, mouth hanging open in utter disbelief. It was Vik, his friend from the factory. A good man, an honest man.

What must he think of me now? Now that he can see the real me, not David Langley anymore, but Jack Kane.

TWENTY-THREE

Warrington Police Station buzzed like a kicked hornet's nest. A gun battle on the streets was unheard of in the town. The shocking event had made the news across the entire country. Craven waited in a meeting room along with the rest of the Serious and Organised Crime Squad. The entire northwest squad had been summoned to Warrington, along with armed response teams and any other units that could be drafted in to help with the investigation.

"It's all kicked off here then," piped Shaw, a thirty-something Detective Sergeant from Craven's unit. He was a short man in round glasses whose cheeks were always the hue of a ripe loganberry. Shaw wore his hair shaved to the skin around his ears and gelled the top in an immaculate side part. He sat next to Craven with a takeaway coffee in one hand and a Danish pastry in the other. "Manchester or Liverpool gangs?"

Craven shrugged, and before he could answer, the meeting room door flew open and swung on his hinges to bang into the wall. The crash silenced everybody in the room, and Chief Inspector Kirkby came stalking in, his face like thunder and his shirt sleeves rolled up. Behind him came the Chief Constable of Cheshire Police, Sarah Coneally. She was a tall woman with a long face and a small mouth. A younger constable scuttled in behind her, clutching a laptop, and with shaking hands, he fumbled with some connection leads at the back wall. Kirkby stared at the young man, whose face turned a deepening shade of red until a projector fastened to the ceiling clicked on, and the pull-down screen showed a Cheshire Police logo.

"We have an armed murder suspect on the loose in Warrington," said Coneally. She nodded at the young constable, who clicked a button on the laptop. A picture of Kane flashed up on the big screen, with the name David Langley written beneath it. Craven sat up straight in his chair. "This man is already the primary suspect in an open murder investigation, and today, he was embroiled in a gunfight in broad daylight. The other individual is in hospital because of a stab wound and will be released into our custody for questioning as soon as possible." Coneally spoke with a Mancunian accent, and her eyes glittered with stern focus.

"Shaw! Put that Danish down. This is serious," snapped Kirkby, stepping forward from behind the Chief Constable with his chest puffed out like a junkyard dog. Shaw lowered his pastry and stopped chewing the piece in his mouth, his eyes flickering around the room as every person in there stared at him. Coneally looked disapprovingly at Kirkby, and he stepped back again.

"He's a fucking muppet," whispered Craven from the corner of his mouth so that only Shaw could hear him.

"I want every available body on this immediately," Coneally continued. "This is a manhunt. No stone is to be left unturned. I want trees shaken. I want every street in this town searched and get patrol cars on all major roads. Stop and search, rattle informants and go door to door at every house within a mile radius of where the gun battle took place."

The younger constable clicked through a series of slides, showing the location of the industrial estate and pictures of the shot-up BMW. He played video footage taken from security cameras showing Kane fighting with a man dressed in black. Finally, he clicked through a series of still pictures showing Kane in the reception area of Warrington Police Station just before he escaped.

"Find this man, but don't approach him alone. If you spot him, call for armed response. He is reckless and dangerous, and I don't want any innocent people hurt or any of our officers injured or worse. Do you understand?" Coneally let her iron gaze wash over the room. There was a low rumble of assent and a few muted '*Yes, Ma'am's*'. The Chief Constable left the room, and Craven rose from his chair but then plonked back down as Kirkby began to talk. Craven tuned him out. He had understood Coneally's message and didn't need to listen to Kirkby grandstanding in front of the officers drafted in from Liverpool and Manchester. His phone rumbled in his jacket pocket, and Craven retrieved it, holding it low so Kirkby wouldn't notice. The text was from an unknown number. Kane had changed his phone again.

Any news? K

Craven put his phone away and stared at the picture left on the big projector screen. It was of a bullet hole in the window of a kids' play centre on the edge of the industrial estate, facing towards the main road. The place was green and had the words *Jungle Den* painted on the sign in orange letters. Nobody was harmed in the play centre, but Craven was concerned that things were getting out of control. He would call Kane, find out what was going on, and maybe even ask him to leave the Deli Boys thing alone. Craven had hoped this would be a quick opportunity to bring down the gang and pin the badge of success to his own chest. Now it was descending into madness. Bullets flying at kids' play centres was beyond the pale.

The briefing ended, and Craven marched out of the room. He wanted to find somewhere private to call Kane, but he felt a hand on his shoulder. Craven turned, and Shaw was there with a worried look on his face.

"We have a room upstairs for our unit, and I'm going to set up a whiteboard with what we know," said Shaw. That was the way their investigations usually worked. The unit would gather around and share information. It would all go on the whiteboard, which they would update every morning as a particular investigation developed. It served as a point of reference, a place to hold regular catch-ups and provide a go-to place with all recent developments in a case.

"Good, I'll be up in a minute," Craven nodded. "I just need to make a quick call."

"Craven and Shaw," a familiar voice uttered, drawling over the names and dripping with sarcasm. It was Kirkby. "You two wasters had better start pulling your weight, or you can piss off back to Manchester. We need coppers who can think on this case, not washed-up has-beens. Get to it. I've got my eye on you both."

"You're right about him, Craven," said Shaw after Kirkby was out of earshot. "Sooner we get back to our own manor, the better."

Craven shook his head and strode towards the exit. He swiped the card on the lanyard around his neck and walked outside the station. Craven took his phone out and called Jacobs.

"Jacobs," came the voice on the other end of the line.

"It's DI Craven. Listen, your boy is fucking running amok in Warrington. Both Kane and the spooks who are after him shot the place up today. There's absolute carnage here. If I can bring him in, can you protect him and get him off the streets?"

"Are you in contact with him, Craven? Do you know where he is?"

"I can contact him, yes." He held his breath.

"Bloody hell, man. Yes, bring him in... for his own safety."

"If I can't bring him in, is there an address I can tell him to go to? I just want this over now, Jacobs. It's a fucking mess."

Jacobs sighed. "Let me think about it. I'll come back to you. For now, if you can talk to him, tell him to come in peacefully and that I will look after him."

"Are his wife and kids safe?"

"They are with me in a safe house, and I am keeping them protected."

Craven hung up the phone. He would attend the whiteboard briefing and then call Kane. He had made a mistake asking Kane to help with the Deli Boys, but he would put it right. He'd get everything straightened out before innocent people got hurt.

TWENTY-FOUR

"The copper just called Jacobs' phone," exclaimed McCann, bursting into the Lymm apartment.

"Finally, a break," said Fowler, getting up from working on his laptop whilst watching the news. "What did he say?"

"Something about the Deli Boys, whoever they are, but that he's going to talk to Kane and ask him to turn himself in. I also have Jacobs' number, so we can get a fix on his location. He's with Kane's family at a safe house. Jacobs' phone had a serious level of encryption on it, almost as strong as one of our own. It's a clean phone – no other data on it. So he's only using it for this op."

"Good work," said Fowler. "Jacobs is clearly MI6 or some offshoot. Be careful with him. We don't want to cause problems up the chain. We're finally getting closer to Kane. Now, before the police get hold of Cole, we need to get him out of the hospital." Fowler turned to Barnes, who sat on the sofa, messing around with a butterfly knife. "Barnes, you and I will grab Cole. McCann, you stay here and track those numbers. Let me know immediately if there's any update on Craven meeting or speaking with Kane. The rest of you stay on alert. We might close this op out today if we're lucky."

An hour later, Fowler stalked through the main entrance to Warrington General Hospital. The hospital had a modern exterior, with orange plated cladding on the outside, grey box-like turrets on the western side and a sleek, flat roof. The entrance reeked of alcohol-based hand sanitiser, and a score of people walked purposefully about the entrance atrium. People on crutches, in wheelchairs, or visitors with worried faces wove in and out of hospital porters and nurses in blue scrubs.

Fowler waited for an old man struggling on a walking frame to shuffle across his path and then stopped to examine the hospital map laid out in bright colours on a plinth by the elevators. He followed the directions around to the A&E department, along corridors of sanitised green and white walls and through a busy waiting room of injured people with glum faces. Fowler ignored the check-in desk and triage area and pressed a square button to open the automatic doors which led into the treatment zone. Fowler strode through the hospital like he belonged there, an old trick to avoid questions, and he moved along plastic-curtained cubicles where folk sat on beds holding injured limbs or pressed thick gauze pads to cuts and wounds. Somewhere, a woman cried, and in a different direction, a couple of nurses laughed.

Two policemen stood guard outside an end cubicle with its pale blue curtain pulled closed to obscure the patient inside. The police officer closest turned and stared at Fowler. He was a heavy-set man with muscled arms beneath his black police polo t-shirt and tactical vest. The police officer saw a tall, well-dressed man approaching and returned Fowler's friendly smile, assuming he might be a doctor or consultant at the hospital. Fowler continued to smile as he drove the flat of his left hand into the policeman's throat with a vicious reverse swing. The policeman's eyes bulged, and he clutched at his damaged windpipe. Reeling from the blow, he stumbled back into the curtain, dragging it from its rail in a crackle of ripped plastic hooks. The second officer's hand dropped to the telescopic baton at his belt, but Fowler leaned into a brutal front kick. His heel crashed into the policeman's stomach, sending him flying across the ward.

Fowler dragged the curtain off its runners and let the choking policeman tangle himself up in its length. Cole peered at him from where he sat upright on a hospital gurney. A petite nurse shook with terror and stepped away from Cole, clutching a bloody wad of bandages. Cole was stripped to the waist with a swollen, raw, but stitched wound on his shoulder. Behind Cole, a policewoman had her hand on a taser gun. The nurse shrank behind her, and the policewoman licked at dry lips, her blue eyes flicking from Cole to Fowler.

"Don't do it," said Fowler as gently as he could. She jerked the taser, and Fowler pointed at her. "Don't do it!" He roared those three words, and the venom of it stunned the policewoman. She took an involuntary step back.

Cole groaned as he jumped down from the gurney. Fowler kept his finger pointed at the policewoman, and the sound of shouting erupted from further along the ward as both nurses and patients caught wind of the assault on the two policemen. The policewoman's expression changed from fearful to one of determined aggression, and she lifted the hand holding the taser. With lightning-fast speed, Fowler closed the distance between them and kicked her in the side of her head. She dropped the taser and fell onto the gurney. Fowler followed his attack up with an elbow to her face and heard the crack of her cheekbone as her skull bounced off the bed and she crumpled to the floor.

The policeman Fowler had front kicked came

stumbling into the cubicle, his shoulder radio crackling and his telescopic baton extended, gripped tight in his right hand. Cole leapt on him, throwing his cuffed hand around the man's neck and pulling him into a choke. The policeman's oval face turned purple as Cole crushed his throat with rapid savagery. Fowler took the keys to Cole's handcuffs from the subdued officer's belt and unlocked Cole's wrists. He punched the officer hard in the gut, and Cole let him fall. Wincing at the pain in his shoulder, Cole threw on his jacket and followed Fowler towards the entrance to the A&E department. At that moment, another policeman came hurtling through the double doors, shouting into his radio. Fowler took two quick steps to meet him, skidded down onto one knee and kicked the officer's legs from under him. The officer fell and banged the back of his head on the hospital floor.

Fowler and Cole jogged out of the building, leaving a scene of sheer chaos in their wake.

"Cheers for that," said Cole in his cockney accent.

"Someone's got to tidy up your mess. We can't have any loose ends. Do you really think Odin would have let them question you?" Fowler replied. "Kane is ripping us to shreds. We need to get at him. Put the bastard down. So get yourself together."

A blacked-out Hyundai SUV swerved around a bend and pulled up in front of the A&E department. The rear passenger door swung open, and Barnes waved them in. Cole and Fowler jumped into the backseats, and Barnes drove off at full speed.

TWENTY-FIVE

Kane packed his gear into the rucksack at the bed-and-breakfast. An enormous silver TV that was at least twenty years old sat on the dresser and played a news channel featuring Kane's face and video footage of the white BMW. Whispering a curse, he reached for the remote control and turned it off. Everything had been going well up to that point. His family was safe under Jacobs' protection, and he had been working towards infiltrating the upper echelons of the Deli Boys gang. But then, as was often the case in the military operations Kane had participated in, his best-laid plans had gone awry.

After the attack, Kane had run through the back streets of suburban Warrington. The area around the industrial estate was thick with post-war fifties housing. It was a maze of densely packed terraced homes with cobble-paved ginnels between the backs of each street. That tangle of cobblestones and wheelie bins had brought him to a pedestrian crossing at a pub called the Rose Inn and then to the banks of a canal. With the sound of distant sirens ringing in his ears, Kane had followed the canal, ambling through parkland and back into the town centre. The walk gave him time to think and reflect on his behaviour. Kane had allowed himself to slide into an imitation of his old life, something he had secretly yearned for throughout his time as David Langley. He loved the action and always had. Kane should have focused on bringing down Mjolnir instead of getting involved with the gang and Yelena's problems. He'd been fooling himself by saying he was going after the Deli Boys for money and weapons to help his cause. Instead, he'd been driven by the danger and thrill. Now, with renewed resolve, he'd decided to sharpen up, to pick up his game, to finish what he had started and then take on Mjolnir.

Kane finished packing his gear and left the B&B, needing to keep moving before the landlady saw the news and recognised his face. He made his way to the train station, and just as he was about to head down the steps to the ticket booth, his phone suddenly rang. Kane stopped and took the burner from his pocket. It was the DI.

"Yes, Craven?" he answered.

"Kane, what the fuck is going on? This is Warrington, not fucking Beirut. There are coppers all over the place looking for you," Craven intoned, the usual belligerent swagger gone from his voice.

"Fowler's men came for me. I didn't start this fight. They did."

"Look, forget about the Deli Boys. I spoke to Jacobs, and he thinks it's best if you come in. Not to the police, to him. He will get you and your family to safety."

"How are Sally and the children?"

"They are safe with Jacobs. You should hand yourself to him; stop all of this madness."

"I can't, Craven. It will never end, not until I put Mjolnir down. There's too much at stake. They'll never stop looking for me."

"That's the second time you've mentioned Mjolnir. What exactly is it?"

"It's the codename for a counterintelligence group, a black ops unit funded by the British Government. They work between the lines of international law to keep the world safe from the really bad elements out there in the distant corners of the world. They take on terrorists and regimes, surpassing even MI6 in their capabilities, using lethal force to keep Britain and the world safe. Or that's what they created Mjolnir for. But having such a lethal force, and access to the vast amounts of money required to fund it, has clouded Mjolnir's moral compass. Oh, and Mjolnir is named after Thor's hammer, from Norse mythology."

"Thor?" Craven spat the word like it was a turd in his soup.

"It doesn't matter. What matters is that I need to finish this once and for all."

"Just leave it, Kane. Call Jacobs and go back into hiding."

Things had become too hot for Craven, and Kane understood that. Criminal violence on the streets was one thing, but the type of violence Kane and Fowler brought was on an entirely different level, and it wasn't fair to keep Craven in the whip of its whirlwind.

"Take care of yourself, Craven."

"Wait!" came a shout down the phone as Kane was about to hang up.

"What is it?"

"The fella who used a machine gun to tear up half of Warrington, the one you stabbed?"

"What about him?"

"Your mate Fowler tuned up his police guard at the local hospital and sprung him out."

Kane hung up the phone and couldn't help but smile. Fowler had gone full throttle – no more pussyfooting around or chatting with the police and pretending to be a regular government investigator. Putting the gunman in the hospital had forced Fowler's hand, and for the first time, Kane felt he had won a minor victory. However, now the challenge was to determine how to deal with Fowler, who would likely be laying low, and also figure out how to get at Mjolnir.

He stared at the station and thought about boarding the next train, whether it be east to Manchester or west to Liverpool. It didn't matter once he got out of the heat in Warrington. Before he set off, Kane dialled Yelena's number on his burner.

"David, is that you?"

"Yes, look, Yelena, I…"

"I saw you on the news. Are you alright?"

"I'm fine…I…" he wanted to tell Yelena that he couldn't help her anymore, but she interrupted him again.

"I have set up the meeting with Oskar for nine o'clock tonight at his flat in Orford."

Kane sighed. "Alright, what's the address?"

TWENTY-SIX

Kane decided to pass the time in a small branch of Costa Coffee, where he opted for a large cappuccino and a scone. Kane's rucksack was placed on the chair beside him, filled with all his gear. He sat at a corner table with his back to the rest of the café so that nobody could see his face, which went against the grain. Usually, Kane's training led him to sit facing the room, scanning for exits and potential threats. He had done that when first entering the coffee shop, but he'd sacrificed having his front to the room in favour of keeping his face as hidden as possible, given that it was splashed all over the news. Of course, it was a risk going in there, but he had two hours to kill before the meeting with Yelena and Oskar.

She had called him at a quarter to eight, and Kane had left the coffee shop and made his way to the address. Oskar's flat was on the ground floor of a two-story block situated next to a strip of road facing a triangle of grassland. Ten flats stretched along the block, each one with old, rotten, wooden facias. The white paint on them was cracked, peeling, and covered with graffiti. Kane had jumped into a taxi at the train station with his head down and taken the route to Orford, a dense suburban area in Warrington close to the town centre. He followed Yelena through an entranceway. It was like an alley, a dark opening in the brickwork between two flats, and she buzzed a keypad on the left-hand side of the entrance. There was no answer, so she buzzed it again.

Kane waited patiently. His plan was to meet with Oskar, warn him to keep away from the Deli Boys and then leave Warrington for good. He felt sorry for Yelena. Kane wasn't sure whether it was her plight, the difficulty of adjusting to a new life, or her pretty eyes. When there was no answer to the second buzz, Yelena looked around at Kane and smiled nervously. She took out her mobile and dialled Oskar's number on the speakerphone. It rang out before cutting to a standard network provider voicemail recording.

"Is he usually late when you two have arranged to meet?" asked Kane.

"No, we are very close," Yelena replied. She put the phone away and shifted from foot to foot, fiddling with a loose strand of her hair. Kane leaned in and pressed another button on the keypad. Each had a number for the flat it related to.

"Yes?" said a woman's voice in a West African accent a few moments later.

"I forgot my outside key. Can you buzz me in?" said Kane. He spoke in a laid-back, confident manner. Too polite would sound suspect, as would a story about a friend needing him to be let in. The door buzzed, and the lock clicked. Kane pushed it, held it open for Yelena, and followed her in. The corridor was dark, an overhead spotlight flickered, and another was out completely. Bike handlebar marks of various colours scuffed the beige-painted walls, and the floor was grey linoleum with dark stains visible in the half-light.

Yelena led him to a dark pine door with a silver number four screwed to the front.

"Look," she said, pointing to the doorframe. The door was slightly ajar, and Kane held his arm out to ease her gently away from it. The situation was suspicious. Oskar hadn't answered his door or phone, and his front door had been left open. Kane had that familiar tingle on the back of his neck, the slight churn in his belly which told him to be careful. "What's wrong?" she put a shaking hand to her mouth, her eyes fixed on Kane. He considered taking the pistol from his rucksack, but the room was quiet and going in armed would likely send Yelena into a fit of terror. Kane judged the risk to be low, and he slowly pushed the door open and stepped inside. Yelena came through behind him, and he reached over her shoulder and pulled the door closed. He wanted to hear it opening if anyone came in behind them.

He followed a narrow hallway with two closed doors on either side and an open door at the end. Kane opened the door to his right first and peered inside. A bedroom with an unmade bed. Kane checked behind the door, and once he was happy the room was empty, he opened the door on the hallway's left side. A bathroom, musty and heavy with damp, but again empty. Now he was sure he wouldn't leave any unchecked rooms behind him, Kane moved ahead. He went through the door at the end of the hallway. It led to a sitting room area, and Kane stepped inside. To the left was a kitchenette, and to the right, there were two sofas facing towards a large screen TV.

Kane stepped towards the sitting room and abruptly halted when he spotted a pale hand draped over the armrest of a sofa. He moved closer and cursed under his breath.

"Oskar!" Yelena cried out. Her brother was dead. He lay on the couch in the foetal position, his legs and arms curled into himself with one hand over the armrest. His skin was pallid, and a needle hung from his left forearm. Yelena howled in sorrow. She stamped her foot, and her entire body shook with the horrifying discovery. Kane pulled her close to him, and she buried her face in his chest. Kane looked over Oskar's corpse as he held her there, feeling her sobs against his body and the wetness of her tears through his shirt. It was a classic drug overdose scene, the needle was still in Oskar's arm, and a belt was pulled tight around his bicep. But Oskar's arm was free of the track marks Kane would expect to see on a drug addict. There would be old needle punctures tracking the veins up the inside of his forearms unless this was Oskar's first time taking heroin or he was new to the drug. But why would he leave his front door open if that were the case?

"Was Oskar using drugs?" asked Kane.

Yelena shook her head and looked up at him, her face streaked with tears, black mascara smudged around her eyes. "He smoked pot, maybe used some cocaine, but so does everyone. He wouldn't take this kind of drug. I know him. He is my brother."

Was your brother, Kane thought.

Oskar's face was as white as fresh milk, but there were contusions around his eye and the bloom of a fresh bruise on his throat beneath his left ear. The coffee table in front of the sofa was askew, a remote control lay on the carpet, along with a beer can. Evidently, a struggle had taken place in the room. Kane noticed a bright green takeaway menu with the name 'Rambo's' emblazoned across the top lying next to Oskar's body on the sofa. The Deli Boys. They'd come to get their money early. Perhaps in revenge for Kane's attacks upon them, but they had killed Oskar and made it look like an overdose. The menu was a calling card that served as a clear warning: mess with us, and we strike twice as hard. Kane had asked them about paying Oskar's debt and had stolen their gang member's car. He had tried to provoke them, and it had worked, but on a scale he had thought was beyond the Deli Boys. He had underestimated them, and that had cost Yelena a brother and Oskar his life. Kane was used to dealing with terrorist organisations, soldiers and government agents, not gangsters. He wouldn't make that mistake again. Craven wanted Kane to leave the Deli Boys alone, to walk away, but he couldn't do that now. Instead, he would treat the gang like he would treat any target in his old line of work.

"Call an ambulance," said Kane. "I am sorry for your loss."

"My brother is dead. How could he do this to us? Take filthy drugs like this? I will have to call my mama. She will be heartbroken," Yelena whimpered through sharp intakes of breath, still crying uncontrollably. She took off her small bag and rummaged inside it until she found a tissue.

She put the bag down on the coffee table and wiped her nose.

"Oskar didn't take heroin, or die from an overdose, Yelena. The Deli Boys did this. They killed him and made it look like an overdose. Get a drink of water from the kitchen and then call an ambulance and the police."

She agreed, then shook her head in disbelief. Yelena glanced at Oskar's body and made the sign of the cross, then shuffled towards the kitchen area. Kane took the folded cash from his suit jacket pocket and counted out four hundred pounds. He placed it inside Yelena's bag and strode out of the room. He didn't look back, didn't stop. Kane left the flats and made for the main road. The Deli Boys were vicious thugs, capable of a greater level of violence than Kane had anticipated. But now he would bring them a war they wouldn't believe.

TWENTY-SEVEN

Craven drank a cup of awful coffee, two and a half spoons of instant with a drop of milk. It was like tar, but it would keep him alert. Craven preferred tea, but coffee was the only way to get him through another whiteboard briefing. He downed the coffee from a novelty Doctor Who mug and left it in the canteen sink. The staff room was empty, but uniformed officers jogged in both directions outside the window, darting around one another, their radios crackling with words Craven couldn't make out through the glass. He left the staff room and set off towards the meeting room allocated to the Serious and Organised Crime Squad.

Jess, the constable from the floor by Kirkby's office, came dashing towards him, wearing her full tactical vest and gear for street work.

"Jess!" Craven called to her. She flashed a quick smile but didn't look like she was going to stop. "What's going on?"

She paused and looked at him, eyes wide with excitement. "They've found Langley."

A stab of panic hit Craven's head as he worried that his collusion with the fugitive might be exposed. "Found him where?"

"A landlady at a B&B recognised his face and called it in. He's staying there. All units are scrambling now." She smiled again broadly and rushed off.

Craven marched through the station and into the whiteboard meeting. Thoughts scrambled inside his head. He considered warning Kane but decided it would be wiser to stay out of it for now. He'd work the case in the hope it would all blow over.

"Did you hear?" said Shaw as Craven sat down next to him.

"I heard."

"Looks like we'll get home at a decent hour this evening, then. Turns out the bugger was laying low in a B&B in Warrington town centre all along, and we've been turning the town upside down."

Craven's phone rang. An unknown number. He ground his teeth.

"What time does this briefing start?"

"Two minutes."

Craven stood up and walked to the back of the room.

"Craven," he said as he answered the phone.

"Detective Craven," came a polished voice with an edge of roughness to it. "This is Fowler. It's time you and I had a proper chat."

Craven massaged his forehead. "What about?"

"About Kane. You know where he is. You've been in touch with him this entire time. Don't try to deny it. I know, so don't waste my time."

Craven glanced around the room. It was filling up, and if Kirkby walked in and found Craven on his phone, he would have a hissy fit. Craven put the phone on his shoulder and marched out of the room into the corridor. Heat rushed into his cheeks, a sudden fear that Fowler had hacked his phone records.

"Fuck off, Fowler," he hissed into the phone, striding away from the meeting room. "I don't know where he is, and you aren't police or MI5, so I don't have to share any information with you."

"That's not very nice now, is it?" Fowler's voice drawled, a mocking tone to every word.

"We're on to you as well, storming the hospital like that. We've liaised with MI5 and MI6, and nobody there knows who you are. You're a fraud, Fowler, and we are hunting you."

Fowler laughed. "Good luck with that. I had hoped we could do this amicably. But I see now that you are nothing more than a fool stuck in a low-ranking job. You have no prospects of promotion; your career has peaked with a whimper. I've seen your file, Frank. Your Chief Inspector is right about you – you're a belligerent has-been. A relic of the old police, back when you could force a confession with a phone book to the back of a suspect's head. You are a fool who thinks it's clever to be rude to your colleagues and superiors and eke out a mediocre career living on former glories."

"Listen here, you jumped up fucking shitbag…" Craven caught himself. He was shouting, and the noise would carry. He hunched into the phone, body tensed for an outpouring of vitriol.

"So maybe I'll pay your lovely wife a visit instead."

Craven almost dropped the phone, and his breath caught in his chest. "What did you say?"

"Barbara. She's a sweetheart. I could pick her up at the school where she works, or better still, meet her at your house. Your garden is lovely, by the way. Maybe Barbara can tell me where I can find Kane?"

"You go anywhere near my wife, and…"

"And what, Craven? Call Kane and arrange to meet him, then give me the location. Do it today and call me back or I'll cut your wife's throat so deep my knife blade will scrape off her spine. There will be so much blood in your house that the walls will need replastering. Think about that, Frank."

Craven kept the phone to his ear even though the call had ended. He was frozen in terror. An image of Barb with her throat cut swamped him. Visions of his blood-soaked house forced their way into his thoughts like a scene from a horror film. Craven's mouth opened and closed silently like a landed fish. After a moment, he put the phone back in his pocket and stumbled back into the briefing on unsteady legs.

"Nice of you to join us, Craven," Kirkby jeered. He stood next to the whiteboard, marker pen in hand and a sour look straining his face.

"Jesus, you look like you've seen a ghost," whispered Shaw as Craven plonked down into the chair beside him.

Craven stared at the whiteboard. But all he could think about was Kane, Fowler, and the woman he had loved for as long as he could remember. Was it even a choice at all?

TWENTY-EIGHT

Kane marched out of Piccadilly station with his head down and a cap pulled low. It was a simple black Nike cap he had bought in Warrington on his way to the train station. Kane's face was plastered all over the newspapers and TV news stations. He was a fugitive wanted for murder and reported to be armed and dangerous. There had been a heavy police presence at Warrington's train station. Armed police with German Shepherd dogs patrolled each platform. Trains ran hourly from Warrington to Manchester and Liverpool, with other services running to Chester, Leeds, Glasgow and Edinburgh. Kane had kept a low profile, wearing his suit and cap, looking like a businessman travelling into the city rather than a jittery criminal on the run from the authorities. A desperate man would run at the sight of the police or try to hide. But Kane blended in like the grey man they had trained him to be. He had bought a copy of the financial times and sat on a bench on the platform, right under the nose of the patrolling officers who hadn't batted an eyelid as he thumbed through the large broadsheet, head down and cap low.

It was dark as Kane walked along Piccadilly Gardens, and the fountains were lit up with bright lights amongst the dancing water. In the evening, the heads down, headphones-wearing commuters were replaced with smiling, laughing groups of students heading for a night out in the city. Kane made the turn away from the polished high street and into the snarl of alleyways and lanes that twisted away from the primary thoroughfare like the back streets in a Dickens novel. Kane's pack held all of his possessions, including clothes, weapons, and spare phones. A cold fury had settled within Kane since the discovery of Oskar's body, and he came to Manchester for vengeance. The Deli Boys were a drug gang, meaning they were cash rich and would carry weapons to enforce their debts and protect themselves from rival gangs. Kane couldn't let his pursuit of the Deli Boys drop, not now that Oskar was dead. But he was sure he could use their destruction to aid his quest to eliminate Mjolnir. He would need all the money and weapons he could get to bring the fight to Fowler and Odin.

The stitching in Kane's shoulder itched with tightness and throbbed with a dull ache. As he walked, Kane rolled his neck and moved the shoulder stiffened by his old wound in a circle to loosen it up.

Mangle Street looked a little better at night than it had during daylight. Darkness cast the iron window bars and floor cobbles in the shadow and gloom that accompanied the underbelly of Manchester. Iron-grey shutters covered the windows of the Polish grocery store, but its neon sign glowed brightly in the twilight. Cars, mopeds and scooters sat outside Rambo's deli, some with motors running and American rap music pulsing from their powerful speakers, others just loitering. Men in tracksuits darted between the vehicles, moving in and out of the deli, phones stuck to their ears or shouting to their friends in a lingua franca of English, Russian, Estonian, and Polish.

Kane drew close, and a tall man wearing a black tracksuit stepped into his path with a scarf pulled up over his mouth and nose – the uniform of the hoodie-wearing gangster Kane had become familiar with since returning to the UK full-time in the protection programme. The Deli Boys were drug dealers and thieves who spent their days terrorising good people trying to go about the humdrum of their daily lives. Lives Kane had tasted in the programme, work, eat, sleep, look after kids, watch TV, repeat. He would be their avenger now, the man to stand up for kids like Oskar, who found themselves stuck in a pit of despair with no way of achieving the affluent, aspirational lives of the people they followed on Instagram, Facebook and TikTok. Kane would defend the builders, the electricians, plumbers, nurses, the people who toiled in offices and schools, banks and hospitals. He could do what the police could not.

Kane kept to his path, letting his shoulder hit the tall man in the tracksuit, and was rewarded with a Jamaican-sounding curse he didn't understand. Kane strode into the deli and tossed his rucksack onto the tiled floor. Faces turned to stare at him from beneath hoods and scarves, gold and silver jewellery glittering under the ceiling lights.

"I'm looking for Aivar and Rasmus," Kane stated, not addressing anyone in particular but speaking loudly enough to talk to them all. They met him with silence, then laughter. A short man with a groomed beard slid from a plastic bench and swaggered towards Kane. The other gang members gathered behind him, rubbing their hands and grinning like hyenas following their alpha.

"Fuck off, boomer," said the short man, his voice deep and heavily accented. He sucked his teeth and looked Kane up and down. "You came to the wrong place tonight..."

The short man could not finish his sentence. The time for talk was over. Kane grabbed a fistful of the short man's tracksuit top, the velvety feel of it soft in his hands, and dragged him into a vicious headbutt; the blow made even more destructive because as the short man came forward, Kane kicked out his right shin so that the thug fell into Kane's forehead. The Deli Boy's body weight caused his cheekbone to shatter against Kane's rocklike skull. Kane kept the short man moving, using the momentum to swing him around, trip his standing foot and throw the man out of the deli window.

The large pane of glass exploded with a crash that sent everyone there diving for cover. Shards of it twinkled on the tiled floor like droplets of ice, and Kane grabbed another Deli Boy and broke his nose with the heel of his right hand. Most of the young men and women in the deli scarpered then, running low, heads down and backs curved, darting away from Kane like whipped dogs. Mopeds and scooters hummed into action as they fled. A muscled man with a shaved head snarled and ran at Kane, wanting to use his bulk to drive Kane down so that he could smother him with his steroid-enhanced chest and biceps. But Kane simply stepped into him and threw the man over his hip, keeping hold of his wrist and stepping over the arm as the thug crashed to the floor. Kane broke the man's arm with an audible crack and left the man crying out in agony. A few braver Deli Boys who had gathered around the muscle man fled, leaving Kane alone in Rambo's, save for four men behind the counter. They were big men, snarling at him with vicious eyes and scarred faces. Men with tattoos rippling up forearms and sneaking out of t-shirts to crawl up their necks.

The counter flipped open on the far right side, a knife blade glinted, and the dull wood of a baseball bat slapped into an open palm.

"Where are Aivar and Rasmus?" Kane asked, only half expecting an answer. His heart pounded, enjoying the adrenaline coursing through his veins.

A skinny man wearing a white vest, with tattoos covering his arms and neck, came at Kane with a kitchen knife. He lunged, and Kane caught his wrist, twisted it savagely, and kicked his attacker in the groin. As the tattooed man doubled over, Kane kneed him in the face and pushed him back into the next man, the thug wielding the baseball bat. The tattooed man fell into him, and before he had time to recover and swing his bat, Kane launched himself into both of them, beating them with his fists, knees and feet. Punching and kicking them savagely until they fell to the floor, curled up in whimpering balls. Kane stepped over them, sweat running down his face from the exertion. At that moment, one of the remaining gang members ran through the rear office and out of a fire door. The only Deli Boy left licked his lips and just shook his head at Kane as if to say 'No thanks'.

Kane pointed at the office, and the remaining Deli Boy complied. There were piles of cash in shoe boxes, a money-counting machine, and an open laptop.

"Put the password in," said Kane, pointing at the laptop. The man was larger than Kane with bright blue eyes and obviously more intelligent than his fellow gang members because he understood what Kane was. He saw a man trained for violence, a soldier and a warrior who had lived his life fighting men similarly trained. He typed the password into the laptop, and Kane took it from him. It was a MacBook Air with several spreadsheets open in the background. Kane reset the password to one of his own choosing and closed the laptop.

"Aivar and Rasmus are at Diego's, their bar in town," said the man, holding his hands up.

"Have you got a lighter?" asked Kane, noting an ashtray thick with stinking cigarette butts on the table. The man nodded and handed Kane a Clipper lighter.

Kane left Rambo's with a blaze kindling in the kitchen, a fire that would tear down the deli and home of the gang who had mercilessly killed Oskar and made Yelena's life a misery. They were drug dealers, pimps and human traffickers, and now it was their turn to suffer. Kane carefully stowed the laptop and as much of the cash as possible in his rucksack. Then, with a determined stride, he marched across town towards the bar, where he could finally find Aivar and Rasmus.

TWENTY-NINE

It was late, and Craven drank another cup of coffee. The enormous tub of Nescafe granules was nearly empty, and the police force would grind to a halt if it ran out. Craven was sure he wouldn't sleep for a week if he drank anymore. He had just left another whiteboard meeting, where Kirkby had thrown a shit fit about their lack of progress in finding Langley. He was especially tetchy since the B&B lead hadn't resulted in Langley's apprehension. The Chief Inspector had raged about how they were making him look like a tool in front of the top brass and how many eyes were on their work at the moment. Although Craven heard the words coming from Kirkby's red, increasingly vein-popping face, the call from Fowler dominated his mind.

Craven's first reaction to the call had been to run for his car and hurtle home to Barb so that he could protect her. But, if Fowler knew where she was and wanted to kill her, she would already be dead. So, instead, he had called his wife, putting on his best act of relaxed boredom and asked if she was alright. His heart had leapt when she answered the phone with the usual.

"Hello love, are you alright?"

Craven then made some small talk and told her he would be working late. Since then, all he had thought of was what to do about Fowler. He hardly knew Kane, yet he loved Barb with all his heart, so the answer seemed simple: set up a meeting, tell Fowler where it would be, and leave them to it. Only it wasn't that simple. Kane was a dangerous man, a killer. What if he got the better of Fowler? Kane would know that Craven had set him up and come looking for revenge. Craven pondered whether he could set Fowler up – a sting. After all, he was a detective. He could send Fowler to a location and spring a trap, maybe pin Kane's murders on Fowler and be rid of the smarmy bastard for good. Craven frowned at the coffee and tossed it down the sink. He needed to think clearly and make the right decision. Craven leaned over and ran the cold tap. He splashed the cool water on his face twice and then dried himself with a sheet of kitchen towel.

"Feeling the burn, guv?" said a polite female voice.

Craven turned and smiled at Jess. Her two

uniformed friends went and sat at a round table in the canteen, and she clicked the kettle on beside the sink.

"I think we all are," he replied, trying to sound upbeat.

"There was another sighting a while ago at a sports shop in Warrington town centre."

"Why are there never sightings reported to us at the actual time when a suspect is present?"

"One of the joys of police work," she quipped dryly and chuckled.

"He's likely long gone by now."

"Do you think?"

"A man like that would hardly stick around a little town like Warrington with all this heat on him."

Craven's phone rumbled in his pocket. He mouthed an apology to Jess and turned away to take the call.

"Craven here."

"Craven, it's Shaw."

"I know it's you. Your name came up on the phone."

"Err, yeah, sorry, Craven. Anyway, there's been a hit on the Deli Boys in Piccadilly."

"What kind of hit?"

"Some fella waltzed in there and nicked all of their cash, roughed them up a bit and burned the place down."

"When?"

"Just now, it came in over the radio, and it got sent over to us because it's the Deli Boys, and they're on our watch list."

"I'll get over there now."

"I'll come with you."

"No, you stay here in Warrington, Shaw. Best if you stay on the Langley thing. I'll head to Manchester now."

"But it could be Langley?"

"I'll check it out I said." Craven hung up. For a heartbeat, he thought about sending a message to Fowler to let him know Kane was in Manchester, but he put his phone away. Kane was doing more damage to the Deli Boys than the police had managed in two years. If Craven could talk to Kane and get a lead on what he knew about the gang, he could make the big collar he needed for his promotion. Maybe he could even persuade Kane to turn himself in. There no going back for Kane now, not after all the carnage he had wrought in Warrington and now in Manchester. But Craven couldn't contact Kane, not whilst he kept on changing numbers. So, he would get himself over to Manchester, get close to whatever Kane was doing to the Deli Boys and hope Kane got in touch with him before Fowler called.

"Fancy working with Serious Crimes?" said Craven, turning back to Jess, who'd just finished up with the kettle.

"Me?" Jess almost stammered, her eyes lighting up like a child on Christmas morning.

"Yes, come on. I need to get to Manchester in a squad car. You can drive. It's all kicking off with a gang we are investigating. There could be a link to Langley."

THIRTY

Fowler stowed his Sig Sauer Pistol and automatic Heckler and Koch MP5 sub-machine gun in a navy holdall with the rest of the team's equipment. Barnes placed a handful of flash-bang grenades on top and zipped it closed. The team all wore dark tactical clothing, combat trousers and t-shirts, and Krasinski held their tactical vests slung over his right arm.

"Ready?" said Fowler.

"Are we sure about this?" asked Barnes, rolling his muscled neck.

"McCann?" said Fowler, fixing Barnes with a hard stare.

"Once we got Jacobs' number from the DI's phone..." McCann uttered, hands on hips and frowning at having to repeat an update she had already provided once before, "...I could track the signal to this address. Jacobs has visited the address three times since I've been tracking him. It must be the place. Satellite imagery also shows a military presence around the building."

"I don't doubt your ability or how thorough you have been," said Barnes. He looked around at the rest of the team. "But this means we are going up against our own. Against MI6, or British Army, or whatever operators Jacobs has protecting Kane's family."

"So?" said Fowler.

"It's one thing doing what we do abroad, but I'm not sure I want to kill our own."

"If you haven't got the bottle, stay here, and I'll report it to McGovern. I'm sure Odin can reassign you to less rigorous work?"

"Hold on, I didn't…"

"He's got a point," muttered Krasinski. He spoke with a broad Welsh accent, was impeccably fit, and had a shiny black beard covering the lower half of his face. "I don't fancy fighting against our own, either. They could be men from the Regiment."

Fowler sighed and massaged his forehead. "Why do you think it's so important that we terminate Kane? He isn't just another target. Kane knows the things we do, what we have done. He was one of us. He's already provided statements, which the Ministry of Defence only just got under lock and key before they saw the light of day. How do you think the new woke world would react to what we did in Sudan? Afghanistan? Syria? Never mind the work in South America. Do you think they would understand? Offer you a medal?" Fowler paused and met each of their eyes. He glanced at the three new recruits to their team. "You three are new, but you're part of the team now. We are a covert unit specialising in counterintelligence ops. We are clandestine, unsanctioned, and beyond the law. But we won't have a saviour or a get-out clause if we are arrested or compromised. There won't be any military protection, either. Our lives will be fucking over, and Odin will gladly take us out. And that's if we even make it that far before another team comes in to put us down. So get your fucking heads together, and let's get the job done."

"But do we really have to go after his family?" asked Nketiah, one of the new team members. She looked at Barnes for support, then at McCann, before returning her gaze to Fowler.

"Not you as well." Fowler stormed across the room and squared up to Nketiah, staring down into her eyes. "We follow orders. No questions asked. You signed up for that to protect your country and your people by any means necessary. To battle all enemies, foreign and domestic. Do you have a problem with that?"

"No, sir." Nketiah squared her shoulders and met his eye, her lips pursing and muscles shifting beneath her cheeks as her teeth clenched.

"Then get in the van with the others. Go. But not you, Barnes."

The rest of the team marched out of the apartment, leaving only Barnes and Fowler.

"I want Kane gone just as much as you," said Barnes. "But don't tell me you are completely comfortable fighting our own countrymen?"

"I never said I was comfortable with it. I hate it. This whole op is a disaster, but we just need to get it done and move on. You said you wanted out after this one? You asked me to talk to Odin about you? How can I do that if you can't follow orders?"

Barnes sighed and shook his head. "After this job, I'm out, but I'd rather go with everyone's blessing."

Fowler placed his hand on Barnes' shoulder. "Remember all the shit we've been through together over the years? Let's just finish this one, and I'll help you get out, I promise. But first, we have to put Kane in the ground."

THIRTY-ONE

Kane left the deli in flames and headed for Diego's, making the twenty-minute walk across the city centre towards Deansgate Locks, which a quick Google search told him was the bar's location. As Manchester's nightlife kicked into full flow, Kane followed the canal westwards and found the bar nestled between two similar establishments beneath the dark brick arches of an embankment. The area was vibrant, with restaurants, bars, and clubs. Uber cabs and private cars thronged the busy roads, and crowds of young people moved from bar to bar, laughing and shouting amongst pulsing music, bright signs and flashing lights.

Kane found an alley two streets away from Deansgate Locks and stowed his rucksack in a culvert behind a racing green dumpster. Kane left his pistol in the bag but took his knife with him, securing it in his right sock in case door security frisked him on his way into the bar. He wore his black suit and jumper and ran his fingers through his hair. Kane took out his burner phone and sent two text messages, one to Sally to check in, asking how she and the kids were holding up, and one to Craven to let him know he had ignored his recommendation and had made his move against the Deli Boys. No doubt Craven and the force could extract some useful information from the laptop he had taken from the deli. He asked Craven if he wanted to meet and put the phone back in his jacket pocket.

Kane approached the double doors to Diego's, which were transparent like glass and fronted by two enormous men in black trousers and t-shirts two sizes too small for their monstrous frames. Even though the evening was warm enough for t-shirts, they both wore black leather gloves and stood behind a thick red rope and golden posts. Rhythmic dance music rumbled from within, and the sign sprawled above the doors like an extravagant signature. The two doormen stared at Kane impassively, both men sporting full sleeve tattoos on their arms and matching shaved heads. He smiled as the leftmost bouncer unclipped the red rope and nodded Kane through the double doors.

The music inside the bar was much louder than anything Kane was used to, and he wondered how any of the patrons held a conversation in the place without shouting at each other. It was more like a nightclub with two floors comprising a bar area, some seating and a large dancefloor on each. Kane could see the first floor and the stairway from the entrance, but the ground floor was filled with people dancing, talking, and waiting to be served at the bar. Kane assumed that Aivar and Rasmus would be in a VIP area on either floor, so he took a deep breath and walked over to the dancefloor. He wove between the gyrating bodies, women in short skirts and tight tops, men in skin-tight trousers and expensive shirts.

A long-haired man slopped beer onto Kane's shoes, but he ignored him and slipped through a gang of women wearing bridal headgear and learner driver plates pinned to their dresses. The hen party was jumping up and down and drinking cocktails, and as Kane made his way through the group, he found the rear of the ground floor but couldn't see any sort of VIP area. To save himself a wasted trip upstairs and just in case there was some sort of backroom in which Aivar and Rasmus might bring their crew to drink, he strolled over to the bar and caught the eye of a young glass collector. The lad leaned forward when Kane beckoned to him to ask where the VIP room was, and the glass collector pointed upstairs. Kane thanked him and returned across the shifting shapes of the dance floor and up the metal stairway.

The first floor was of a similar layout to the one below, a long bar on the left-hand side and a dancefloor area, but beyond the bar was a raised platform where two huge bouncers stood guard on either side of a red rope which marked out what looked like a VIP area. Kane couldn't see between the gyrating bodies on the dancefloor or through the flashing darkness to make out who was in the raised area, but then again, he didn't know what Aivar or Rasmus looked like. All he knew was they would suffer for what the Deli Boys had done to Oskar and Yelena.

Kane went to the bar and waited to be served behind two women in shorts. The pair bought gin and tonics and nodded their heads in time with the pumping music as they made their way towards the dancefloor.

"Bottle of Bud, mate," Kane said to the barman, leaning over to be heard above the din. The barman turned and pulled a red-labelled bottle from a back bar fridge.

"Fiver, mate," nodded the barman with a smile. Kane pulled a ten-pound note out of his jacket pocket and handed it over.

"Who're the VIPs then?"

"The owners, mate."

"Who owns this place, then? They must be making a fortune?"

"Estonian lads. I'd give them a wide berth if I were you."

"Thanks. Keep the change."

The barman nodded appreciatively, and Kane glugged back a mouthful of beer. There could be no stealth in this type of environment, no strategy or plan of attack. Just like his attack on the deli, the only way to get this done in a busy bar was by using brute force. Kane walked along the length of the bar towards the VIP area, and the crowd cheered as a new song came over the speakers. Kane didn't recognise it. Just as he neared the end of the bar, a commotion on the dance floor caught his eye. Kane turned to see a group of four men in tracksuits bustling through the sea of people, pushing the dancers out of the way and making a beeline for the VIP area. It was the Deli Boys. Arriving, at last, to bring their leader news of the attack on their headquarters. The four men gesticulated at the bouncers, who removed the red rope by its golden clip and let them in.

Kane approached slowly. Inside the VIP area, several men were standing around while a group of people were sitting on velvet couches, five of which were glamorous-looking women. The Deli Boys were talking to a large man in a black suit. He had a broad, flat face and dark eyes with heavy black rings beneath them. The man beside him was smaller and wore chinos and a polo t-shirt with a gold chain around the collar. He struck one of the Deli Boys hard enough to make the man stumble, and the slapped man held a hand to his face, glancing behind him at the people on the dancefloor, checking if anyone had witnessed his humiliation and damage to what the man probably thought was his bad-boy reputation.

Kane stopped and leant against the bar holding his beer, and as the slapped man turned to face his bosses again, his eye caught Kane's. It was one of those brief moments across a busy room, a fleeting connection, but there was recognition in it. The slapped man's hand fell away from his face and pointed slowly at Kane. His lips moved, mouthing the words, 'That's him'.

Kane froze, the dance music dimming to a dull thump in his head. The familiar heat in his belly churned with the onset of unease, the knowledge that men who wanted to hurt him had spotted him. Instinct told Kane to fear the violence to come. The inbuilt human reflex was to run away from the risk of broken bones, cuts to his skin, and the likelihood of suffering or death. They were all feelings Kane was used to, feelings that his training had taught him to welcome. Kane could turn them into a heightened state of awareness, using the threat against those who would harm him. So, as the men inside the VIP area surged to their feet and the brutish bouncers lunged in his direction, Kane did not run. He attacked.

THIRTY-TWO

Fowler rapidly crossed the field double time, holding his sub-machine gun in front of him with its barrel pointed downwards. He wore night vision goggles on his forehead, utilising the natural moonlight to navigate through the channels cut into the soil. His gun had a torch fixed to the barrel, but to shine that now would let everybody at the farmhouse know that Fowler and his team were coming. To his left and right, the team advanced in the same way, a fast-moving crouch with their weapons ready, continuously moving their barrels in sweeps to cover the surrounding area.

They came within two kilometres of the farmhouse, and the team fanned out into a triangular formation without Fowler having to issue an order. They were experienced, professional, and moved like a spear with Fowler at the tip. Fowler pulled down his night vision goggles, which sometimes were a pain to wear because the sight it gave could be distorted depending on how busy the area was. They were perfect for use in an enemy house, base, or compound with walls and human targets, but in the jungle or forest, there was often too much background movement for them to be completely effective. These particular goggles, however, also had body heat sensor technology so Fowler could make out three glowing figures patrolling the farmhouse perimeter, but he could not see beyond the house itself or what lay beyond surrounding structures. McCann's satellite imagery had shown two large barns and a long stall for horses on the western side of the farmhouse.

Fowler sensed the team moving outwards, broadening the width of their line to encircle the farmhouse and its building, securing the perimeter before they entered the house itself. Fowler led seven operators across the heavy field, four of his trusted team plus the three newer bodies; Nketiah, Anderson, and Nolan. None of them had anticipated this kind of mission when they'd first enlisted in the Army or Navy and later joined the Special Operations forces. When Fowler had signed up for the army officer training programme after leaving school, he had certainly never envisioned himself attacking a farmhouse in the UK's northwest and attempting to take a woman and her children hostage. But he had been young then, naïve about the world and the actions required to keep his country safe. This was just another job, and one Fowler would execute with his usual ruthless efficiency.

A glowing figure emerged from a dark, sprawling structure ahead which looked like a tree through the distortion of Fowler's night vision goggles. He was within a kilometre of the farm and moved swiftly and silently towards it like a wolf descending on a flock of sheep. His heart thumped evenly, the sound of it echoing in his right ear beneath the earpiece of his headset. Each operator in his team wore a headset, but they would work in silence unless a dire need for comms arose.

Within half a kilometre, Fowler paused, waiting for a glowing figure to amble past the tree again. A guard on his or her rounds. Then, Fowler closed the distance at a run, keeping his weapon raised and ready to strike. The glowing figure grew larger, and Fowler clicked off the safety of his weapon and squeezed a quick burst of three shots. The MP5SD spat the subsonic rounds out of its integrated suppressor, and the glowing figure crumpled to the dirt. Another guard to that sentry's right fell shortly after.

Fowler lifted his night vision goggles to the resting position on his forehead and leapt nimbly over the gorse hedge which separated the field from the farmhouse yard. His right boot slipped slightly on the muddy dirt track that served as the farm's driveway. He paused momentarily, waiting for the team to complete their sweep of the farm and its buildings. So far, everything had followed the plan that Fowler had laid out earlier that day. The guards were neutralised, and all that remained was the house itself. Despite his misgivings about fighting on home turf, Fowler had felt nothing when he shot the sentry. It had been just like shooting on the range.

Fowler had been combat active for so long that it was just one long string of numbness. Only his first few kills had resonated with his conscience. In Afghanistan, there had been sleepless nights when Fowler had killed his first enemy soldier. Sorrow for the taking of a life, wrestling with the morality and significance of the man's death. Fowler had imagined the man as a father and a son, as being a good man loved by his family, who was simply fighting to protect his homeland. The more experienced hands in the Regiment had quickly disabused the younger Fowler of those sentiments. It was just another Terry Taliban who needed putting down – a threat and a potential terrorist. Two more kills, and Fowler became numb to it. He was simply a tradesman. After all, does the fisherman feel remorse for every fish he catches?

The farmhouse sat in darkness save for a light in the hall behind the front door. A security light reflected the moonlight on the right-hand side of the property, ready to activate upon any approach towards the house. Two black SUVs were parked ten paces from the door, reminding Fowler that he would have liked a day to properly reconnoitre the place before attacking, but time was against him. There could be anything from two to ten armed operators inside the house, and they would need to be careful in the inevitable fight inside the front door. Fowler's priority was to keep Kane's family alive. Their capture would quickly bring this entire sorry episode to a close. A simple bait-and-catch operation. Kane wouldn't be able to resist coming to his family's aid, and when he did, Fowler would send his old friend to hell.

The hall light switched off, and Fowler clenched his back teeth. McCann had cut the power to the building as planned. Time to go. Fowler swore under his breath for allowing himself to think of Kane as his friend. He remembered looking at pictures with Kane in a base camp deep in the desert, snaps of Kane's wife and his babies. They had smiled together at how much Kane's daughter resembled Sally and how Kane was excited to get back and see his family. Fowler had never met Kane's wife or kids, but suddenly the operation became more personal, harder. For a moment, Fowler wondered if he'd really needed to go to this extreme level so soon and whether he should have waited for Craven to arrange the meet-up with Kane.

"Ready?" hissed a voice. Fowler turned, and Barnes stared back at him, his camouflage-painted face dark, his scarred lip twisted away from his teeth.

Fowler exhaled the doubt from his body. Kane was his enemy, the enemy of his country, and he had orders to bring him down by any means necessary.

"Ready." Fowler ran towards the farmhouse and broke procedure. Rather than wait for his team to follow him and execute a proper door entry, he let his anger swell, and he kicked the front door open, throwing a flash-bang grenade inside. Barnes followed him, and they pressed themselves against the outer wall. The grenade went off, followed by shouts and groans from within. Fowler readied his finger on the trigger and resolutely went inside.

THIRTY-THREE

The first bouncer reached Kane with a glint in his eye and a snarl on his sunbed-tanned face. His muscled shoulders bunched beneath his t-shirt, and he came on running, aiming to tackle Kane to the ground with his monstrous size. Kane sidestepped him and smashed a bottle of Budweiser on the bouncer's face. The bottle shattered as glass met skull, and the big man crumpled to the ground. The second bouncer slowed his approach, stunned by the vicious ease with which Kane had dispatched his colleague. Kane kicked the second bouncer on the inside of his knee and punched him hard in the solar plexus. The big man's eyes bulged as he clutched at his throat, desperately trying to suck in a breath.

Kane ducked as a magnum of champagne hurtled at him from the VIP area. The glass wall behind the bar smashed as the large bottle crashed into it. The dance floor erupted into a welter of screaming and running, people pushing and scrambling to escape the sudden outburst of violence. Kane darted to his right and came up, wary of other missiles coming his way, but there was nothing but a throng of Deli Boys gathered at the edge of the VIP area. They held themselves there like a baying mob, shouting abuse, yet reluctant to engage with Kane after what he had done to the bouncers and their men at Rambo's. One of their group came forward, a mid-sized man, lean and calm. He approached Kane with his fists raised in a boxer's stance, chin low and light on his feet. Kane raised his own fists as though he would meet the boxer at his own game, but at the last moment, Kane front-kicked him in the stomach.

The thug bounced away from Kane's kick and threw a right-handed jab at his face, glancing off Kane's ear with a dull sting. Kane tried to grab the man's arm, but it whipped away too quickly and punched Kane in the ribs with his left hand. Kane doubled over and just managed to raise his arms as another attacker ran at him and aimed a kick towards his face. The shoe connected with Kane's forearm just as the boxer punched him in the side of his head. Kane fell to one knee.

Time to stop fighting fairly.

He pulled the knife from his sock and stabbed it viciously into the boxer's foot and then deep into the thigh of the man who had kicked him.

Kane lunged to his feet. The boxer hopped and howled, trying to nurse his injured foot, whilst the second man fell to the dancefloor, holding his thigh as blood pulsed from his wound and around his hands. Kane kicked him savagely in the face and stabbed the boxer in the shoulder and stomach with his knife in short, rapid bursts.

"I'm here for Aivar and Rasmus," Kane shouted above the music and pointed the blood-stained blade of his knife at the VIP area. "Anyone who doesn't want to die should leave now."

Two of the Deli Boys took a step back from the leaders, and the big man in the suit pointed at Kane and barked an order at his men. Three of them came for him, and one in a t-shirt and gold chain pulled a butterfly knife from his pocket, flicking it around elaborately until the glinting blade showed in his fist.

"What the fuck do you want?" asked the man wielding the knife, holding the other two back from their advance.

"I want Aivar and Rasmus. For what you did to Oskar in Warrington and what you tried to do to his sister."

"I'm Rasmus," he said with a smirk. "Who the fuck is Oskar?"

"He's the prick over in Warrington who owed

us money," piped a thug to Rasmus' left, sporting a tattoo of a tear on his cheek. "Aivar sent a crew to send a message after this one attacked Kris and stole his car."

Rasmus shrugged as though he didn't care about Oskar's death. There was no remorse for how his men had made the murder look like a drug overdose and no concern about the pain it would cause Yelena and her parents back home.

"So what do you want?" Rasmus asked again. "Money?"

"Kill the bastard," shouted the big man in the suit. The pumping dance music stopped just before he opened his mouth, so the words came out ridiculously loud. He was the leader they all deferred to. He was Aivar, hulking and malevolent in his fury.

"Vengeance," Kane said as he launched himself at the three men. He moved like his old self, swift, sure and skilled. He cut and slashed with his knife, holding the blade underhand. Rasmus reeled away, clutching a gash to his stomach. The man with the tear tattoo fell to the ground with Kane's knife in his kneecap, and the blade was so deep in the wound that his fall yanked the weapon from Kane's hand. The third man came on, and Kane allowed the Deli Boy's momentum to draw him into a throw across his hip. A bottle smashed at Kane's feet, and he rolled the falling man over to use his body as a shield. Aivar ran past him, followed by the rest of his group, leaving Kane to break the fallen man's arm with a savage twist.

Rasmus came on with his knife, the blade slashing in front of Kane's face. Dark blood soaked Rasmus' t-shirt, and his expression twisted into a rictus of hate. Kane let the knife go by him and kicked Rasmus' legs from under him. He fell to the ground, and without hesitation, Kane stamped the heel of his shoe down hard on the gangster's throat, crushing his windpipe. Rasmus turned purple as he struggled to breathe, and Kane left him to choke to death. He ran after Aivar, hurtling down the stairway and out of the bar's front door.

Blue lights lit up Deansgate Locks, and a crowd thronged the pavement and road. Kane paused as the door swung closed behind him. A clutch of five uniformed police officers approached with batons and tasers at the ready. Behind them, Craven loomed like a bear. He paced back and forth as more uniformed officers handcuffed a struggling Aivar and bundled him into the back of Craven's car. Craven locked eyes with Kane and shook his head subtly, but enough to show that this wasn't the time to be taken into custody. Immediately, Kane seized the red rope and golden poles that served as the barrier to enter the bar and hurled them at the officers before swiftly retreating back into Diego's. He burst through the doors, heart pumping, and raced back up the stairs. Kane ran past Rasmus' corpse and crashed through a set of emergency doors beyond the VIP area. Behind him, footsteps hammered on the stairs and the dancefloor, police officers shouted for him to stop, but Kane was not done yet. The Deli Boys were broken, but now he had to bring down Mjolnir, and Kane wouldn't let the police take him yet.

THIRTY-FOUR

Sally jackknifed in her bed, the sound of an explosion ringing in her ears. She sprang from underneath her duvet and ran for her bedroom door. Her bare foot slapped on the cold wood flooring of the upstairs landing, and panic flooded her senses as though she was underwater. Smoke drifted up the stairs, acrid and thick, and Sally flung open Kim's door and dashed inside. Kim was sitting up in bed, her face pale and mouth open in shock. Her tiny hands were wrapped around her ears, and a solitary tear ran down her cheek. Sally ran to Kim and scooped her up.

"It's alright, it's going to be alright," Sally whispered, half to reassure Kim and half as a prayer. She wasn't sure what had caused the noise or the smoke, but then two gunshots cannoned loudly from downstairs, and Sally let out a small, involuntary whimper. They come. Whoever it was that Jack had feared would find them, they'd arrived. "Danny!" she screamed, and a moment later, the boy came running through into Kim's room wearing his Liverpool Football Club pyjamas.

"What's going on, Mum?" he said, sobbing with fear, his mouth drawn into a terrified half-moon.

More gunfire pealed out, and all three of them jumped at the same time. Sally held her children close. She needed Jack. Violence had come for his family, and he wasn't there. Sally forced back her tears. She had to be strong for Danny and Kim.

"Wait here," she said and ran back to her room.

"No, Mummy, don't leave us!" Kim wailed after her, but Sally ran into her bedroom and grabbed her phone from the bedside table. Turning on her heel, she sprinted back towards the children and found Kim staring at her with wide, terrified eyes. Sally pulled Danny and Kim down onto the hardwood floor beside the bed, and they sat against the wall, holding each other tightly. The chaos continued in the distance with more shouting and then another burst of gunfire. The shots were loud enough to hurt Sally's ears, even though they were being fired downstairs. She had one arm each around Danny and Kim and pulled their heads into her chest. Both children had their hands over their ears, and she could feel the trembling fear pulsing through their tiny bodies. She shifted the phone in her right hand, keeping her elbow close to Danny's back. She found the last text message Jack had sent and hit reply.

The safe house is under attack. Guns fired. We are scared. Where are you?

She typed the words quickly, the clickety-clack of the letters like a tiny typewriter. Another explosion rocked the farmhouse, and Sally closed her eyes tight. She forced down a scream and held the children tighter as they wailed with terror.

"Sally," said a woman's voice from the smoke-filled hallway outside Kim's room.

Sally recognised Sarah's voice, the agent who had welcomed her and helped the kids settle into their rooms.

"In here," Sally called, and Sarah came in through the doorway. She walked backwards, a handgun held in both hands and pointed out towards the hallway.

"Stay down," Sarah said, turning to glance at Sally, and nodded when she saw that they were crouched beside the bed beneath the window. Heavy footsteps came banging up the stairs, and then another gunshot echoed, followed by the sound of a body falling on the timber staircase and sliding downwards, a groan of pain. Another shot rang out, and then silence.

"What should we do?" Sally screamed, but Sarah didn't reply. She stood in a shooting position, legs braced and her gun held out before her, trained on the stairway. Sarah's head jerked downwards, and she fired her gun. Sally couldn't stifle her cry this time. The sound of the gun firing shocked her, and Sally bit her tongue. More gunfire ensued, and plaster fell like snow from the ceiling, sprinkling on Sarah's hair.

A monstrous crash above Sally's head made her roll onto the floor, pulling Danny and Kim beneath her body. Shards of glass from the smashed window peppered Sally's back, and glistening chunks of it littered the surrounding floor. Boots thumped onto the hardwood floor less than a metre from her head, and a strange spitting sound cut through the air. Sally turned and found herself staring past a pair of black boots and saw Sarah's face as she lay on the floor. A man had come in through Kim's bedroom window and shot Sarah with a muffled weapon. The only person standing between Sally and those who had come for her was down. Horrified, Sally's gaze was fixed on Sarah's eyes, but they were empty of any spark, cold and lifeless, like those of a shark. Sarah was dead, and a trickle of blood seeped from her mouth to drip onto the wooden floor.

The boots in front of Sally turned, and she

looked up into a man's face. He had scarred lips, and his entire face was smeared with dark brown, black and green paint, like a ghoul from a nightmare.

"You're coming with us," said the man, his voice a low growl. He reached out with a gloved hand to grab Sally's shoulder. Kim screamed uncontrollably, her tiny body convulsing with fear. In his other hand was a long machine gun-type weapon, smoke drifting lazily from one end. If the man could kill Sarah so easily, Sally knew he might kill her children. Trembling, she tapped a button on her phone to record a voice memo to Jack.

"Help us!" Sally screamed.

She threw the phone onto the floor and punched the scarred man in his groin. He howled in pain, and Sally threw herself at him. Her children's lives were in danger, and she would not let this murderous bastard hurt them. She lunged at him again, but the man slapped her hard across the face. Sally gasped at the pain and fell to the floor. She went for him again, grabbing his leg and sinking her teeth into his thigh. He roared and grabbed a fistful of her hair. The scarred man tore her off his leg by her scalp and tossed her aside like a rag doll. She leapt up, screaming incoherently and maddened with white-hot rage. He stood between her and her children, and Sally howled at him, scratching, punching and kicking. She grabbed his gun and raked her nails down his face. He roared again and punched her in the stomach. The air whooshed out of her, and Sally fell to her knees, desperately trying to suck in mouthfuls of air.

"Bitch," the scarred man growled.

Sally went for him once more, trying desperately to grab his gun, but he twisted her around and pushed her away. Then, as she tried to turn back to the fight, the spitting sound filled the air, and a force threw her forward as though a horse had kicked her in the back. Sally collapsed to the floor. The dull thump in her back grew like a black hole in a space movie, its darkness creeping through her body. The strength seeped from her, and she couldn't stand up. Sally pushed her hands onto the floor, but they slipped in a thick, warm liquid. She could taste iron in her mouth. Blood. Sally gasped and twisted her head towards Danny and Kim. Her eyes became heavy, and a sadness swamped her beyond any suffering she had experienced in her life.

The scarred man picked the children up by the scruff of their pyjamas. Kim screamed and wailed and held her arms out towards Sally. Danny was stiff and silent, his eyes drinking in the horror of the farmhouse bedroom. Sally's eyelids flickered. She couldn't move. Darkness came for her, and Sally knew she was dying. A killer had taken her children, and there was nothing she could do to defend them.

Jack, please get my message. Help us...

THIRTY-FIVE

Craven looked on as twenty uniformed officers poured into the front door of Diego's in pursuit of Kane. More officers ran along the front of Deansgate Locks to get around the back and cut him off. The scene was a flurry of bright green jackets, pounding boots, sirens, and shouting that filled the air as Kane's actions brought the full force of Greater Manchester Police down upon himself.

Kane had looked straight at Craven when he appeared at the doorway, and for a disturbing moment, Craven had thought the fugitive would shout at him for help and that his scheme to enlist Kane's assistance in bringing down the Deli Boys would unravel, leaving Craven in a disastrous world of shit.

"Who is this bloke?" asked Jess. She shook her head, staring at the vast number of police cars, vans, and ambulances congregated outside the bar.

"He's fucked now, whoever he is," said Craven. There was no way Kane could escape such a heavy police presence in the city centre. He only had a few minutes' head start on the officers chasing him. "I expect they'll frogmarch him out of the front door soon enough. Now, let's get this arsewipe back to the station."

Aivar struggled against his handcuffs. Two burly men in uniform wrestled with him against the side of the police car in which Craven and Jess had travelled from Warrington to Manchester. Aivar had his back to the car, and the officers grimaced and groaned as they tried to move him away from the vehicle so that they could open the rear passenger side door and bundle him inside.

"Is he coming back with us, sir?" asked Jess, taking a step back as Aivar bucked against the officers again. Aivar spat and cursed at them in his native tongue, his voice deep, run through with gravel like the valley of a desert ravine.

"Yes, we'll get him back to Warrington. My squad is there for the Langley manhunt, so it makes more sense to take him there rather than hold him in Manchester." Craven wanted Kirkby and the rest to see him bring Aivar in. He wanted it known that the Deli Boys were his collar. It needed to be on his record for when the next opportunity for promotion came up. If he brought Aivar to Manchester, the top brass would descend like beggars on hot chips to take the glory for themselves. Craven would be nailed on for a bump-up with such a high-profile scalp under his belt. A promotion meant a better pension, which meant his and Barb's dream of a home in Spain would become a reality. Cleaner air and recovery for Barb and a peaceful retirement for Craven. He imagined himself reading books and drinking chilled wine in the sun.

"What are you charging him with?"

"For now, just possession of a weapon," he replied, snapping out of his daydream, "and then I'll go through his file, which is almost as thick as his arms, and see which of the hundreds of crimes we can stick to the bastard."

"So he's a big fish, then?"

"You could say that, yes. He founded and runs the Deli Boys, one of Manchester's dominant gangs involved in importing and distributing cocaine, heroin and marijuana. They also dabble in prostitution and human trafficking. The Deli Boys saw off some fairly grim Russian mafia gangs here in the North West and are rumoured to have beaten the fucking Triads into submission. So, that, my dear Jessica, is a genuine bad guy."

"Well, he certainly looks the part."

Aivar stepped up his struggle with the officers, driving his knee into one's groin and kicking him towards the pavement.

"For fuck's sake," Craven huffed. He punched Aivar in the liver. Aivar was taller than Craven, which meant he was a shade over six foot one and much broader across the chest and shoulders. Craven hadn't been in a gym in his life. His bulk was entirely down to genetics, meat and potato pies, and creamy pints of Guinness. Aivar, however, had the musculature of a bodybuilder and the face of a demon. The liver punch doubled him over, and Craven grabbed his meaty head, slamming it into the side of the police car. Aivar fell to his knees, dazed.

"Is that allowed?" gasped Jess, staring at Craven with a look of incredulity on her face.

"Technically, no," said Craven, standing upright and rubbing at his right shoulder. "I think I've put my bloody shoulder out. It's not in the handbook, Jess, but everybody's got their eyes on the bar and Langley, and we need to get this vermin out of here. So it's allowed in my book."

The officers bundled Aivar into the back of the police car, and Craven jumped into the passenger seat. Jess turned the engine on, and they pulled away from Diego's, heading towards Warrington. They drove along a dual carriageway without the siren or lights on, adhering to every red light they passed nearing the motorway. Jess hummed along to a Bee Gees song on the radio, and Craven sent a message to Barb to check how she was. It was late, and she might be in bed. Fowler's threat still rattled around Craven's head like a ball inside a whistle. He couldn't get rid of it. As guilty as it made him feel, Craven hoped they caught Kane in Diego's and brought him into custody. It would be over then. There would be nothing he could do to help Fowler apprehend Kane because he would already be in custody. So, Barb would be safe, and this entire sorry affair would be over.

A voice crackled on the police radio, but it was too low to make out. Craven turned the music off and turned up the volume.

"... on the rooftop. Officers in pursuit. Many injured suspects in the bar. One man dead, a known criminal names Rasmus Kask. All units form a secure perimeter around Deansgate."

Craven glanced over his shoulder at Aivar, and the gangster stared back at him through hooded eyes with an arrogant curl to his top lip. Kane had held up his part of their arrangement because the Deli Boys were effectively ruined. One of their leaders was dead, and Craven had the other in cuffs.

"Looks like your mate Rasmus is dead," said

Craven.

"He was like a brother to me," Aivar replied. He spoke slowly, carefully enunciating each word in his thick accent.

"A brother in crime. How many people had Rasmus hurt in his time? You reap what you sow."

"Rasmus came from nothing, just like me. We are Russians, born in Estonia, to live like beggars. We came to this country and built an empire with our bare hands. The man who killed my brother will suffer."

"It's going to be hard to do anything like that where you're heading, son. I'll make sure they bang you up for life if I can."

"Good riddance to bad rubbish," muttered Jess.

Aivar suddenly exploded into a rage. His head bounced off the car roof, and he bucked and spat in the backseat. "You don't talk to me, whore! I put you to work! I pimp you like you deserve. A bitch like you can't insult me. I'll fucking kill you." Aivar carried on wailing in his own language, spittle flying from his mouth like a madman.

"Calm down, you fucking idiot!" Craven shouted so loudly that Jess jumped.

Aivar snapped out of his rage and peered out of the car window. He grinned at Craven in the rearview mirror as the car came to a stop at a set of traffic lights.

"Maybe we should put the sirens on, sir," said Jess. She shifted uncomfortably in her seat and shot a glance at Aivar. "Get him into a cell?"

"Aye, go on then," nodded Craven just as a sudden movement caught his eye, and he turned to see Aivar stuff himself into the small foot space between Craven's seat and the backseat.

"What the fuck are you..." Craven began but didn't have time to complete his sentence. Bright headlights appeared from the driver's side window, illuminating Jess like an angel. Then, the sound of a car engine erupted into a deafening roar just before a vehicle slammed into the side of the police car. Craven heard the crunch and grinding twist of metal before he felt the impact. He was thrown around the cabin as the police car spun and then rolled onto its roof. Craven gasped, blacked out for a few seconds, and then awoke to find himself hanging upside down from his seatbelt.

It took Craven a few heartbeats to get his bearings, and then he noticed Jess hanging next to him. Her head flopped at an unnatural angle, and blood dripped from her ear. The rear passenger door opened a finger's width and then creaked as someone dragged it open against the press of the damaged chassis. Hands reached inside and pulled Aivar from the vehicle. Craven struggled against the seatbelt. Being upside down had sent blood rushing to his head, and he couldn't work out how to find the button to unclip himself. Aivar crawled out of the car before turning to look back at Craven and Jess through the open door.

"You were right. You reap what you sow, and the mouthy bitch is dead," spat Aivar, then he smiled at Craven and disappeared into the night.

THIRTY-SIX

Kane pushed open a heavy hatch that led to the rooftop above Diego's. The cool night air hit his face like a splash of water, and he clambered out onto the hardtop. Just as Kane let the hatch fall back into place, he caught the shouts of the pursuing police officers. They were close and would be up and out on the rooftop within minutes. Kane surged into a sprint across the rooftop. His weapons and equipment were stowed in the alley in his rucksack, but he would need to come back for that later. Killing one of the Deli Boy's top men was his way of avenging Oskar's death, but their leader yet lived. Now, the police had descended upon Deansgate like there was a giveaway at Dunkin' Donuts.

A knee-high brick wall separated Diego's roof from the next one across. Kane leapt over it and onto the next one. He headed towards an overhead railway bridge. It was huge and ran across the lock arches themselves and over the canal into the city centre. The hatch creaked and burst open behind him. Torch beams, followed by shouting, lit Kane up as he ran. His ribs and head throbbed from the fight inside the bar, and he needed to get away from the police quickly. Kane leapt over another rooftop divider and noticed that there was a significant gap between the end of the rooftops and the beginning of the railway overpass. Kane didn't hesitate. He picked up speed, pumping his arms, and drove his legs forward.

He searched the onrushing overpass pillar, picked his spot, and leapt. Fresh air wafted through his hair, and his legs moved as though he were still running. Kane collided with the old brickwork with a thud which rattled his already injured ribs, and he grasped for a black power cable with both hands. He swung to his left and scrambled his legs on the brickwork pillar, desperate to find purchase. The sound of his pursuers grew louder, and torchlight illuminated the overpass. Kane's left shoe found a nook in the brickwork, and he pushed himself upwards, using the cable to move hand over hand towards the summit. He looked down, which he had been trained not to do when climbing, but that was one thing he'd never adhered to.

The canal shone, reflecting the bright lights of Manchester at night, and onlookers thronged the pavement. Most had their phones out, videoing his escape. A fall from this height wouldn't kill him but would certainly shatter his ankles. Kane thought about dropping into the canal and swimming along its length away from the police, but it was a bad idea. They would have units everywhere and could locate him wherever he exited the water.

The rumble and screech of an approaching train rose like thunder in the distance, and Kane had to hurry. He moved from the pillar and towards the overpass itself. The thick, black cable ran the length of the concrete structure, and Kane swung across it like a monkey. His wounded shoulder burned from the exertion, and his heart leapt into his mouth as part of the cable sprang away from the iron fixings which attached it to the railway bridge. There was a gasp from below as he fell a foot, but fortunately, the cable held. He threw a leg up, jammed the toe of his shoe into the join between two enormous concrete sections and used the cable to haul himself up. Kane got his right hand onto the surface of a rough concrete slab and pulled himself up and over it. He risked a quick glance behind him. Twenty police officers stood on the rooftop from which Kane had jumped. They contemplated following him, but the leap and subsequent climb put them off, so instead, they shouted at him to halt and shone their torches at him. Kane set off again at a flat run, racing parallel to the train track. The train approached, rattling the tracks in a low hum, and the overpass shuddered beneath Kane's feet.

The train would be upon him in moments. He could cross the track in front of it and try to escape down the opposite side of the overpass, but there could easily be more police waiting to scoop him up as he descended. There was no time to think, and few options were available to him. From his rail journeys into Manchester from Warrington, Kane knew that the train approaching was most likely one of the chugging versions that stopped at every small station on the line between Liverpool and Manchester, not a super-fast intercity type of train. He kept up his pace, his breathing still even, but his muscles were aflame with exertion.

The sound of the train became like an avalanche behind him, and then it was beside him. Kane looked to his left and ran closer to it, resisting the pull on his body as it hurtled past him. If he hesitated, the train would pass, and they would catch him. So Kane let one window pass, then another, catching the time with his strides, and then threw himself at the train.

Kane's right hand gripped the bottom corner of a window. His fingers curled around the warm rubber seal just as his left leg hooked around the metal step of the carriage's door. The wind flew in his hair, and he gasped at the sheer desperation of the jump. Kane tried to get his right foot in the same position, but it banged against the side of the carriage. In a horrifying moment, just as he thought he would fall and tumble beneath the train to be crushed into oblivion, his left hand found a hold on the side of the doorway. Kane hauled himself into the space where the door would slide open to allow passengers to alight. He crouched in that space, faces staring at him openmouthed from inside the carriage. The police retreated into the distance behind him, their torches shining beneath the night sky.

"Next stop, Deansgate," came a woman's voice over the tannoy inside the carriage. Kane banged his fist on the carriage door in frustration. The next stop was a moment away, and the police would undoubtedly be on the platform waiting for him. The train slowed, brakes squealing. Kane twisted himself in the door space and reached upwards, finding a hold in the metal carriage frame, and pulled himself upwards. He planted his feet in the doorframe to thrust his body upwards and scrambled on top of the train carriage. The train slowed, and Kane knelt on its top, the city whizzing by below. Somewhere behind him, cutting through the din of the train, came the thrum of helicopter blades. Kane had to move and get under cover. The police had mobilised one of their choppers, and once it got a bead on him with its heat-sensitive night vision, there would be no escape.

The train slowed, and Kane crouched lower to stop himself from sliding off the roof. He readied himself as Deansgate station appeared below and above, its Victorian brickwork glowing orange under the city lights. Kane took a deep breath, and as the train pulled in, he made the short jump onto the station's corrugated roof. Kane kept low, moving as silently and carefully as he could, conscious that if he ran, his feet would hammer on the metal structure and give him away. He leapt over the end wall and down onto the hard, black top of the passenger entrance to the station. It curved down and away from his position, and Kane followed its contour to the lowest point. He lowered himself over the edge and dropped onto the pavement.

Kane found himself away from Deansgate's primary thoroughfare and ran across the street into a gap between two tall buildings. There were no streetlights, just shadow-dark alleys and a scrap of wasteland. Kane ran around a corner and pulled up sharply as he came face to face with the bright yellow of a police officer's uniform.

"You're him, aren't you?" said the Asian man staring back at Kane from beneath his policeman's cap. He licked dry lips beneath a silky black beard, and his hand crept towards the baton at his belt.

"Don't do that," Kane uttered. But the officer shook his head slowly. His radio crackled, and Kane shot himself down and forwards, knocking the policeman's legs out from under him and tackling him to the ground. Kane moved around his body, twisting on the hard pavement so that he came around the falling policeman's back and grabbed him in a rear chokehold. Kane locked his left forearm around his right, pressing down on the policeman's head whilst his other arm choked his throat. The man's legs scrabbled and kicked until he fell unconscious. Kane sighed. He didn't want to fight the police, but he was desperate not to be taken until he had removed the Mjolnir threat from his life. The copper would be fine when he woke up, just a bit of a sore head to go with the embarrassment of having his gear stolen.

Kane stripped the officer of his cap, tactical vest, luminous yellow coat and stab vest. He slipped the items on over his suit, pulled the unconscious policeman to the closest wall, and left him in the recovery position. The radio crackled and hummed as Kane clipped it into place on his shoulder, and he marched back the way he had come, towards Deansgate station. Kane passed the station, strolled out onto the main road and walked towards the tangle of police cars and yellow barrier tape around Deansgate Locks. He didn't hurry, nor did he amble. He simply moved as though he was supposed to be there. A regular police officer patrolling the scene of a major crime and manhunt.

The alleyway near the locks and canal was empty, and Kane found his rucksack where he had left it. He pulled his police cap further down to cover his face, slung the bag over his shoulder, and walked into the night. Other officers walked past him in groups of three or four, and whenever they did, Kane would talk into his radio and walk briskly as though he was responding to an urgent call or order and therefore had no time to stop and chat with fellow officers. Kane kept moving until he became lost in the city's warren-like back streets.

Kane stopped in a tight lane which ran behind a street filled with restaurants and takeaways. He ducked down low behind the various large bins and piles of rubbish bags and stripped off the stolen police uniform. Kane threw it into a wheelie bin and checked inside his bag. Everything was there: the gun, money, laptop, spare clothes and the rest of his equipment. Kane pulled out his burner phone and saw a message notification. It was a voice memo. Kane pressed play and put the phone to his ear.

The first sound was heavy breathing and

dim sobbing, like children crying. A hole of apprehension opened up in Kane's stomach.

"Help us!" Sally's voice screamed down the phone. There was a distorted muffle, then the sounds of a struggle and a man's voice somewhere in the melee. Finally, a silenced gunshot. Kane would recognise that sound anywhere. He had fired the same shot himself countless times. Sally and the kids needed his help, the only things he loved in the world, and he was miles away from the safe house. Kane rocked back against a wall and closed his eyes. Dark thoughts ran through his mind, desperately wondering if Sally, Danny, or Kim could be hurt or worse and whether Mjolnir had taken them to use against him.

He had to get to that farmhouse, yet it might already be too late.

THIRTY-SEVEN

Craven had escaped any serious injuries in the car collision, but Jess hadn't been so lucky. He stood at the side of the road whilst a paramedic dabbed cleaning solution on one of the many minor scratches on his scalp caused by the shattering car windows.

"What happened?" asked Shaw as he ducked under a line of yellow tape.

"Your eyes look like piss holes in the snow," said Craven, and Shaw adjusted the glasses.

"It's the middle of the night," he said. His cheeks flushed redder than usual, and despite it being two o'clock in the morning, Shaw's hair was immaculately gelled in his straight side parting. "Aivar, the big fish, got away?"

"His cronies smashed into our car. He must have been wearing some sort of tracking device small enough to be missed when his pockets were searched." Aivar's struggle outside of

Diego's made more sense now. He had made enough trouble to make their search urgent and difficult. Mobile phones, tracking devices and satellites. Technology had advanced so much during Craven's time on the force that policing had changed entirely. He often wondered what the surly old detectives he had started out with would make of things today.

"Poor girl," said Shaw, nodding to where the paramedics solemnly pushed a gurney towards a waiting ambulance. A sheet covered the body it carried. Jess' body. Craven rubbed his eyes and thanked the paramedic as she left him alone. The gut-wrenching shock and horror of Jess' death was hard to take. It left him hollow.

"She was one of the good ones." Craven shook his head. "I brought her along to give her a taste of what plain clothes work is like. Now she's gone."

"It's not your fault, Frank. These gangsters are scum. I've never even heard of anything like this before. Ramming a bloody police car moments after an arrest. I don't envy the person who has to tell her family."

"It will devastate her mother and father. She wasn't married, still so young, with her whole life in front of her. Jess was as bright as a button. She could have gone far in the force. We see so much shit on the streets, Shaw. The human race is crumbling. Do you ever feel like that? We are sinking into a mire of apathy and cruelty. There's no sense of community anymore. All people give a shit about is money and possessions, what pictures they can put up on fucking Facebook or Twitter or whatever bloody social media is the most popular these days."

"Insta."

"What?"

"Instagram, it's the most popular social media app now."

"Whatever. People are just so fucking entitled. Ninety per cent of our time is spent chasing around after druggies who rob houses and cars to get money for their next fix and then trying to stop the bastards who sell them the drugs in the first place. Life must have been so much easier in the old days. No technology, no email or mobile phones. Just fucking letters. People used to help each other and care for each other. Then, to top it all off, things like this happen. Good people suffer and die, whilst the scum thrive and sail through life."

"I nicked a fella last month, a coke dealer, out in Oldham. Making a fortune and still claiming benefits. He had five kids with four different women, and they're all on benefits as well. But at least the Deli Boys have seen a bit of rough justice these last few days. Weird that it's Langley who's been dishing it out, though? Is it linked to the woman at the factory?"

"Must be."

"No coincidence that we found her brother dead from a suspicious-looking overdose, and then all this kicked off today. You think Langley is bringing down the pain on them for that? Getting back at the scum?"

"They are scum, and we have to stop them. Aivar's escape just shows how little respect they've got for the fucking law if they dare to pull off something like this."

"Kirkby's going to have a shit fit when he finds out."

"More than likely. Let's hope he's more concerned that Kane got away."

"I heard that on the radio. You mean Langley?"

"Yeah, Langley."

"He's a slippery bastard, that one. All we know about him was that he was involved in a national security issue?"

"That's what his man Jacobs said, yeah. I know we've had a hundred fucking whiteboard meetings, but I wasn't listening. What else do we know about Langley?"

"Nothing. Only that Langley isn't his real name, obviously. So he's Kane, then?"

"Yeah, I think so. Maybe that pompous prick Jacobs let that slip."

"Any first name? Then we could run a proper check, find out where he's from, what his background is."

"I only know as much as you, Shaw."

Craven's phone rang. The Warrington station number.

"Craven," he said as he answered it.

"It's Kirkby. There's been another gunfight. At a farmhouse this time. Langley's wife is dead, as are Jacobs' men. It's absolute carnage over there. Langley's kids are missing. I heard about Jess and the crash, and I'm sorry, Frank."

"Thanks," said Craven, surprised at the gentle tone in Kirkby's voice.

"Things are getting out of control. Can you get over to the farmhouse?"

"I'm on the way." Craven hung up the phone. Kane's wife had been murdered, and his children had been taken. For once, he agreed with Kirkby. Things had spiralled out of control. If Kane could tear up half of Deansgate in revenge for the Estonian girl and her dead brother, what lengths would he go to now?

THIRTY-EIGHT

Kane raced down the M62 motorway in a stolen Volkswagen Golf GTI, pushing the car to its limits. His knuckles were white where they gripped the steering wheel. He reached down to his phone and played the message again. The sound of Sally's voice cut into his chest like a knife. There was potent fear in it, the terrible fear a person cannot understand until they have come face to face with death. That horror when, in a split second, you question your beliefs about death and the afterlife. That momentary existential crisis where you wonder about God, the people you love, people you've lost before. Kane knew that feeling and had experienced the horror of it more times than he could remember. They were dark memories locked away in the vault of his mind. He was good at that, burying things. It was a skill he had honed throughout his life. If something hurt, he'd bury it deep inside and never let it see the light of day again. But with Sally, it would not be that simple.

He used the same burner phone to dial Jacobs' number for the fifth time since he had heard Sally's message, but it rang out again. Kane should have thrown the phone away after the fight at Diego's. But he couldn't now that it contained Sally's voice message. He tried Craven, desperate for any news on his family's fate, but again, no answer. The motorway sped by as Kane pushed his foot harder on the accelerator. He thundered past the exit for the M56 and North Wales, and just as he passed Burtonwood services, his phone rang, and it was Jacobs.

"Jacobs?" said Kane.

"Yes, it's me, Jack," his voice was solemn but level.

"What's going on, Jacobs, are Sally and the kids safe?"

"There's no easy way to say this. But there was an attack on the safe house. My agents were all killed. Jack, listen to me. I have some bad news for you. Sally has died. They've taken Danny and Kim."

The world stopped. Kane was aware at some level that he was driving, but it was as though he had left his body. Part of him had known she was gone, but hearing Jacobs say it was unbearable. The car swerved, and Kane almost vomited. He took a breath and came back to himself. He tried to think clearly but failed.

"Kane, can you hear me?" said Jacobs.

"I heard you. You were supposed to protect them." He wanted to shout, rage, fight, and tear the world apart. But he had to remember his training, what he had learned from a lifetime of living on the edge of death. "Was it Mjolnir? Was it Fowler? And who has my children?"

"I had a team with your family, but they were taken out. It can only be Mjolnir. Where are you now?"

"Heading to the farmhouse."

"I'll meet you there. It will be safe. The police are there, but I'll move them out."

"I'll be there in fifteen minutes."

Kane fought down the lump in his throat and swallowed the urge to cry. A vision of Sally on the day they had first met flashed before his eyes. Kane loved her instantly; she was so funny and so beautiful. Her parents had disapproved of him, to begin with, and they had been right about that. He was just a squaddie back then, a kid in the Parachute Regiment before he had gone through selection for the SAS. Other memories came to him so thick and fast that he almost raised his hand to waft them away. The birth of their children, and the loss of his parents. He hadn't deserved a woman like her, and she had deserved a better man than him. Now she was gone.

Jacobs had promised them safety, that upon entering the programme, Mjolnir would fold, and that he and Sally could live a life in peace. But Mjolnir was still going strong, still running black operations all over the world, and everything Kane had sacrificed had been for nothing. Sally had given up her life, career, friends, and even contact with her parents. All a waste. The worst of it was, as her death throes rattled around in Kane's skull like a haunting, he recalled how he had become bored within the programme.

Kane had so wanted to be a family man, to work a regular job, play with his kids, and be content with that. But he'd yearned for his old life. Kane told himself that it was the action he missed, the travel, and the sense of patriotism from protecting his country. But the darker side of him, the thoughts that come to a person in the deep of night when the mind digs up its recesses, challenged his sense of self, telling him that it was the violence he missed. Kane recognised that truth now that he was back in the thick of life-threatening combat. Violence was his drug, it was what made Kane feel alive, and he was ashamed of that. If he had been a better man, a better father, Sally would still be alive, and Danny and Kim would be safe. He'd helped Yelena because he could and had wanted to. He had wanted to fight her attackers and had taken pleasure in their defeat.

Anger and despair quickened Kane's pulse, and he fought with himself to control it. He had to think clearly. Sally was dead, and there was nothing he could do about that now. But he could get Danny and Kim back, and he needed to be able to work towards that with a rational head on his shoulders. Only Mjolnir would have the strength and audacity to pull off an attack on Jacobs' safe house. Jacobs was MI6, so an attack on him was an attack on the British Government, an act of terrorism.

The whole point of Kane going into the programme was his testimony detailing the illegal operations he had taken part in across the world. Kane had always followed orders, unquestioning and unflinching in whatever they had asked him to do. The morality or justification for any of it had never entered his head until Jacobs had approached him. A mission had gone wrong. They had sent Kane's team to eliminate a high-value target. Kane had shot the HVT, but his unit was all but wiped out in a calamitous horror beneath enemy tunnels in a distant country. He and Fowler had escaped, but it had been a political shitstorm, a coup to overthrow a government in favour of better lithium mining concessions. Mjolnir was operating with international impunity. Jacobs had said they were no longer under the control of the British Government.

Kane had provided his testimony, attending gruelling depositions before suited bureaucrats who knew nothing of combat or war, and then he had been shipped off to the North West and his new life with no information about Mjolnir's fate. He hadn't cared. Kane had done his bit for his country. He had done what was asked of him in the field, and he'd also brought Mjolnir's actions to the fore. But nothing had changed, and Kane could not believe that Fowler was involved in Sally's death or the kidnap of Danny and Kim. Kane had loved Fowler like a brother. They had been through hell together.

The Golf leaned into the exit ramp as Kane left the M62 at Great Sankey and sped through a chain of roundabouts west towards the farmhouse. Whoever had Danny and Kim would suffer. Kane was resolute in his determination. He would get his children back, and if they had been harmed, Kane vowed that those responsible would pay the price with their lives.

THIRTY-NINE

Fowler buttoned up his shirt and stared at his reflection in the bathroom mirror. His piercing blue eyes stared back at him, and Fowler tore his gaze away from their judgement. He splashed cold water on his face and dried it with a fistful of paper towels. Fowler took his suit jacket from the back of the cubicle door and pulled it on, noticing a patch of camouflage paint on the back of his right hand, which he rubbed off with his thumb. He left the bathroom and came into the vastness of the aircraft hangar.

A chill night breeze blustered in through the open hangar doors, and the unit waited in a small room cordoned off from the wider hangar by thin partition walls. Fowler opened the door and went to grab a glass of water from the sink. The team sat on the selection of cafeteria-type chairs and old armchairs whilst the two children sat on a cracked, old brown leather sofa. Fowler couldn't look at them.

"How much longer until the jet arrives?" asked McCann, her forehead wrinkled into a frown. She looked as sour as he felt.

"A couple of hours," he replied. "Barnes, outside."

Fowler left the room, followed by Barnes.

"What's up?" asked Barnes, fiddling with the cuffs of his shirt. His thick neck bulged at a too-tight collar, and he wore a shoulder holster and gun without a jacket to cover it. His right cheek bore three lurid scratch marks like a cat had attacked him.

"So, what happened with Kane's wife?"

Barnes shrugged. "She attacked me like a fucking mad woman. She went for my gun, and it went off. I didn't just shoot her in cold blood." He pointed at his cheek and threw his arms up as if to say his version of events made it obvious that he had been left with no choice but to kill Sally Kane.

"She got the better of you, did she? All nine stones of her?"

"What does it matter? We have the brats. He'll come for them. All you've got to do is tell Kane where to find them, and the trap is baited."

Fowler stared into Barnes' eyes. There was no point explaining to him that he had seen pictures of those kids when they were babies, that he had listened to Kane talking lovingly of his wife and kids for hours on end, and that he had never gotten bored of it. Kane had something that Fowler could never have – love and a family of his own. Fowler was too far gone for that, and he knew it. An orphan brought up in foster homes, some good and some horrific, straight into the army as soon as he was old enough, and then the Regiment. Fowler had never known love, had never been loved. When he had joined Mjolnir, they had told him he was the perfect recruit. No family, no ties. Cold, borderline sociopath, which had come as little surprise. He gestured his head towards the room, and Barnes walked back inside. In the mire of awful things that Fowler had done in the name of his country, and there were many, Sally's death hurt him the most. She was someone he knew, not in person, but through his old friend's constant chatter about her. It was personal now, a real human being with an actual family, not some greedy warlord or terrorist with blood on their hands.

The door to the room opened, and Nketiah poked her head out.

"Phone for you," she said.

He had called in the mission report earlier on a secure line, and there would be a debrief when he returned to London, yet he had expected this call. It wasn't that he dreaded the dressing down to come but more so that he was tired of it all. Fowler was exhausted with all the blood, secrecy, loneliness, and never-ending pointlessness of his life. He reached out and took the mobile phone from her hand.

"Hello?"

"This is McGovern," said the stern woman's voice. "Is that you, Thor?"

He sighed at the use of his codename. This was an official call, then. "This is Thor."

"Your orders were to find Jack Kane, a known threat to national security. You have failed in that mission. I have Odin on the line."

"Thor?" said a clipped voice that unmistakenly revealed a background of public school and Oxbridge. Fowler had never met Odin, the leader of the Mjolnir agency, but knew him by reputation.

"Yes, sir."

"The jet will fly you to London. Take the children with you. You have the woman's phone. Call Kane on it and set up a meeting. If he turns himself in, the children can go free. If he doesn't come to you at the appointed time, tell him you will cut his children's throats. I will join you in London with another team to ensure the job is done properly this time."

"Yes, sir."

"Thor?"

"Yes, sir?"

"Don't fuck up again. I will hold you personally responsible if Kane isn't handled this time."

FORTY

Kane approached the farmhouse lane with the car lights off. There were no blue lights flashing, and Kane couldn't see any sign of a police presence around the building. He pulled the vehicle to a halt on the dirt road at the corner, where it turned right into the farmhouse's driveway. Police tape cordoned off the entrance, but Kane could see no officers on duty. Jacobs had been as good as his word and used his wizardry to clear the place. Kane exited the car and pulled his rucksack off the passenger seat. He took out his pistol, stowing it at the small of his back in the waistband of his trousers. The weapon had fifteen bullets left, and he still had the Deli Boys' laptop and a bag full of their cash.

He picked his way along the dirt track road. There were no streetlights, but the moon was bright enough for Kane to avoid the worst of the muck and puddles. He rounded a corner heavy on each side with hedgerows that loomed above him in the darkness. There was a light on in the farmhouse, and as Kane approached, he felt a strange foreboding. This was where Sally had died, where his children had been taken. Kane had scouted the place himself, and it had looked safe. Yet now they were gone. He questioned his own decision-making again. If he had just turned himself in when Jacobs had asked him to, then Sally might still be alive. Then again, knowing Mjolnir's malevolent ruthlessness, she might still have been killed and Kane alongside her. At least Danny and Kim were alive, or he hoped they were alive.

Kane used the darkness to hide while he quickly circled the house. It was empty, except for one room with a light shining from a rear window. Kane made his way back to the front of the house. The door was ajar, and Kane pushed it open. There were chalk circles on the hallway floor and little yellow numbered pyramids next to spent bullet casings. The air inside the farmhouse was acrid, like the smell of an old fire. Kane strode along the hall until he reached the room from which light flooded out onto the floor tiles. He walked carefully along the hallway, noting the bullet holes in the walls and ceiling in the half-light. There was a blood spatter against a pine doorframe, and Kane turned away, hoping it wasn't Sally's.

"Is that you, Kane?" came an upper-class voice

from inside the room. Kane stepped inside to find Jacobs sitting on a dining chair, smoking a cigarette. The tendrils of smoke rose and sat below the ceiling like a foul-smelling fog.

"Is she really gone?" Kane asked. He hoped Jacobs would say that there had been a terrible mistake and that Sally was still alive.

Jacobs put his cigarette out in a coffee mug on the long dining table and uncrossed his long legs. He stood and approached Kane, putting a hand on his shoulder.

"I can't tell you how sorry I am, old boy. She was a brave woman and a splendid mother," said Jacobs.

"You were supposed to protect them. To protect us all."

"There was a fully armed unit here, Jack. This should not have happened. I don't know what to say. Sally should have been safe here."

"But she wasn't, and now she's dead. How could you let that happen?" Kane shouted, his fists balling.

"I didn't let it happen," Jacobs spoke slowly and carefully, his voice measured and calm. "We had heavily armed, experienced operatives in this house."

"Why weren't you here to protect them?" Kane demanded, pressing his fists to his forehead.

Overcome, the same question plagued him:

Why wasn't I here to protect them?

"I can't be here the entire time, Jack," Jacobs replied gently. "They were here because…"

"Go on, say it."

"Well, they would only have been here until you came in, then I would have moved you all to a different location. Scotland, Wales, or Cornwall. Somewhere far away, new job, new identities."

"They should have been safe, Jacobs. Now Sally's dead, and my children are gone. What the fuck are you going to do about it?" Kane un-balled his fists. His shouting had grown into a roar, and he fought to remain calm.

"We will find your children. You have my word."

"What was the point of all this anyway if Mjolnir is still active?"

"You did a brave thing for national—"

"Don't say national security, Jacobs. Not today. If my testimony didn't bring Mjolnir down, didn't stop all that black ops bullshit, then what was the point?"

"Your sacrifice and testimony led to real change, Jack. You must believe me when I say that. There was a change in the way Mjolnir is run, how its operations are selected and how they are reported to the government. The funding is under wiser control now, the agency runs the right ops in the right countries, and its links with the Americans and other allies are stronger than ever."

"Whatever you say, Jacobs. You said that many of the operations I ran, the people I killed, were not in the interests of national security. You said that corrupt politicians and MI6 agents were sending Mjolnir on jobs for money. That they were being paid by revolutionary juntas, magnates and criminal organisations. That's the only reason I agreed to testify against the agency. But nothing's really changed. How can you say it has when Mjolnir has just killed my wife on home soil? When they are running wild in Northern England with military-grade equipment and special forces-trained operators? So, was it Fowler who did this? Where are my children?" Kane was tired of it all. He couldn't care less anymore about what happened to Mjolnir. But if Fowler had killed Sally, he wouldn't be able to let that go unavenged.

"It was Fowler. He brought a team here and killed my men."

"How do you know it was him?"

"One of my operators survived for a time and identified Fowler."

"My children?"

"He must have them. He'll offer them in exchange for your life. They won't have forgiven you, Jack. Mjolnir wants you quiet, no more surprises."

"How do I contact him?"

"He'll contact you, I imagine." Jacobs took a few steps back and reached inside his jacket pocket, likely to fish out another cigarette, Kane expected. "Your testimony and everything you know about Mjolnir – did you write any of it down, type it up, or record it somewhere for safekeeping?"

"What do you mean?" Kane was thrown off by the question for a moment. His thoughts were preoccupied with Sally's death and the plight of his children.

"Did you keep a record of what you know about Mjolnir anywhere? Details of the operations you took part in?" Jacobs still had his hand inside his jacket, and if he didn't know the man better, Kane would have thought he had his hand on a gun.

"Why are you..." Kane stopped talking and spun around as the front door creaked on its hinges. He dropped his rucksack and drew the pistol from behind his back, pointing the barrel at the entrance to the kitchen.

"Jesus, put that away," tutted Craven, seeing the gun barrel pointing at him and holding up his hands. Craven's police radio crackled, and he made a slow gesture to show that he was going to answer it. Kane nodded and shoved the gun back into his trousers.

"This is Craven," he said, taking out the black radio from his jacket pocket. There was a response which Kane couldn't make out. Craven had the thing to his ear. "I'm at the location of the multiple murder scene now. With Jacobs, tell Kirkby that. He knows who he is. From here, I'll go home and report to Warrington station at nine tomorrow morning."

Jacobs hissed as though Craven had irked him by answering his radio. Kane turned to him, and the tall government man sat down in his chair again, all languid limbs and aloof weariness in his eyes.

"Sorry about that," said Craven, putting his radio away. "I have to report in for a debrief. You caused no end of shite in Manchester tonight."

"My wife is dead, and they have kidnapped my children," Kane responded flatly.

"I heard. That's why I'm here. I'm sorry for your loss. Truly, I am."

"Has Fowler been in touch with you since you met him at the station?" asked Kane. Craven's eyes flickered from Kane to Jacobs. "It's OK, you can trust him, speak freely."

"Yes. He threatened my wife and tried to blackmail me into arranging a meeting with you. To set you up."

Kane stared at Craven, assessing the policeman in a fresh light. It took bravery to deny Fowler. He was a frightening man, a killer not to be trifled with. It also told Kane that Craven was a person he could trust, and there were few people he could say that about.

"Did he give you a number to contact him on?"

"Yes. I have it here somewhere." Craven dug his meaty hand into the pocket of his overcoat, pulled out a KitKat wrapper and stuffed it back in, then pulled out a bent business card. "Here you go."

Kane took the card. No name or agency details, just a number.

"So, what happens now?" asked Craven.

"Kane, come with me. Let me bring you in, and we'll send a team after your children," said Jacobs.

"I'm going after them myself. You can help by giving me men and weapons. Otherwise, stay out of my way," Kane intoned. "Thank you for your help, Craven. I hope the Deli Boys are damaged enough for you to bring them to justice now."

"They are, but their leader escaped custody. His thugs crashed into my car and killed an outstanding young officer."

"Find him, Craven."

Kane spoke more harshly than he'd intended, but he feared for Yelena, for what Aivar would do to her now that he knew it had been the Deli Boys' mistreatment of her and Oskar's death which had set Kane against him.

"I'm not sure I can let you walk away from here, Jack," said Jacobs, rising from his chair. "Come in with me, and we'll get your kids back."

"You can't stop me. I've done my bit. I gave you the information you asked for. Sally gave up her life for your cause, and now look at us. I'm not going anywhere until this is over, Jacobs. Then I'll come in."

Jacobs stared at Kane, then smiled in his upper-class laconic way and strode out of the room. Kane watched him go and then took out the Deli Boys' laptop, placing it on the table.

"I have something else for you, Craven." He opened the laptop and connected it to the farmhouse Wi-Fi.

"The power has only been back on here for the last hour or so. The lines were cut. You're lucky that's working."

Kane gestured to a chair, and Craven sat down. Kane went through the Deli Boys' laptop. It was a MacBook, and he could gallop through the various spreadsheets which contained details of the Deli Boys' finances and their various accounts and businesses. Kane opened a cryptocurrency account, where the username and password were pre-populated from previous use. The Deli Boys might have been skilled at drug distribution and human trafficking, but their online password security lacked finesse. He sold two hundred and fifty thousand pounds of Dogecoin and emptied an online shares trading account. Kane transferred the money to his own emergency offshore account in the Caymans. He traded another eight hundred thousand pounds worth of Bitcoin and passed the laptop to Craven.

"This will give you everything you need to put Aivar away. The laptop has details of cash received and distributed. They've kept a spreadsheet as a sort of ledger to keep track of it all. The entries are coded, but I am sure you can figure it out. Give it to your tech people. Also, I've put some money aside there for you personally. In case you ever need it."

"I've never taken a bribe or dirty money in my life, and I'm not about to start now."

"I know, I know. I've moved the money into a secure account, one of a few dummy online accounts I had set up in the old days, which you can access and use without the money being traceable. If you don't want it, that's fine, but I'll write the location details down for you now, and you can either use it or leave it there. Think of it as a retirement fund. Let the Deli Boys' money go to someone who deserves it."

Craven just stared at him with an open mouth. Kane went to the kitchen island and found a pen and an old envelope in a drawer. He wrote the location of the crypto account and pushed the envelope into Craven's hand. Kane left the detective there and strode outside. One last thing to do, and then it was time to call Fowler.

FORTY-ONE

Kane sat in the stolen Volkswagen Golf and reclined in the driver's seat. It was half three in the morning. Stars shone in the sky above him on a clear night, casting the hills and fields around the farmhouse in textured shadow. There was a chill in the air, and Kane turned the key in the ignition to switch on the warm air conditioning. He massaged his stinging eyes with his knuckles and allowed himself a long yawn. Kane took his phone out of the rucksack. Just before he dialled Fowler's number from the card, he quickly checked the locator app for Yelena's tracker. The green dot blinked slowly on a map of Warrington. He zoomed in and saw her location was in a suburb south of the town centre and a fifteen-minute drive from his current location. He would call Fowler on the way.

He drove away from the farmhouse, and the strangeness of Jacobs' demeanour struck him again. There had been an edge to the ordinarily friendly government man, a sort of underlying anger or frustration. Even after entering the programme and through all the different phases of his testimony, he still wasn't sure what government agency Jacobs worked for. Jacobs could belong to domestic MI5 or MI6 or some other civilian administrative agency. It was strange that Jacobs hadn't batted an eyelid when Kane had lost his temper. If there had been any change at Mjolnir since he had given his evidence, there was certainly nothing to show for it as far as Kane could see. If anything, the agency was even more brazen and out of control if they could pull off a military-style special forces attack on a farmhouse in the UK. Their typical theatres of operations were war zones or places teetering on the edge of becoming war zones. Sally was dead, and their lives were ruined, and in the pit of his stomach, Kane knew it had all been for nothing.

He punched Fowler's number into the burner phone and put the handset on speaker so it wouldn't impede his driving. The Golf was a manual transmission, and Warrington was a place of a thousand traffic roundabouts. The phone rang three times before a familiar voice answered.

"Yes," said Fowler. A voice Kane had not heard for years. In his old life, hearing that voice would have made Kane smile. Memories of operations they had conducted side by side came flooding back, days they had spent together waiting for an operational green light. Other hazy memories of nights out drinking together all suddenly came to Kane in a flash of flitting images.

"How could you do that to Sally and take my kids?" said Kane.

"I wondered if you would get this number or if I'd have to call you. Very resourceful, as always."

"Where are my children?"

"Safe. But only if you hand yourself over to me."

"My wife is dead, Simon. Or should I call you Thor instead?"

"What, for old times' sakes? Sally's death was an accident. We didn't go there to kill her, just to take her."

"You tore up that fucking house like it was a terrorist bolthole. What did you think was going to happen?"

"Don't come on all innocent with me. We've both seen our fair share of collateral damage, Kane. It's part of the job, and you know it. Whenever we go to war, we go prepared to kill, and sometimes civilians get caught in the crossfire."

"Don't call Sally collateral damage. Where are my kids?"

"With me. Come and meet me, and I'll let them go unharmed. You have my word."

"Your word? We were friends, and you killed my wife. Look how far you've fallen, Simon. We were in the Regiment, SAS operators. We were government agents, the tip of the spear. Now you're killing women and kidnapping children?"

"Just following orders, Jack. Don't judge me. You brought all this on yourself when you turned into a grass. When you betrayed your comrades and stabbed me in the back."

"I had no choice. Things were getting out of hand."

"All you did was give Odin more power. They mugged you off, and you sold out your brothers in arms. And all for a semi-detached house in some shit-hole town and a job in a factory?"

"What's the point of it all, though? Why are you so blindingly loyal to the same bastards who sent us to die on missions where we shouldn't have survived?"

"But we did survive. And I serve my country with honour. When I retire, I'll do so with pride. People sleep safely in their beds across Britain because I do my job. I do the hard things, the things that other men would flinch from. I am all that stands between the darkness and the light. I do what I do so that the people of this country can live their lives in peace."

"Do you really believe that shit? Do you think that killing a politician in Sierra Leone or inciting a military coup in Bolivia keeps people in England safe in their beds?"

"Fuck you, Kane."

"Where are you now? I want my kids back, and I want to know they are safe."

"They're safe. I'll meet you in a car park, at a place between Warrington and Liverpool. Lots of lights and cameras, no need to be afraid. I'll text the postcode to this number."

"Bring Danny and Kim with you." Kane had no choice but to meet Fowler, even though he would be outnumbered. The car park was a good strategic location for Fowler and his crew. It would be brightly lit, even at night time, and would allow Kane's enemies to see him approach from a distance and assess if he was armed or not.

"I don't think so, Kane. Do you think my head buttons up the back? We will keep the children at a secure location, and once you hand yourself over to me, they will go free."

"I don't trust you."

"What choice have you got?"

"I want to know they are OK. Now."

Fowler sighed. The background on the phone rustled, and people spoke in muffled tones so that Kane could not understand what they said.

"Dad?" said Danny. His voice was higher-pitched than normal like it had been when he was a toddler and wanted to get into Kane and Sally's bed at night. Kane swallowed a lump in his throat.

"Danny. Are you and Kim OK?"

"No, Dad, they took us. They hurt Mum. Are you coming to get us?"

Kane controlled his breathing, forcing himself not to allow the heart-tearing sorrow to show in his voice. "I'm coming, son. Look after your sister."

The phone rustled once more, and Danny was gone.

"Meet me at the car park, Kane. I'll be there in ninety minutes. If you try anything, or I don't return, your children will die, Jack," said Fowler.

"I'll kill you for this. I'll kill you all," Kane shouted, his anger and fear spilling over despite his best efforts. He shook the car steering wheel, took one hand off and punched the roof above his head. He slammed his foot on the accelerator, and the car screamed along an empty dual-carriageway.

"Just be there." Fowler ended the call. Kane's shoulders sank, and agonising sadness overwhelmed him. Sobs erupted from deep inside his chest, wracking his body and shuddering his torso. Kane howled like a wounded wolf inside the speeding car. Fat, heavy tears rolled down his cheeks, and he wept with the pain of a bereaved husband and a father who knew that his children's lives were in the greatest peril.

FORTY-TWO

Kane pushed the stolen car to its limits, racing along dual carriageways and Warrington's streets as he followed the signal from Yelena's tracker. He had time before his meeting with Fowler, and Kane had to use that time to tie up loose ends. His mind was like a butter churn, turning over his multiple problems. Worry for his children and rage against Fowler and Mjolnir. He owed it to Yelena to fix her problems, and he had to do it before he settled with Fowler. Once he had his children, Kane would disappear. He would use his old training and resources and simply fade away in a different country where his family could be safe. The pain of Sally's loss ached like a lost limb, drowning the physical pain of his shoulder wound into insignificance.

The streets were empty and dark, and Kane turned into a sprawling estate of terraced council houses from the 1970s with flat roofs and cobble-locked driveways. Yellow streetlights lit up an empty warren of streets and cul-de-sacs, and Kane drove into a courtyard. He parked in front of the three-storey block of flats, one of which was Yelena's. A black SUV reversed out of the car park at such speed that the tyres shrieked with protest when the jeep turned sharply to face Kane's direction. The entire chassis lurched as the SUV screeched around in a half circle and sped past Kane, its driver and passengers hidden behind blacked-out windows. Local thugs at their night's work, Kane expected. He gathered himself and wiped the tears from his cheeks with his shirt cuff. He had wept for Sally and his children throughout the journey, but it was time for calmness and control.

Kane jumped out of the vehicle and brought his rucksack with him. He ran along the pavement and into the dark entranceway, which ran in between two blocks of flats. The entry door was closed, but the latch was on, which prevented it from locking. Kane went inside and leapt up a flight of stairs. He checked his phone locater app to see which flat was Yelena's, but Kane stopped running when he noticed the green flashing dot showing her position was moving away from him at speed. He shook his head in disbelief. A door stood wide open ahead of him, and Kane instinctively made for it. He kept one hand on the Glock in the waistband of his trousers and moved into the doorway. The hallway lighting lit up the flat, and the sitting room was a disaster with an overturned coffee table and an armchair on its side. Kane moved inside cautiously. He cast his eyes on the brown, heavy carpet as something crumpled under his shoe. It was a takeaway restaurant menu.

"No," Kane whispered as he bent to pick up the menu. He scrunched it and tossed it into the sitting room when he read the word 'Rambo's' on the menu's header. It was the Deli Boys, and they had taken Yelena. Kane raced back along the hallway, out of the block of flats and to his car. He leapt into the driver's seat and turned on the ignition with a roar. The tracker app signal pulsed. The vehicle carrying Yelena wasn't far away, and it had to have been the black SUV he had passed on the way in. Kane reversed out of the parking space and spun the steering wheel around under the palm of his hand so that the Volkswagen Golf turned to face the exit. He could catch them. They only had five minutes on him, and the Deli Boys would surely head for the M62 motorway and Manchester. But time was against him. He had to meet Fowler in an hour, and it had taken thirty minutes to drive to Yelena's flat. There was simply not enough time to chase Yelena's captors and get to Fowler in time.

Kane swore and slammed on the brakes. The engine ticked over, and he watched the blip on the tracker app getting further away. The Deli

Boys were taking Yelena to Manchester because Aivar wanted his revenge. He knew she was Oskar's sister, and Aivar would finish what he had tried to do the day this whole shit storm had begun. He would turn Yelena into a prostitute to pay off Oskar's debt and to spite Kane in return for the chaos he'd brought upon Aivar's gang. Kane had come to Yelena's flat to give her access to a portion of the funds he had taken from the Deli Boys' bank accounts, to give her the financial freedom to have options. She could leave Warrington, return home, or go wherever she wished and live the rest of her life in peace and comfort. But, now she was in an SUV being sped towards Aivar and a life of pain and suffering. It was a terrible, heartrending decision to make, but Kane had to think of his own family first. So he sped the vehicle away from Manchester towards Liverpool and the address Fowler had sent via text message. For now, he would have to leave Yelena to her fate, and that decision tore at the very fabric of his being.

FORTY-THREE

Kane made it to the designated car park for the meeting with Fowler within forty minutes. The retail park it served was a square of shop units, a pet store, a DIY store, an electrical outlet, and a bowling alley. The car park linked them all, and at four o'clock in the morning, it was empty save for half a dozen random vehicles left there overnight. Six tall posts with umbrella-type arms lit up the black tarmac, which was cut into neatly laid out rows and lanes separated by hedging and raised kerbstones. Kane left the stolen Volkswagen in a bus stop layby half a kilometre away from the retail park and walked the short distance to the car park with his rucksack over one shoulder.

The Glock pistol sat snug at the base of his spine, and the retractable knife was in his right sock. Leaving Yelena to her fate sat like a sour stone in Kane's belly, but when it came to deciding whether to prioritise his children's safety, there had really been no decision to make. He marched up a grass bank to the left of the pathway leading to the retail park, and the nighttime dew soaked through the soft leather of his shoes to wet his feet. Kane vaulted over a waist-high timber fence and waded into a thicket of gorse which separated the retail units from the road. He crouched there in the cover, and though a heavy blanket of darkness still cast the world in shadow, the retail park itself was lit up as bright as the hottest summer day.

Fowler had the advantage because he had set the location. But Kane wouldn't simply walk into a trap like a fool. From his position in the gorse bushes, Kane quickly assessed the location. The vehicles left in the car park overnight were mostly Fords and Vauxhalls over ten years old and were of little value. Kane thought they were most likely left by store employees who had gone over to the Toby Carvery pub for drinks after work and left their cars overnight. The exception was a brand new navy blue BMW 5 series parked in the north corner. Kane called Fowler.

"I'm here," said Kane as soon as the call was answered.

"I know," replied Fowler's voice. Kane had given up replacing his burner phone after each call, even though Mjolnir had the current number. Fowler knew Kane would come to the meeting for the sake of his children, so it made little sense to dump the phone despite being aware that its signal could easily be traced. Letting them have that knowledge of his whereabouts might serve him later, so he kept the phone in his pocket.

"I'll meet you outside the pet shop in two minutes," said Kane, and he cast his eyes around the tops of each retail unit and then across the road where the front of a Toby Carvery pub poked through a line of sycamore trees. "And tell your snipers to stand down. If they get an itchy trigger finger, you'll never know where I've squirrelled away copies of my transcripts. If anything happens to me, my transcripts will be automatically emailed to a selection of journalists at multiple publications. Details of all the ops we've run, the places we've fought. A diplomatic time bomb."

"There's nobody here but you and I."

The door to the BMW opened soundlessly, and Fowler stepped out of the driver's side. He wore a dark suit and a black overcoat. Fowler strode languidly towards the pet shop. Kane waited and scanned the place again. There was no gleam from a rifle sight or any noise to give away a sniper's position. But he knew they would be there, weapons trained on him as soon as Kane showed himself. The tracker they had on his phone signal would tell them he was at the retail park, but not precisely where he was.

Kane hoped that the threat of his written transcripts seeing the light of day would be enough to keep a bullet from his head long enough for him to save Danny and Kim. He pushed his way out of the gorse and stood on the car park tarmac. The hairs on the back of Kane's neck bristled, a sure sign that they had trained rifle sights upon him at that very moment. Kane walked at a regular pace, resisting the urge to run and get close to Fowler before the shot to end his life came for him. What would happen to Danny and Kim then? The naïve part of him hoped Fowler would turn them in to the authorities, into the care of the state. But he knew their fate would be far more ruthless than that. Someone would kill the children and leave them in a shallow grave once Kane was dead and the threat of exposing Mjolnir's operations was over.

"Jack," Fowler nodded in greeting as Kane approached. Fowler's blue eyes shone beneath the artificial light. He was an inch taller than Kane, broader across the shoulders, and looked fit and strong, just as he always had. Fowler wore a white earpiece in his left ear to communicate with the rest of his team.

"Take me to Danny and Kim," said Kane, his tone clipped and forceful.

"All in good time. You say you have made transcripts of your evidence? First, you are going to give me the location of those files. Once I'm happy that we have access and that they are the only copies, I'll let your kids go."

"The minute I give you that access, I'm a dead man."

Fowler shrugged. "You should have thought about that before you grassed on me and your brothers in arms."

"After what happened to Smithy, Carl, and the others in those tunnels, I'd had enough. When the government came to me with a way out, I took it. For my family. Can't you understand that?"

Fowler kicked a pebble across the pathway's paving stones. "That op was a mess, and the top brass made a mistake sending us into that hellhole. But how many times have we been on ops that went tits up? I've lost count. You never turned grass before."

"The lads died, Simon. They left us there to rot, but you and I got out. Why were we there anyway? For a fucking lithium mine? What's that got to do with keeping Britain safe?"

"They died following orders, and you betrayed their memories and the memories of all the men who died before them."

"Don't you ever stop to think about the things you're doing? About who is giving the orders, and why?"

"Never. I follow orders. Now, tell me where those transcript files are, or I'll see my orders through to the bitter end."

"What about Sally? How could you do that to her, to me and the kids?"

Fowler shook his head and wiped his hand down his chin. "I didn't kill her. One of the team pulled the trigger after she attacked him. It was a mistake."

"Which one of the team?"

"It doesn't matter. Give me the location of the files."

"Were we ever really friends? Remember all the times we bled together, looked out for each other on the battlefield? How many times have you saved my life and me yours? Just give me back my kids, and you'll never see me again. You can tell Odin that I'm dead, and I'll disappear. This whole shitstorm goes away, and you get the kudos for a job well done."

"It's not that simple, though, is it? You'd turn up again in the Scottish Highlands or some back arse town in Wales or Ireland. Local hero stops burglary, or brave neighbour rescues kid from fire. It has to end here. I'm tired, Jack. Just give me the files."

"So you can give them to your masters like

a lackey? You're a fucking idiot, Fowler. A hired assassin, doing whatever he's told by fat cat businessmen and politicians. You haven't done an honest day's work for this country since the day they pulled us from the Regiment to work for Mjolnir. You're not a soldier anymore. You're just like the people they sent us to kill."

"The files." Fowler's long fingers curled into fists, and his jaw muscles worked as he ground his teeth.

"I'll give you the files' location, then we are going to walk to your car, and you are going to take me to Danny and Kim?"

"That's the deal."

Kane pulled the rucksack from behind his back. Fowler reached inside his coat, and Kane knew that his old friend's fingers were touching his shoulder-holstered weapon. He couldn't see the gun, but it would be there. In that split second, Kane ran through his options. He could take the pistol from his back and kill Fowler, but Fowler's team would gun him down before the bullets left the barrel, and Danny and Kim would die. He could try to tackle Fowler and take him hostage in return for his children's freedom, but Mjolnir was a ruthless organisation, and Kane couldn't be sure that the order wouldn't come through to kill both him and Fowler just to get the job done. Odin had always been a merciless commander, utterly focused on achieving the objective, even at the cost of the lives of his operatives.

Kane unzipped his bag and reached slowly inside as though he were going to take out a drive containing the files. Suddenly, the pet shop window thrummed, and Kane instinctively dropped to one knee. He glanced to his left, where a bullet had passed straight through the window without shattering it, and the hole was only an inch away from where Kane's head had been a moment earlier. There was no bang or report from the weapon, so the shot was silenced, and Kane's choices evaporated as Fowler drew his hand out of his jacket pocket.

FORTY-FOUR

Kane leapt forwards with his rucksack still in his hands. He cannoned into Fowler, pinning his gun hand to his chest as the two men thudded into the shop window. Fowler's knee came up into Kane's gut, and he twisted his torso just in time to avoid being winded.

"Hold your fire," Fowler grunted. He didn't need to shout. His earpiece would pick up his voice easily and relay the message to the wider team.

Kane punched Fowler in the groin and forced his left hand between the press of their bodies to grip Fowler's gun hand. The window banged and cracked, another bullet hole punching through it just to the left of Kane's head as the grappling men swayed back and forth. This time, however, cracks spread along the shop window like it was ice buckling under too much weight. Kane dragged Fowler back two paces and then drove him at the window with as much force as he could summon. The weight of their bodies crashed through the glass, and the sound of it was like a hundred bottles smashing on the floor.

Fowler fell onto his back, and as he went down, he kicked out with his legs to bring Kane down with him. The two men scrambled on the hard shop floor, feet kicking and hands tussling for holds. Lights from the ceiling kept the windows bright at night to advertise the shop's wares, but they kept the inside dark. Blood rushed in Kane's ears, and Fowler's arm jerked towards him so fast that Kane only just pushed the limb aside with his wrist before Fowler's pistol fired inches from his head. The gun firing so close to Kane's ears was deafening. A dull ringing in his skull caused by the ear-splitting bang replaced the blood rush of panic. Kane brought his right hand over to catch Fowler's gun hand, but when he tried to reach around to his back for his own gun, Fowler punched him in the face.

Kane reeled from the blow, twisting at the hip and rolling off Fowler and onto the arm with the gun. Fowler followed him and hooked his knees around Kane's waist. Kane elbowed him in the jaw and pushed himself to his feet. As Kane stood, Fowler's knees lost their grip, and Kane stamped down hard on Fowler's wrist. He yelped, and the gun slipped from his grasp. Kane scrambled and kicked it away, and the weapon slid along the shiny floor under a block of shelves. Kane ran deeper into the shadows of the pet store before Fowler's team could fire a bullet into his head, and then he waited.

Fowler sprang to his feet. "Barnes, if you fire again, I'll fucking skin you alive," he hissed. Kane noted the name. Whoever this Barnes was, he was obviously a shoot-first, trigger-happy operator, and Fowler had said that Sally's death was an accident. A too-quick trigger finger. Fowler slowly removed his overcoat and draped it over a toppled window display. He kicked aside a tub of fish food from his path and walked cautiously into the shop's dark interior.

"You should have come quietly," Fowler growled and shot his cuffs beneath the arms of his jacket.

"Your team fired first. All I want is my kids back." Kane leant into a single security light shining from the store's interior ceiling so that Fowler could see him, and then he darted quickly back into the darkness. Fowler smiled and came on, fists raised for the fight.

Kane dropped his rucksack, kicking it behind him, and then Fowler was upon him. Fowler sprinted the last three steps towards Kane and bellowed with rage as he sprang into a flying kick. Kane deftly caught his leg and threw Fowler into densely packed shelving. Fowler fell to the floor, the contents falling with him. Kane kicked Fowler in the ribs, yet his enemy surged to his feet, swinging a flurry of punches, and the two men came together in a whirlwind of fists and kicks. A brutal punch connected with Kane's injured shoulder, and as he folded with the shock of pain, Fowler brought the flat of his hand down on Kane's ear. Kane fell to one knee, and Fowler punched him in the eye.

At that moment, darkness swallowed Kane, lights sparking from deep inside his brain. Fowler was faster and stronger, while Kane was out of shape and out of practice. It was as though he moved through treacle, and Fowler's limbs were supercharged. In the fog of semi-consciousness, Kane sensed Fowler's hands around his throat and the sensation of being hauled backwards until his back crashed against a wall. It was like he was drowning underwater, struggling to cling to some level of alertness as Fowler throttled the life from him.

Danny and Kim needed him. If Kane died, they would surely follow. The ruse of his evidence being emailed to journalists would not stop Fowler at that moment. Kane's eyes flickered open, and hate burned in his old friend's pale blue eyes. Fowler's lips curled back from his teeth in a feral snarl, and Kane forced himself to wake up. By sheer will, Kane regained consciousness. The pull of his children's defencelessness and dependency on him flooded his senses and body with strength. Kane reached to his back and pulled the Glock free of his waistband. Fowler saw it just in time and jerked his head away as Kane fired from the hip up at his face. Fowler grabbed Kane's arm, and they wrestled for a heartbeat in that position.

Car tyres skidded on the tarmac outside, and there were only moments before Fowler's team came in to put Kane down. He raked his foot down Fowler's instep and twisted his body so that Fowler's arm came around in a wide circle above his head. Once Fowler was off balance, Kane kicked him backwards and shot Fowler in the chest. The bullet's force threw Fowler from his feet, and he rolled on the shop floor, turning, gasping and clawing at his torso.

Kane cursed at himself for not taking a headshot as Fowler ripped open his shirt to reveal a bulletproof vest. Bright lights blinded Kane. It was the full-beam headlights from a car, and Kane turned away as machine gun fire ravaged the shop, tearing up shelving and products and filling the air with debris. Kane ran, keeping as low as possible. He scooped up his backpack and crashed through a door on the rear wall. Kane emerged into a tight corridor and then a staff locker area.

The machine gun fire halted, and the door to the shop burst open. Kane leant around the door and aimed low, shooting an onrushing operator clad all in black. He shot the attacker first in the foot and then in the head, learning the lesson from his failure to kill Fowler and recalling his old reflexes. Bright blood and white bone fragments splashed onto the beige-painted walls, and Kane edged down the corridor. He moved away from the shop and locker room, keeping his Glock trained on the door. A creaking sound behind him snapped Kane's head around, and he leapt to the floor just as another figure in black came through an emergency exit door at the end of the corridor. The muzzle of an MP5 flashed, and silenced bullets spat along the walls so that plasterboard rained down onto the floor and Kane. Kane rolled and shot his attacker in the arm, who emitted a female cry of pain. Kane ran at her and pistol-whipped her across her skull. He leant and took her earpiece, but her MP5 was fastened to her body by a strap. Before Kane could unclip it, the door towards the shop opened, and another shot rang out.

Kane dashed for the exit and burst out into the chilly night. He ran for his life, making for the ring of thick bushes around the car park's perimeter. His heart thumped in his chest, and as he quickly ducked under the branch of a tree, an impact thudded into his arm, spinning him into the undergrowth. The bullet had passed through the meat of Kane's arm beside his bicep, and hot blood pulsed from the wound. Kane rose and kept running. The searing pain burned in his arm like a bonfire, and his body screamed at him to stop and lie down. But to stop was to die, and he had to get to Danny and Kim, no matter what.

FORTY-FIVE

Fowler dragged himself up the wall by his fingernails. He sucked in gasps of air to fill his empty lungs. The vest had saved his life, but the force of the bullet at short range was like being punched by a heavyweight boxer. Blood pooled on the linoleum floor where Nolan lay in an awkward position, dead with a bullet wound on his forehead.

"Nolan's dead, McCann's wounded," Fowler sighed. He grimaced at the shooting pain in his stomach and the ache in his eye socket, gifts from the fight with Kane.

"We're here now," said Barnes' voice in Fowler's earpiece. He crashed through the door behind Fowler and into the corridor holding his MP5.

"Why did you open fire?"

"I thought he was reaching for a weapon in his bag. I saved your life."

"You cost us our target. We could be on our way out of here now, mission completed. Instead, we've got to fly those kids to a new location and arrange another meeting with Kane – if he is still willing to meet, that is. Not to mention we'll feel the wrath of Odin and McGovern for another failure."

"He's wounded," Nketiah spoke up through Fowler's earpiece. "I winged him."

"We can still catch him," said Barnes. "She shot him."

"He's gone by now. Besides, we need to get this fucking mess cleaned up. Your mess. You've always been quick to pull the trigger, Barnes. Kane would have come quietly. He'd do anything for those kids." Fowler realised he was shouting, and he straightened his back to ease the pain in his chest. "Call it in. Get a cleaning crew out here. Someone will have heard the gunfire, and the police will be here soon."

"Me call it in? Get one of the new guys to do it. Let me out there. I'll hunt Kane down inside thirty minutes."

"You call it in. One of the new guys is dead, and McCann is wounded. We need to regroup. You don't get it, do you? Kane is rusty. I felt it when we fought, but he's getting sharper. Old reflexes are returning. He was the best of us once. Even in the Regiment, he was different. Don't let the family man exterior fool you, Barnes. Kane is a killer, and if you go out there after him, it'll be your body in a black bag next to Nolan's."

"He's not that good. I could take him."

"No, you couldn't. He's killed more people than you've had hot dinners. He's wounded, but he's also armed. We regroup back at the hangar. Follow orders."

"That's right, Fowler," Kane's voice crackled in Fowler's ear over his team's communications system. "Regroup. You harm one hair on my children's heads, and I'll kill you all. I'll find you and burn your entire operation to the ground."

"How did he..." murmured Barnes, and then McCann pointed at her ear as she sat up, cradling her wounded arm.

"I came to meet in good faith, and you tried to kill me. The only way this ends is if you let my children go. But next time, I want to see them go free. Otherwise, I go public with everything I have on Mjolnir. That means the end for you bastards, your team, Odin, the whole merry band of nicknamed wankers."

"Come back now, Jack. We can sort this out here and now," said Fowler.

"No chance. I trusted you, Fowler, and you tried to blow my head off. Next time we meet,

I'll have my files with me. You can take me, but I want to see my kids released."

"I'll cut your fucking brats from neck to groin," Barnes said, his face twisted in a rictus of hate. "I'll piss down their dead throats if you don't turn yourself over to us now."

Fowler could have hit Barnes then, and he fought with himself to remain calm.

"See?" Kane uttered. "We need a better meet. An exchange. Me for my kids."

"We'll be in touch," said Fowler.

FORTY-SIX

Kane ran across a football field, the wet grass slippery under the smooth soles of his shoes. The sun crept over a skyline of factories and housing estates, just a slither of pallid yellow and orange under a slate grey sky. The bullet wound had been numb initially, but now pain throbbed from his arm. He felt his ribs burning like a fire, and he noticed that the stitches in his shoulder were torn and leaking blood.

He gritted his teeth against the fatigue in his legs, blood loss and lack of sleep taking their toll, and made for a pathway leading into a dense housing estate. Darkness kept him hidden on the football field, but as his shoes hit the pavement, he moved into the glare of streetlights. Kane darted left into an underpass beneath a road bridge. He cannoned into the wall and let himself slump to sit on the cold concrete. Kane pulled the earpiece free and tossed it into the gutter with a collection of crisp packets and plastic drink bottles. He reached inside his jacket and felt gingerly at the wound. It was ragged and would need proper care. The bullet had passed through the edge of his arm and was not stuck there. But tiny scraps of his clothing and whatever oil or particles of dirt were on the bullet itself would fester inside the wound. Kane had seen such wounds gone bad in the field before, and they were as deadly as an enemy grenade. He needed medical attention.

The hospital was out of the question. They would arrest Kane the moment he stepped inside the A&E department. He could wait for the shops to open and find a nearby pharmacy to get the supplies he needed to treat himself, but he could already feel weakness overwhelming him. Blood soaked Kane's shirt, it clung to his skin like a wet blanket, and if he lost much more, he could lose consciousness. Kane opened his rucksack, took out his phone, and dialled the only number he thought could help him. The line rang out, and Kane hung up before it went to voicemail. He slammed the handset into his thigh, cursing himself. There had been a chance to get Danny and Kim away at the car park, but he'd made a mess of it. Now that Kane had killed or injured members of their team, Fowler and his crew would not treat them well. He rested his head against the stone wall and closed his eyes, tiredness washing over him. A vibration in his hand snapped Kane awake, and he put the phone to his ear.

"This is Kane," he answered.

"Kane, I've only been asleep for a fucking hour. What is it?" said Craven, his voice deep and groggy from sleep.

"I need your help, Craven. I'm wounded. I need you to pick me up."

Craven sighed so loudly that it sounded like a wind storm down the phone. "Where are you?"

"I'll text you a location now, but from a different phone."

"I'll be there as soon as I can."

Kane took his spare burner phone from his bag and switched it on. He keyed in Craven's, Fowler's, and Jacobs' numbers. Just before he threw away his old phone, Kane clicked on the tracker app. Two dots blipped on the screen, a green dot in Manchester showing the location of Yelena's tracker. A red dot also blinked, moving away from Kane's location towards Liverpool.

Kane smiled because, for the first time in this whole sorry episode, he had done something right. In the seconds before his fight with Fowler, Kane had taken his spare tracking device from his rucksack. Fowler had thought Kane was reaching for his transcript files, but he had grabbed the tracker to buy himself an extra few seconds to think. The bullet had then smashed into the window. During the struggle with Fowler, Kane had slipped the tiny tracking device into the inside pocket of Fowler's overcoat. So Kane had two signals, one from a woman who desperately needed his help and one for his enemy, the man who had taken Kane's children.

FORTY-SEVEN

The sun was up as Craven turned his car into a housing estate on the border between Widnes and Warrington. It was a dull morning with heavy clouds moving quickly over a wind-swept sky. A man in a white van passed Craven and stared at him through his open window, a cigarette hanging limply from his mouth. Craven drove along the narrow streets between rows of cars parked on either side of the pavement. He wondered what he was doing and whether it would have been easier to just ignore Kane's call and leave him to his fate. The whole thing had gotten way out of control, anyway. He had a meeting scheduled with Kirkby later that day to discuss the Deli Boys' case. Though the gang had been dealt a blow, they weren't defeated by any means, and while arrests had been made at Diego's, Craven couldn't take the credit for it.

He had left Barb sleeping soundly in their bed. She slept little these days. Worrying about her cancer kept her up most nights if the pain didn't. Craven couldn't see a way to promotion without the Deli Boys' demise squarely pinned to his lapel. That meant that his dream of clean air and a new life in Spain was nothing but a pipe dream – unless he used the money that Kane had taken from the Deli Boys. He feared using it, though. Craven prided himself on being a clean copper. Despite seeing such things going on throughout his career, he had never taken a bribe or falsified evidence. Craven hadn't mentioned the money to Barb, or anyone else for that matter. He hadn't checked the account or done anything about it at all. He'd simply tucked away the slip of paper with the account details in his leather wallet behind his warrant card, and there it would stay. Not thrown away, but not accepted either.

Craven turned left and stopped at a crossing to let a teenager amble across the road, long hair swinging and head bowed, phone out and headphones on. Standard teenager behaviour. He drove past a newsagent just as a portly man in a green cardigan pulled the noisy shutters up from the window. Craven followed the road around the bend and pulled into where a pathway cut through the tarmac to lead down to an underpass. He clicked on the car's hazard warning lights and ran down the sloping pavement to where Kane was slumped in the shadows like a homeless person.

"Kane?" he called when he was close, and a pale face turned towards him.

"I'm wounded," said Kane, his voice ragged.

"Fucking hell," Craven tutted as he lifted Kane to his feet. "You look like you've gone ten rounds with Mike Tyson." Cuts and swelling distorted Kane's face. However, the dark stain on the shoulder of Kane's suit jacket was far more worrying. "You need a hospital, mate."

"No hospital," Kane croaked. "Just get me somewhere I can rest... and some water."

"Did you find your kids?"

"Mjolnir still has them. They tried to kill me."

Craven hooked his arm under Kane's uninjured armpit and walked him slowly towards the car. Kane stumbled, his skin pale and waxy. Craven opened the passenger door and helped Kane slide into the seat. He quickly ran to the other side, got into the driver's seat, and turned the car around. Craven drove back the way he came, stopping outside the newsagents.

Craven walked inside and bought a bottle of water and an energy bar before returning to the vehicle. His mind worked overtime. If he was found with Kane, he would lose his job and would probably be arrested. If he didn't get Kane to a hospital, there was a real danger of Kane dying, which could still lead to Craven losing his job and probably being arrested. Nevertheless, he and Kane had been through something together. Craven felt a sense of loyalty to the man. It wasn't that he owed him anything, simply that Kane needed his help and was worthy of it. Craven had asked Kane to bring down the Deli Boys, and he had done it. It was Craven's fault that he hadn't been able to take credit for their downfall. The plan he had devised on the spur of the moment had been terrible from the outset. He'd sensed an opportunity to exploit Kane's brutal skill with violence for his own benefit. But now, Kane needed Craven's help and Craven, despite his many shortcomings, was a good judge of character.

"Drink this and eat that," Craven said, handing the water and bar to Kane. "I'll take you to my place. You can rest there."

"Are you sure?" asked Kane as he slowly twisted the top off the water bottle, grimacing at the pain from his wounds.

Craven didn't answer because he wasn't sure. Barb would lose her mind when she saw the state Kane was in, but she would help him. It was a risk. How would Craven explain it away if they found Kane in his house? The man was the subject of a manhunt larger than any Craven had seen in his entire career. A suspected murderer, a man that Craven should not only arrest on sight but also report his sighting to headquarters.

If Craven understood correctly, Kane was also a government agent, a secret agent. A former special forces soldier and government agent on the run. What if this Mjolnir crowd found Kane at Craven's house? He shouldn't put Barb in that kind of danger. But Craven always followed his gut, and it told him that Kane was a good man, and sometimes a man had to do the right thing.

Thirty minutes later, Craven parked his car in the driveway of his house.

"Wait here," he said, and Kane nodded, his head lolling against the headrest.

Craven exited the car and opened his front door.

"Barb?" he shouted into the hallway, closing the door behind him. It was seven thirty in the morning, and she would be up by now.

"Yes, love?" she called from the bedroom.

"I have a friend with me who is in trouble. Don't be alarmed when I bring him in. He's hurt, and he needs our help."

"What do you mean he's hurt?" Barb appeared at the top of the upstairs landing. She wore her fluffy blue dressing gown and had a towel wrapped around her head to cover her hair, wet from the shower.

"Don't worry. Get ready, and I'll bring him in."

Craven returned to his car and helped Kane climb out of the passenger seat. Kane leaned heavily upon Craven's arm, and he crept towards the front door. Kane slipped as he tried to step into the house, but Craven pulled him over the threshold.

"Bloody hell," gasped Barb, covering her mouth with her hand. She scuttled off into the bedroom, and Craven worried again that he was making a terrible mistake. He dragged Kane into the kitchen and sat him down on a dining room chair. Craven took the rucksack from where Kane clenched it tightly in his left hand.

"It's alright," Craven said. "I'm going to help you." He reached around and took Kane's suit jacket off. The wounded side clung to the shirt beneath, and Kane gasped in pain as Craven tugged it free. He ripped Kane's shirt open and winced as he pulled the shredded corners away from the bullet hole. The wound trickled with dark blood, and the surrounding skin was already purple and swollen. Craven went to the sink, grabbed a clean cloth and soaked it in water. He returned to Kane and held the cloth to the wound.

"Oh my God, Frank," Barb exclaimed from the kitchen door. "What happened to him? Shall I call an ambulance?"

Craven turned and walked over to her. He put a

hand on each of her shoulders and looked her in the eye. "Barb, I love you, and I need you to trust me. This man is Jack Kane. He's my friend, and we need to help him. He can't go to the hospital, and I can't call it in."

"Isn't he the man...?" she began, her eyes widening as she recognised Kane's face.

"Yes, but it's not what you think. He's a good man."

Barb nodded and smiled. "Alright then, let's have a look at him."

She knelt in front of Kane and inspected his injuries. She tutted as she removed the cloth from the bullet wound, then rose and fussed around the kitchen, searching for their medical box and grabbing clean tea towels. Craven watched her, and in that moment, he was reminded of how he loved her completely. She trusted him to the point where she accepted a dangerous fugitive into their house, even though the consequences of assisting such a man were mind-blowingly life-changing.

FORTY-EIGHT

Kane awoke like a forest creature coming out of hibernation. His head rolled on a soft pillow, the warmth of the bed comfortable and welcome. His eyes opened a crack, and he closed them shut again, the light too bright. He licked at dry lips, and then, as his senses adjusted and his mind kicked into wakefulness, Kane shot upright. A knife-like pain stabbed into his arm, the agony so acute that bile rose in his throat. He raised his good arm and rubbed the sleep from his eyes with the back of his hand.

Memory returned from the fog of sleep, the fight at the car park, Craven picking him up from the underpass. He remembered little after that. Kane looked at his watch. It was eleven in the morning, but he wasn't sure how long he had been out. The dressing on his arm was fresh and bound well, and the stitches in his shoulder were secured with a clean bandage. Kane yawned, and the muscles in his face moved around the swelling. The fight with Fowler and his team had been desperate, and Kane was lucky to have escaped with his life.

Kane lay in a double bed, the duvet a soft quilt patterned with summer flowers. Eggshell-painted walls surrounded him, with pictures of mountains and lakes hanging here and there. Pastel curtains framed a window from which sunlight bathed the bedroom and warmed Kane's bare torso. He was at Craven's house, and he remembered then that it had been the Detective and his wife who had cared for his wounds. He glanced to his left, his rucksack rested against the bedside table, and his burner phone lay face up on the pine tabletop, a charger extending behind it. Kane reached for it. No messages. He breathed a sigh of relief when he remembered he had dumped his old phone and switched on a new burner in the underpass.

According to the date on the phone screen, he had slept for an entire day and night. The kids. Kane unlocked the phone.

We need to meet. Prove my kids are OK, or I'll go public.

Kane sent the text message to Fowler's number and stared at the screen for a minute, but there was no answer. He opened the tracker app and logged in from the new phone. Yelena was still in Manchester, but the tracker he had placed in Fowler's coat was now in London. Another minute, and still no answer.

The bedroom door opened, and a small woman crept in, her movements exaggerated like she was in a comedy movie. She wore a yellow roll-neck jumper beneath a navy gilet, matching trousers, and an electric blue scarf tied around her head. She smiled when she saw Kane was awake.

"You had a good sleep," she chimed warmly. Her voice was gentle and kind, and her face was open and round. "You needed it. Frank's at work, but he asked me to keep an eye on you." She set a glass of water down on the bedside table. "I just need to check your dressing, then I'll make you something to eat."

"Thank you," Kane said. The heavy worries weighing on his mind like an anvil made it impossible for him to return her smile.

"My name is Barbara. But everybody just calls me Barb."

"Thank you, Barb."

She perched beside him on the bed and reached over towards Kane's wounded arm. Barb sucked at her teeth as she removed the dressing. She bent to retrieve a shoe box brimming with medical supplies from the floor and dabbed at the edges of the bullet wound with a cleaning wipe.

"I used to be a nurse, once upon a time," she said. "Saw nothing like this, though. Lots of cuts and gashes, burns and the like."

Barb cleaned the wound and placed a fresh dressing over his shoulder. She smiled at him again and left the room with a promise of some food. Kane ground his teeth, angered by his failure to protect his children and inability to help Yelena. Everything he had tried to set right had failed. Things were unimaginably worse than they had been. Sally was dead, and Danny and Kim were in Fowler's hands. God only knew what Yelena was being put through by the malevolent Aivar and the remnants of his Deli Boys. The only way to set things right was to kill everybody involved with Mjolnir and eliminate Aivar and his Deli Boys. Kane would do what he did best. He'd kill them all.

Kane tensed the wounded arm and flexed his hand. He could move it. Kane raised the arm, and even though it screamed in painful objection, it still moved. He thought of the man he had once been. That man would never have allowed himself to end up in this predicament – licking his wounds in a housewife's spare bed while Sally's lifeless body lay cold somewhere at the hand of his enemies. He had to get up and about and start moving. He had to go on the attack.

Kane had to become his old self again. He had to step back into his old boots. He reached inside his bag and checked the gun. Eleven bullets remained. His knife was still there, as was his change of clothes. The trackers he had bought from the tech shop in Manchester were deployed, and the bag was crammed with crumpled bank notes stolen from the Deli Boys. Kane rolled his neck and set his jaw. He was even thinking like his old self. To end this, for Kane to raise his kids without looking over his shoulder at every turn, his enemies had to die. No compromises or half measures. No forgiveness or pity and no exceptions.

If he was going to end this, to finish Odin, Mjolnir and Fowler and get Yelena out of Aivar's world of prostitution, he would need supplies and weapons. Lots of weapons.

FORTY-NINE

"So we think he's dead, then?" asked Shaw, staring at the whiteboard incredulously with his arms folded.

"It doesn't matter what you think. It's over and closed. Word came down from on high, from Westminster. Case closed," said Kirkby, and he smiled for the first time in days. "The Chief Constable commended our efforts on the manhunt and assured me that the matter had been closed by MI5 or MI6. Doesn't matter, really."

"So are we off back to Manchester then, guv?"

"Back to Manchester," Kirkby nodded. "And back to the gangs and the drugs and its never-ending drudgery. Pack all of this shit up. I want to be out of Warrington today."

Craven waited for Kirkby and Shaw to finish their discussion and then followed Kirkby towards his office.

"Can I have a word, sir?" Craven asked, knocking on Kirkby's door just as he sat down.

"What is it?" Kirkby said, a frown darkening his cheerful demeanour when he realised it was Craven who wanted to talk to him.

"The Deli Boys, sir. I should have them all wrapped up soon. I've worked them for a while, and I think it's a brilliant collar for me and the team. A good opportunity to look at getting a bump up to the next rank and I just wanted to see if you would support my application to…"

Kirkby chuckled and shook his head as Craven spoke, raising a hand to stop him mid-sentence.

"Hang on a minute, Craven. Langley brought down the Deli Boys with his gun-toting madness. It had nothing to do with you, so don't try to take the credit. Two years you've worked their case, and you haven't got near them. You've got more chance of shitting in the Queen's handbag than me supporting your promotion. You're a dinosaur, Frank; you're finished. No use to anyone. If I had my way, you'd be off this team, but apparently, you still have some friends in high places."

Craven stepped into the office and closed the door. "Listen, sir," he began, but Kirkby stood and raised his hand again.

"I never told you to come in. Get out. Pack your

shit and get back to Manchester."

Anger welled inside of Craven. Kane had given him enough money to live comfortably and leave the UK for Spain with Barb. He didn't want to use those funds, money taken by a gang from those they preyed upon. But someone who had tried to live a good life should use the money rather than a gangster who would squander it. Craven could sell his house, add those funds to the Deli Boys' money, and never look back.

"You are a fucking weasel, Kirkby," said Craven. He took two long steps to position himself next to Kirkby's desk, on the side closest to where Kirkby stood, so that he towered above the smaller man. "You are everything that's wrong with the force nowadays, and I'm sick to the back teeth of swallowing your shit."

"Back off, Craven, you're out of order." Kirkby licked at dry lips as he stared up into Craven's eyes. His face flushed red, and Craven grinned at him.

"I'm going to walk out of here now, Kirkby, and I'm never coming back. I can't work with you anymore. You're not police. Not like we used to be. The force used to be good men and women, honest people grafting to make the streets safer for people to live in. Now the force is infested with shit bags like you, only interested in promotion and climbing the greasy pole. Well, you can stick your job and your pole up your arse, you little shit."

Kirkby stammered for a few seconds and stepped back out of Craven's shadow. "I'll have you up on a disciplinary for this, threatening behaviour or…"

"I'll give you something more to put in your fucking report then, you miserable little twat." Grabbing a stapler, Craven yanked Kirkby's black tie down towards the desk, securing it with the stapler, and then took a clear glass jug of water and poured it over Kirkby's head. Craven marched away and flicked his middle finger over his shoulder as he left Kirkby raging in his office.

FIFTY

Fowler sat in an armchair, staring at a painting on the wall. It was an oil painting of a Napoleonic-era battle; he wasn't sure which one, but it depicted a cavalry charge down a valley, and the soldiers wore glorious uniforms and rode to battle with sabres drawn. It reminded Fowler of his years in the army when he had served his country with pride and honour. First in the Parachute Regiment and then in the SAS, that pinnacle of the British Army, which all soldiers aspired to. The soldiers in the painting had stern faces, strong chins and pride in the regimental colour that fluttered behind them.

The room was small, just the armchair and a sofa around a glass coffee table. A thick, teak-painted door led to the room beyond, into which Fowler waited to enter. The day they had asked him and Kane to move from the SAS into the mysterious Mjolnir agency had been a day of celebration. They had thought at the time that they would become James Bond-type spies, moving into the higher-paid echelons of the defence forces. That illusion had slowly dissolved in the reality of their new roles. They still worked to protect Britain's national security but in the shadows and in between the lines of morality and international law. Kane's words from the botched meeting had stung like a slap across the face, and they hadn't left Fowler's head since. It had been a long time since Fowler had been proud to serve his country.

The door opened, and McGovern strode into the waiting room. She was tall and slim, her angled face stern beneath the hard lines of her black, bobbed hair.

"Are you ready?" she said.

"Good morning," Fowler piped, flashing her a wide grin, more to annoy her than as a pleasant greeting. He rose from the chair, took his overcoat from the back and slung it over his arm. Fowler wore a tailored, double-breasted suit, shirt, and tie. It had been less than twenty-four hours since the plane from Liverpool had landed, and Fowler had to mask the pain of his bruises as he stood.

"Looks like you've had a busy time in the field?" McGovern flicked her eyes at the bruising on his face.

"You should try it sometime."

"Well, I certainly couldn't be less successful than you, Thor." McGovern turned on her heel, and Fowler followed her into the room beyond. A man in his fifties sat comfortably on a tufted, dark leather chair. One long leg hung over the other, with an expensive pair of black loafers glinting in the sunlight. He wore an Italian-style suit, perfectly tailored, a crisp white shirt and a striped military tie. His face was long and chiselled, with a patrician nose protruding from it like the prow of a ship. Behind him, a large window provided a sprawling view of the River Thames winding away past the Houses of Parliament.

"Thor," said McGovern, "This is Odin, Commander of Mjolnir."

"Sir," Fowler barked, coming to attention with his body perfectly rigid, eyes straight ahead, and arms held stiffly by his side. He came to attention more out of habit than necessity. Mjolnir wasn't part of the army. He could tell Odin was a Rupert from the moment he laid eyes on him. Rupert was the nickname soldiers gave to the top brass, the commanders and officers who invariably came from the upper echelons of British society. They always had public school accents [A1]and the air of entitled nobility to go with them.

"At ease, Thor," Odin uttered in a languid drawl. "We aren't in barracks here. You contacted

Kane?"

Fowler relaxed, but only by shuffling his feet slightly further apart and clasping his hands behind his back. "Yes, sir. We met in the early hours of yesterday morning, but the situation turned violent, and he evaded my team."

"Your orders were to kill the target, were they not?" said McGovern, her lips pursing.

"They were. But intelligence came to light that Kane had copies of the statements he provided to the government concerning our operations. I thought it prudent to establish the whereabouts of those copies before completing the mission."

"So you disobeyed a direct order?"

"No, ma'am. The situation changed, and I adapted."

"Does he have copies?" asked Odin. He uncrossed his legs and reached for a crystal glass resting on a table.

"It could be a bluff, but I don't remember him ever being much of a gambler, sir," replied Fowler.

"If he releases what he knows to the press, it could cause us problems."

"Him turning on our agency did little damage when it happened, sir."

"That's because it wasn't meant to, Thor."

"I don't understand?"

"You aren't paid to understand. You are a blunt instrument, a tool to be wielded," McGovern said, venom dripping from her like a serpent. She turned to Odin. "What is the truth these days, anyway? Any truth can be made to look like the ramblings of an online troll or a chat room conspiracy theorist. And any falsehood has the potential to be meticulously moulded into a seemingly undeniable truth, radiating with the brilliance of divine revelation. People will believe anything, or not, depending on what the media, or more specifically, social media, tells them."

"Now, now," Odin smiled. He took a sip of whiskey from his glass. "I agree with you. The truth has become fluid. But in our line of work, I think the righteous left would lap up details of our operations and use them against the government, so I would prefer to err on the side of caution. Thor has been a stalwart operator for some time, so maybe he deserves an explanation."

"Thank you, sir," said Fowler. The corners of his mouth twitched in a stifled smile as McGovern sat down in her chair, her face calm but rage festering behind her eyes.

"Getting Lothbrok, or Kane, to provide testimony about Mjolnir was a counterintelligence operation. Not the type of operation you usually take part in, not a high-value target in a war-torn country, or a foreign junta to destabilise. This was an operation against a domestic threat."

Odin stopped talking, and the silence became awkward.

"So it was us who made Kane testify?" Fowler's face reddened, and his gaze shot between Odin and McGovern. He spoke slowly, concerned that what he said was foolish or that he had missed the point entirely.

"Yes. We convinced him to give evidence detailing the nature of our operations," said McGovern after frowning at Odin. She spoke hurriedly, annoyed that Odin had opened up to Fowler about Kane's testimony. "He was our most prolific operator, responsible for multiple kills and missions beyond the pale. Activities in direct contravention of international law. We used that evidence against mandarins in Whitehall to increase our scope of influence and operation. Senior civil servants, men who had worked in intelligence since the Cold War, were moved aside based on Kane's evidence. No more oversight, no more weak men looking over our shoulders trying to control our funding and activities."

"But he turned after the operation in the tunnels went wrong – when our team was massacred?"

"Fortunate timing, or not, depending on your point of view. The world has changed, Thor," said Odin, waving a hand as though the thing was obvious. "But British intelligence had not moved with it. We needed a change at the top, and Kane's evidence shifted that in our favour. McGovern, here, whilst not strictly part of Mjolnir, is our woman on the inside. She secures our funding, and we do what must be done to protect this country."

"So why do we want Kane dead if him turning traitor helped our cause?" asked Fowler.

"Do catch up," McGovern sighed. "He was supposed to disappear, never to be heard from again. Clearly, he had other ideas if he was so willing to get his hands dirty and expose himself. Getting mixed up with prolific Eastern European criminals suggests he's living more than a quiet life. We've had to reassess the situation. If he was prepared to testify once, he could do so again, perhaps even on a larger, more public stage. And if he has made copies of his evidence, well..." she shook her head and shuffled back in her chair.

"So why not kill him back then, after he had made his testimony?"

"Because we aren't as utterly ruthless as all that, Thor," said Odin with a smile that sent a shiver across Fowler's shoulders. "Lothbrok served his country well, and he believed that his evidence would never see the light of day. He also believed that he was riding off into the sunset into his new life of drudgery up north, and we were happy to let a decorated warrior have his retirement."

"Until he popped up again."

"Until he popped up again," Odin agreed. "If he can't keep quiet, then he has to go. His family was secure, and he might have joined them until you tore into that farmhouse and killed Kane's wife. We could have kept this all quiet and dealt with the family all together. You got us into this mess, Thor, and we must tidy it up. Now you tell us he's written his evidence down, and we can't have that."

"I warned you at the time that you were too sentimental towards Kane. So, does he have the bloody files or not?" McGovern barked, looking at the expensive watch on her wrist.

"Well, we have his children, and he would do anything to get them back," Fowler answered.

"So we set up an exchange," said Odin. "His kids for the files."

"And then what?" asked McGovern.

"Then, I'm afraid, my dear McGovern, they must all die. Only this time, I will be there personally to ensure the job's done properly."

"You, sir?"

"Yes, you bring what's left of your team, and I will bring along another team. A kill squad. We must eradicate all traces of Lothbrok and his family. It's hard and cruel, but it's a matter of national security. If we aren't out there, working in the shadows to protect this country from the increasing threat of terrorism, cyber-attacks, and the ever more sophisticated international criminal organisations, who will keep the country safe?"

"Three lives for the sake of millions, sir," said Fowler.

"Can we contact him, or do we know where he is?" asked McGovern.

"He sent a text message to one of my secure numbers today."

"Set it up then, Thor. And this time, let's do it right."

FIFTY-ONE

Kane stared at his reflection in the mirror as he shaved. He ran a hand down his pale skin and peered at the dark rings around his eyes. His cheeks appeared sunken, bones sharp and prominent. The dressing on his arm covered the bullet hole and the stitches in Kane's shoulder, but his chest, ribs and face were littered with purple and blue welts. The bruising intermingled with other scars, crisscrossing his body like a memoir. They told the story of his life, the places he had been and the things he had done for his country.

A burn scar twisted and crawled across the left side of his chest and stomach, and Kane remembered the terror of the Chinook helicopter coming down behind enemy lines and the pain of the flames licking across his body. He rinsed the shaving foam from his face with hot water from the bowl in Craven's bathroom. Other scars tried to get his attention, to scream their stories at him, but he banished them to the darkest corners of his mind. Knife wounds, bullet holes, shrapnel from IEDs. Each had a tale to tell, and he didn't want to hear it.

Kane dried his face with a hand towel and checked his phone again. Still no reply from Fowler. He pulled on a white t-shirt, carefully slipping it over his wounds. The worry for Danny and Kim's safety made his head ache. It was like a permanent hammering inside of his skull, and he had to find a solution, to figure out a way to get them back. Kane still hadn't grieved for Sally. There had been no time to think about or process her loss. They had been together for most of his adult life, and now she was gone. No funeral was arranged, and with their names protected by the programme, he wasn't even sure if they had notified her parents that she was gone. How would anybody other than Jacobs know who to contact? Was her body just waiting on a cold slab for somebody to come and claim it?

The front door downstairs opened and closed, and Kane heard voices talking in the kitchen. He pulled on the tactical combat trousers he had bought from the army surplus store in Manchester and made his way down the stairs.

"Just a bit of time off, that's all it is. No need to worry," said Craven, his voice carrying from the kitchen out to the hallway.

"They've never given you time off like this before. Are you sure there isn't something else going on, something you aren't telling me?" asked Barb. Kane held back, waiting at the foot of the stairs to avoid disturbing their conversation.

"I'm owed a ton of holidays, love, and I have to take them. They won't let us roll them over to the following year anymore, so I need to take them now. You've been saying we should go on holiday. So, now we can go. Let's go to Spain for a bit. Have a rest."

"You do work very hard, and a holiday would be nice. But, first, you turn up with our friend upstairs who has been injured, shot by a gun of all things, and now this talk of time off. I'm worried, Frank."

"What else would he have been shot by?"

Barb chuckled, and Kane imagined Craven pulling her into a cuddle. Craven was a gruff old-school police detective, but he loved Barb with the tenderness of a poet.

"You would tell me, wouldn't you? If there was anything wrong?" she said, speaking softly.

"Of course, I would. Now, why don't you nip into town and have a look around the travel agents and see if they've got any deals on?"

Kane walked into the kitchen and smiled, unable to help feeling guilty for imposing on

Craven and his wife. Everything was not alright, and they were in danger. Killers were hunting Kane, and if they knew where he was, they would descend on Craven's semi-detached house with all the fury of a military strike. It would be as though the place was a terrorist hideout. They would come with full, uncompromising force.

"You should rest in bed," said Barb, scolding him but smiling at the same time. She wore a green scarf and her usual outfit of gilet and smart trousers. "I've left soup in the fridge. You just need to warm it up, and there are fresh bread rolls on the counter."

"Mrs Craven, I..." Kane began, but she tutted at him to stop as she took her car keys from a drawer in the kitchen island.

"Call me Barb, please."

"Barb, then. I just wanted to say thank you. You have been very kind, and I'll be gone today."

"Nonsense," she replied matter-of-factly. She kissed Craven on the cheek and headed out of the front door.

"How did you get so lucky to find a woman like that?" said Kane after she had gone.

"She's lucky to have me, lad," Craven retorted, puffing his chest out. "I used to be a catch. Women from here to bloody Manchester lined up for a date with me. I played Rugby for Wigan

Schoolboys, and I wasn't half bad."

"You seem surprisingly chirpy today?"

"Aye, well. That's because I decided you were right. I will use that money you took from the Deli Boys. So, I've left the force."

"You've left the police?" said Kane in shock.

"That's what I said. I am now a man of leisure. I just need to find a better time to tell the Mrs, that's all. When you've gone, maybe. We can sell this house and get the place in Spain she needs for her chest. Get Barb the best cancer care money can buy."

"That's good. At least the money will go to good use."

"Any word on the children?"

"No. But I know where Fowler is, so I'll head in that direction today." The tracker in Fowler's coat still pinned him in London, so Kane would go after him.

"I'm with you. Where are we headed?"

"No, Craven. You've been in enough danger. Stay here. Forget about me now. Move to Spain and look after your wife."

Craven fixed him with a look that would curdle milk. "Don't you dare say that to me after all we've been through. I've no kids of my own, but I'm going to help get yours back. That's the end of it. And we can't leave that young girl to that bastard Aivar. God knows what he's subjecting her to at this very moment."

"I can do it alone. There's…"

"That's enough now. Where are we headed?"

The burner rumbled in Kane's pocket, and he took it out. It was a text message.

"It's Fowler. He wants to meet."

FIFTY-TWO

Craven drove his Ford Mondeo hard down the fast lane of the M6 motorway, heading south. He had called Barb to tell her he was driving Kane to some friends down south and that he would be back the following day. She hadn't liked it, but she understood. They drove past motorway services ten miles out from Birmingham, and Kane sat in the passenger seat fiddling with his handgun.

"Do you think we'll need that?" Craven asked.

"We might," said Kane. He took out the magazine and cast an expert eye over its contents. "But we only have eleven rounds left, so hopefully not."

"So, were you in the army, then?" Craven knew very little about Kane besides the crumbs of information Jacobs and Fowler had provided at the station. He also knew next to nothing about guns. Britain wasn't like the US. Craven had never carried a gun, and nor had he wanted to.

There were armed response units in the British police force, and some of the lads Craven had come up through the ranks with had gone to those units, but it hadn't been something which had ever interested him. Craven's calling was more the investigation and arrest of criminals who made honest folk's lives a misery. He enjoyed the thrill of the arrest, of seeing nefarious bastards being put away behind bars. But for every successful collar, there was another criminal who got away. Craven would send a file of every arrest to the Crown Prosecution Service. If there was even a sniff that evidence hadn't been gathered to the absolute letter of the law or that there wasn't sufficient evidence to prosecute the case, it wouldn't go to court, and the criminal would go free. Even criminals Craven had waved off to prison often got out on technicalities. Their lawyers would find some loophole or challenge the process of how the police had built their case. He was well rid of his job. Once he helped Kane out, he would be in Spain drinking sangria.

"Yes, in the past," said Kane. He clicked the magazine back into the pistol.

"Marines?"

"Parachute Regiment, then special forces."

"Jesus, Kane, it's like getting blood from a stone. We've at least an hour and a half before we get there."

"I joined the army after school and did well. I loved the Regiment after the Paras. We fought in Afghanistan and other hostile locations."

"So you're well used to firing guns, then?"

"You could say that, yes."

"You think they're going to ambush us down there?"

"Last time I met with Fowler and his team, it didn't exactly go peacefully. So, we plan for the worst. Our only aim is to get Danny and Kim away in one piece."

"They want to meet at a train station in Cambridge, right? With so many people around, they can't exactly open fire and gun us down."

"Hopefully not, but what if the station platform is deserted? What if they have snipers on the roof or in an adjacent building? This is Fowler's suggested meeting location. It's where he wants us to be, and he's picked it for a reason. It's probable that the station has good exits, has elevated positions for his team, and he feels he can control it. They want the files of my testimony, so I hand them over, and they hand over Danny and Kim."

"Do you have the files they're looking for?"

"Not exactly."

Craven turned his body so sharply that he almost crashed the car. "What do you mean?"

"There are no files. I have no records of what I gave in evidence. I spoke, and they wrote it down. But Fowler is expecting me to hand something over and will want to verify that it's the only version. They can't do that. What's to stop me from handing them a drive with the data and then having another copy stored elsewhere?"

"If that's the case, why don't they just kill you?"

"They should, but they are nervous. If I have statements and make them public..."

"They're fucked," said Craven, finishing the sentence in his own style.

"Yes. So, I have to give them something. I have a file location which they'll no doubt want to access before releasing the children. They'll likely have a laptop with them to do that when we meet. We have four hours until then, so take the exit for a town on the way. Not a city, maybe Rugby or Kettering. We'll stop and find a cybercafe so I can create some files before we get to Cambridge."

"Sounds a bit flimsy, if you don't mind me saying so. Create some files? Won't they just look shit, and Fowler will see right through them?"

"You just drive. Leave the files to me. First, though, we are going to meet Jacobs."

"If he was going to help you, wouldn't he have done it already? Seems to me he hasn't much power at all. He's just a pencil pusher. He can get you a new identity, but he can't save you from Fowler. Your wife died on his watch."

"He got me out of a world of shit once before... when everything went bad for me. When my team was massacred, Jacobs gave me a way out. We were on a job in smuggling tunnels. The tunnels were dark and close. It was horrific fighting down there. Crawling through tight spaces, not knowing what lay around the next corner. Our intel was bad, and we stumbled into an ambush. Good men died; only me and Fowler survived. There was a shitstorm after that, with civil servants asking questions about what we were doing there and who authorised the operation. Jacobs helped me then. Maybe he can again. And if I die, I need to know that someone can take care of Danny and Kim."

FIFTY-THREE

Kane stepped out of the Ford Mondeo and onto hard-packed earth. Craven got out of the driver's side and frowned as he looked around the car park, which was empty aside from one other vehicle, a black Jaguar saloon.

"That must be Jacobs' car. Why in God's name does he want to meet here?" asked Craven.

"It's private," said Kane with a shrug. He glanced around the surrounding woodland and waterways. Jacobs had agreed to meet and had suggested Fen Drayton Lakes, a wildlife reserve network of lakes and rivers northwest of Cambridge. It was on Kane's way to the arranged meeting with Fowler, and so he had agreed. Jacobs had talked about Kane handing himself in again, of letting the authorities go after Danny and Kim, but there was no merit in that course of action. If Kane went quietly or didn't show up for the meeting, Fowler would kill the children. Kane was in no doubt about that now.

They followed a pathway leading from the car park towards the waterways. A timber bridge extended from the car park shore to an island thick with dark trees. A red-breasted bullfinch caught Kane's eye on a clutch of brown-topped reeds, and as his boots stepped on the flexing walkway timbers, he saw a man in a suit leaning against the trunk of a silver birch tree. Craven pointed at the figure, and Kane nodded. Kane's suit had been ruined in the fight inside the pet store, so he wore the fatigues and boots he had bought at the army surplus store back in Manchester. The Glock pistol rested in the rear waistband of his trousers, and he had taped the knife inside his sock. Craven wore jeans and a casual jumper rather than his usual high street suit.

Kane reached the end of the walkway bridge and set foot on the island's soft grass. To his left and right, waterways stretched away, pitted here and there by forested islands similar to the one Kane now walked across. Jacobs stood with his back to the car park side of the island. He stared out at the sunlit waters where ducks and cormorants made their homes.

"Jacobs," nodded Kane as they drew close.

"Ah, Kane," Jacobs replied. He turned and raised a surprised eyebrow when he noticed Craven. Jacobs was tall and lean, his long face framed by a pair of sunglasses. "Have you thought any more about coming in?"

"Yes, but I need to be sure Danny and Kim will be safe. If I come with you now, who will..."

"Do you have copies of your evidence, Jack? Have you written and stored statements relating to your time as a Mjolnir operative?"

"That doesn't matter. You have what you asked for. I gave all my evidence at the time. If I come in now, who will look after my kids, Jacobs?" Kane's stomach rolled over, a warning tingle of fear kindling there. Something was wrong. How did Jacobs know he had threatened Fowler with exposure of his written evidence?

"You keep calling me Jacobs," he took his sunglasses off and smiled at Kane. "You really shouldn't. You used to call me something else, Jack."

"What are you talking about? Can you help get my kids back or not?" The burning hollowness of fear rose from his belly to his chest. Kane's heart rate quickened.

"Tell me where the files are, Jack, and this ends here. You have my word your children won't be harmed. They'll be taken care of, but this is the end of the road for you."

"How do you know about the files?"

"Jacobs, what the fuck are you talking

about?" Craven snapped, and he stepped forward towards the tall government man. "Can you help the kids or not?"

"Now," said Jacobs, turning his head a fraction. Six dark figures rose from the undergrowth like demons. They wore black combat fatigues and tactical vests, their faces covered with camouflage face paint. Each one carried a rifle, and each weapon pointed at Kane. Kane took a step back, and Jacobs smiled. "I wouldn't," Jacobs drawled as Kane reached for the Glock at the small of his back.

"Jacobs, what the…" stammered Kane, confusion raging in his mind.

"I told you to stop calling me that. Call me Odin, just like old times."

FIFTY-FOUR

Shock hit Kane like a bullet. He reeled, mouth opening and closing like a landed fish. "Odin?"

"We never met during your time under my command. But I am Odin, just as you were once Lothbrok. Now, do you have records of your evidence or not?"

Kane stumbled, thoughts swimming as the shattering knowledge that Jacobs was Odin overwhelmed him. The Commander of Mjolnir was also his protector and the man who had provided new identities for Kane and his family. Jacobs was the man Kane had trusted to protect his loved ones, yet the very thing he had wanted to shield them from. He couldn't make sense of it. The armed figures closed in, moving in controlled, short steps, weapons levelled and aimed in his direction.

"What's going on?" said Craven. He held his hands up and backed away from the gunmen, who had appeared so suddenly from the fen.

"Why get me to testify, Odin?" asked Kane.

"To make us stronger. And you did well, but now it's over. If you help me now, Agent Lothbrok, I will ensure your children are well provided for. Make it difficult, and they might turn up in that lake there with crabs crawling out of their little eyes."

"What about my team? Smithy, Carl, Wisdom, Nidge? Did you set us up as well? Just to get me to give evidence?"

"Collateral damage. For the greater good. The files?" Odin's tone grew serious. Up to that point, he had spoken with the self-righteous tone of a powerful man explaining something to a fool. The Mjolnir armed operators closed their circle so that they surrounded Kane with five paces between him and them. Some dripped water from where they had crouched in the lake, but all had darkened, impersonal faces. Even though he couldn't see their features beneath the camouflage, Kane knew them all. Not personally, but he knew them as Mjolnir killers, men like him. Ruthless and brutal.

"Was Sally collateral damage as well?"

Odin shrugged. "You popped your head up. You should have stayed quiet. I could have disposed of you after you gave evidence, you and your little family. But I let you live. You'd earned it. None of this would have happened if you'd stayed quiet. But you had to throw your weight around, show that little Estonian girl what you could do. Once your name was flagged up, we had a problem. You made things... inconvenient for me." At that moment a strange look crossed Odin's face. "I tried to get you to come in peacefully, but you wouldn't listen. Sally and the kids were safe at the farmhouse. It was your belligerence that forced Thor to send his team after them. You just couldn't stay quiet and wouldn't come to me as I asked. So you are as responsible as me for your wife's death. Do you think I wanted this? Mjolnir agents fighting on home soil when we could be out there protecting this country?"

There was no time to reach for his gun. They would pump him full of automatic rounds before Kane's weapon left his trousers. Rushing them would be futile as he was totally outnumbered. There was no way out. This was it. Kane would die here, and his corpse would show up days later, found by a dog walker or a bird watcher, floating face down in the fen.

A movement from the corner of Kane's eye drew his attention, a sudden jerk from his left. He twisted his head just in time to see Craven fire a taser from his hip, and the operative close to him seized up under the electric shock. They had been so focused on Kane that the agents had failed to keep weapons trained on Craven. Time slowed, and the tasered man jerked in slow motion as white teeth showed in his camouflaged face. His arm snapped out to the side, and his weapon spat a silenced burst of three rounds. The soldier opposite him yelled as a bullet tore through his knee. Another crumpled in half as a second stray bullet cleaved his thigh, leaving a mist of crimson blood in the air.

Kane leapt towards the fallen men and drew his Glock pistol in the same motion. He landed on his side, firing a shot at Odin, and the Mjolnir Commander fell backwards. Rolling towards the operator who'd been shot through the knee, Kane kicked out his leg, and the wounded men fell. The grass next to Kane's head burst open, spraying him with dirt as a bullet ripped into the earth. Kane rolled the fallen man on top of him, pressing his Glock pistol underneath the man's bulletproof vest and firing another shot into his flesh. The man's body jerked, and his green eyes stared into Kane's as he blew his fetid breath into Kane's face. His body shook as bullets fired from his own team riddled his legs and torso instead of Kane's. Kane let his arm rest on the grass and closed one eye. He aimed carefully and fired at a gunman who was locked in a close-quarters struggle with Craven. The man's face turned to red ruin as the bullet smashed through his mouth, sending a spray of blood and mangled teeth across Craven's front.

The body Kane had used as a human shield lay lifeless and heavy, and Kane struggled to unclip the MP5 from the man's shoulder strap. Another bullet slapped into the man's body armour, and Kane felt the automatic weapon come free. He took the submachine gun in his left hand, fired three shots at the enemy, and rolled out from under the corpse. He quickly sprang to his feet and ran towards Craven, firing another burst of three rounds from the weapon as he went. A bullet sang perilously past his head, so close that it took Kane's breath away. He cannoned into Craven, sending him spinning into the lake and away from the gunshots. Kane turned and charged at the Mjolnir gunmen, too close now for them to fire without hitting one another in the crossfire. He smashed the MP5 into one man's nose and shot another in the groin at close range with the Glock.

Kane turned to fire again when a hand batted the MP5 aside and grabbed his right wrist as he tried to raise the Glock. It was Odin, recovered from the gunshot to his vest. Odin crashed his head into Kane's face, and his elbow cracked across Kane's jaw. Kane stumbled, reeling from the pain, and Odin front-kicked him in the stomach. Kane tried to raise his pistol, but Odin punched him hard in the face causing Kane to stagger backwards, the gun flying from his hand. Odin stood on the MP5's barrel, and Kane released his grip on the weapon. In a flash, Kane retaliated, slamming the flat of his hand into Odin's throat, and then leapt for the water.

Gunshots sliced through the ice-cold water, and voices shouted behind him. Kane dragged Craven with him deep into the lake, diving beneath the surface into the murky darkness. Slimy plants and weeds slopped past his face and hands as Kane clawed at the water to propel himself faster. Craven was beside him, both men rising to gasp for air and then diving again, desperate to escape the attackers and move further into the water.

FIFTY-FIVE

A train rumbled away from the platform. It was a multi-carriage, slow-moving relic which would stop at every town on its journey towards Norwich. Fowler leaned against an iron girder and cast his eye over the handful of people hurriedly making their way to the stairwell that would lead them away from the platform and out into the station.

"Any sign of him?" he said quietly, knowing that his earpiece would pick up his voice.

"Negative," came Barnes' response.

"Nothing from the roof either," added Nketiah.

"Be vigilant," Fowler repeated for the tenth time. "Kane won't simply stroll in here and leave himself vulnerable to an ambush. Don't let him take you by surprise."

"Let the bastard try," Barnes growled, and Fowler clenched his jaw in frustration. Even the man's voice annoyed him.

"Watch that itchy finger. Let's not have a monumental cock up like last time. Be calm and use the comms. Work as a team. Let's get this operation finished."

The train disappeared out of sight, and the platform returned to its usual peaceful self. Layers of chipped paint on the iron structure revealed the station's age, and the nearby litter bins were packed with rubbish left by the early morning commuters. It was midday, the rush was over, and aside from Fowler, only two people were waiting for a train – a pair of students sat on a bench, scrolling through their phones.

The conversation with Odin and McGovern nipped at Fowler's thoughts like an overzealous puppy. The revelation about Kane and his testimony being an inside job, a setup, raised suspicions in Fowler's mind. It led him to contemplate whether the botched operation in the tunnels had also been deliberately orchestrated. He wouldn't put it past Mjolnir, especially considering how things had appeared during his meeting with Odin. Good men had died that day in sweltering tunnels, searching for a high-value target that might never have existed. Fowler never questioned who their HVTs were, and in truth, he didn't care. The order came in, and he followed it. However, the abject failure of that mission and the bitter loss of their teammates had tipped Kane over the edge.

If he closed his eyes, Fowler could hear the explosions of IEDs ripping through the tunnels. He could taste the dust and the iron tang of blood, accompanied by the agonising screams of his comrades as they died in the darkness. So, he kept his eyes open.

Fowler told himself to stop thinking about the strange warp of how Odin had engineered Kane's testimony against Mjolnir. It was a thing best left to the top brass. Kane had turned grass, no matter what the situation or excuse was. And that could never be forgiven. Yet amidst the chaos and confusion, the one positive note was that Odin had actually allowed Kane to ride off into the sunset. That would be Fowler's next step. He'd see this job through, then ask to retire. He had enough money to live a good life. Fowler could go wherever he wanted, buy a house by the sea or a lake. He would buy a boat, fish every day, and swim in the water. Perhaps he could find a woman and settle down. Even Barnes wanted out, but Fowler wouldn't mention that to Odin until he'd sorted his own future out first. He just needed to get the job done, the worst job Fowler had worked in his career. Even crawling through dank tunnels on his hands and knees in the dark had been better than this. He would take jungle fighting any day over fighting his old friend on home soil.

Fowler's phone rang, so he took out his

earpiece. The display was a protected number, a secure line.

"Thor," he said, using his codename to answer the call.

"Thor, get your team together and meet me at headquarters with Kane's children ASAP," Odin ordered. His voice came in bursts between sharp intakes of breath, and the background noise indicated that he was running.

"What's going on?"

"Kane called, so we set up a last-minute meet in the fens. It went badly. We have men down, and Kane is loose in the field."

"What? We were supposed to meet at Cambridge station? It was all arranged. I'm here now with…"

"He called en route to Cambridge, and I met him with a team. But he got away before we could achieve our objective. Scramble all operatives to HQ now. I want every Mjolnir gun pointed at Kane. Every able body we have is to work on this case until Kane is dead."

The phone cut off, and Fowler slid his earpiece into place, then gave the order. Mjolnir headquarters was a facility on a vast swathe of land on the Wessex Downs. It was primarily a training base for Mjolnir teams, with a firing range and acres of land for training ops. At its centre was a stately home with offices and barracks on the grounds. Odin had acted rashly, meeting Kane without contacting Fowler first. Odin was Commander of Mjolnir and didn't need to consult Fowler about anything, but they were supposed to be working as a team to bring Kane down. It was getting messy and unprofessional. Kane had faced another attack and had managed to escape once more. He would be angry and desperate to get his children back. An animal can be at its most dangerous when it's wounded and desperate. If he were Kane, he would expect Mjolnir to hold his children at the headquarters. It was secure, well-defended, and it would be impossible for Kane to get into or make any attempt to recover the kids. Odin would have to find an alternative approach to draw Kane out since he would likely refuse any further meetings after the previous two had ended in ambush and bloodshed. Whatever plan Odin cooked up, this had to end soon.

FIFTY-SIX

Craven crawled out of the stinking mud; his clothes hung from his shivering body as though they were dragged down by rocks. The filth of the lake bed squelched through his fingers, and his teeth chattered uncontrollably. As slick wetness turned to dry grass, he flopped onto his back, staring at a sky thick with dense clouds. His muscles ached from the exhausting half swim, half scramble through the weed-heavy fen waters. Kane strode out onto the shore beside him and turned to stare across the lake.

"They'll hunt for us," said Kane, pulling a long strip of glistening green sedge from inside his t-shirt. The once-white garment was now brown and soaked through, with spots of blood showing on Kane's arm and shoulder.

"How the fuck did we get out of that?" gasped

Craven.

"Your taser took them by surprise. And as for me, I'm not sure if what I did was very brave or very foolish. Come on, we need to keep moving." Kane reached out a hand, and Craven grabbed it to let Kane haul him to his feet. Craven followed Kane across the breadth of the island. They waded into a thick clutch of rushes in the deep fens until Kane bent low and pressed a finger to his mouth. Craven knelt with him, cold water covering his legs to the waist. They waited there, and Kane scanned the expansive waterways in silence. A heron flew overhead, its broad wings like an aeroplane, as it circled and landed in the shallows twenty paces away from them.

Kane tapped Craven on the shoulder, and he followed his finger as it pointed towards the water. Craven squinted. His eyes weren't what they once were, and he cursed under his breath at the figure creeping inexorably through the lake. The man's face was obscured and low to the waterline, his weapon held just above the lake, sweeping in wide arcs as the Mjolnir agent came on. Craven hugged himself, doing his best to stop shivering.

"We need to warm up," said Kane, and Craven frowned at him for stating the obvious. "Hypothermia will kill us as easily as their bullets."

The cold bit and snapped at Craven's fingers and toes. His legs were warmer than his torso, so he edged deeper into the water to submerge himself further. It was spring, and even though the weather was becoming milder, the waters were ice cold.

"I'm too old for this," he whispered. Kane ignored him. Craven watched the man in the water move away from their island. He looked like a floating log or a crocodile with his camouflaged skin and his gun on the waterline. After waiting until the gunman had disappeared from view, Kane led Craven back into the water and across to the next island. A dark wooden walkway linked all the different islands and waterways, but Craven assumed Kane avoided it to remain hidden. They headed away from the car park and Craven's car. Mjolnir agents would be at the vehicle, ready to put a bullet in their heads if they tried to reach it. Kane pointed ahead at a timber box-like structure on the edge of the next island along. A hide for bird watchers. They waded towards it, and once they reached the hide, Kane stripped off his clothes and gestured for Craven to do the same.

Kane took his clothes and wrung them until his muscles bulged like cord on his lean body. Craven followed his lead and scrunched his clothes as tight as he could to remove every last bit of the filthy water. They pinned their clothes around the structure, tucking hems into the small gaps between the wood planks, and then huddled together in a corner. Craven tried his best not to stare at the pattern of scarring and burns heavy on Kane's body and refrained from asking Kane about their origin. It was obvious the man was a soldier and a fighter who had seen a lot of action.

"We'll wait here for dark," said Kane.

"Thank fucking Christ it's not winter," Craven muttered, and Kane just shook his head.

They shivered and huddled in the hide for hours. Kane remained vigilant, his eyes fixed firmly on the fens for any sign of Mjolnir agents, but none came close. Craven shook uncontrollably. His fingers and toes felt like they could snap off, and the filth of the lake bed smeared his skin with grime. The two men endured the long day in silence, waiting in fear as they anticipated their enemies arriving in a storm of bullets. Craven imagined his corpse floating for days in the foul water before being discovered, and he worried about how Barb would manage without him.

The day drew on, and their clothes slowly dried on the hide's walls. Craven eventually warmed up, and although he was hungry, thirsty, and cold, he was alive.

"So Jacobs wasn't on your side after all?" he

asked. It had surprised Craven as much as Kane to learn that Jacobs wasn't the mild-mannered government Mr Fixit he had purported to be.

"No, he wasn't. He ruined my life."

"Turns out he's actually the gun-toting leader of a network of secret fucking agents hell-bent on seeing us both dead."

"Something like that," Kane peered through a slit in the hide wall. The long, thin open window provided a place to rest binoculars while watching wildlife in the fens and islets.

"So he lied to you?" Craven pushed Kane to elaborate. He clearly didn't want to talk. But Craven was on the verge of freezing to death, and talking took his mind off it. Besides, he needed to know what kind of war he had got himself tangled up in.

Kane tore his eyes away from the lakes and stared at Craven. There was a hollowness to his brown eyes in that moment, the haunted look of a man who had seen or experienced too much in the world. Craven had seen that look before, usually in detectives who had spent too long working undercover or had worked on the sex offender's squads and become ground down by the horror of society's underbelly.

"Jacobs approached me after a Mjolnir operation went wrong," said Kane. He glanced out at the distant, still water and then back to Craven. "I'd served as a Mjolnir agent for years, working with different teams, sometimes alone. I had been working with one team for over a year on a series of kill operations. This job was to infiltrate a network of underground tunnels where a high-value target was hiding out. We went in. It was tight down there, dark, and hard to breathe. Like something from a nightmare. We were deep in the tunnels when IEDs started going."

"Improvised explosive devices?"

"Yes. Tunnels collapsed around us like an old coal mining disaster. The fear of suffocation was overwhelming, and we were pinned down by relentless gunfire. It was catastrophic. Aside from Fowler and I, the entire team died in the carnage as we tried to dig and fight our way out. After that, Jacobs came to me and offered a way out. He said that the government knew about Mjolnir's activities and errors and wanted to bring them to justice. Jacobs said that the operations they had been running were for money and not national security; Mjolnir had gone rogue and become a mercenary organisation available to the highest bidder. To my disbelief, a drug cartel funded the tunnel operation. So my team fought and died for nothing. We thought we battled to protect the people of Britain, that our suffering allowed normal people to sleep safely in their beds each night. So, when I found out that we were actually working for the same guys we were supposed to be fighting against, it sent me into a head spin. Jacobs asked me to give recorded testimony about the places I had fought in and the things I had done, and in return, he would give me and my family a new life."

"And he did, right?"

"Yes. But that all turned to shit. My wife Sally had to give up her life and was never happy afterwards. The kids were fine. They were small and adapted well to their new schools and names. It was like a game for them. But me and Sally ended up splitting. She couldn't bear to have me around anymore. I think she blamed me for her life changing. When I was in Mjolnir, she complained I was never at home. Yet once we moved up north, everything she'd worked for was gone, and she seemed to lose all sense of herself. I was miserable, working menial jobs for bad money, and I withdrew into myself, which created some distance between me and Sally. I got to see more of the kids, though, which was the only good to come out of it all. Sally started training at a gym and found a man who showed her a bit of attention."

"She cheated?"

"She didn't even try to hide it. I don't think she

actually slept with the guy. I think it was just a couple of dates. Our lives had changed so much; I think she just wanted some love, and I couldn't give it to her."

"And it turns out that your own organisation tricked you into giving evidence against them?"

"So it seems. Jacobs, or Odin as we now know, duped me. They used me to strengthen the Mjolnir agency. As if I hadn't done enough for them. My hands and soul were drenched in blood, and they still wanted more from me. Mjolnir killed my wife, and they've snatched my children. They've taken everything from me."

"Your children are still alive," said Craven. He hadn't seen this side of Kane before. Kane, as tough a man as Craven had ever met and with war skills beyond the comprehension of ordinary folk, suddenly looked small and sad. Kane wasn't a big man anyway, nowhere near Craven's own height and weight. He was average, which, Craven supposed, was probably the point. Kane wouldn't stand out in any crowd; he looked like an everyman.

"Danny and Kim are only alive because Odin and Mjolnir believe I have a record of my evidence ready to send to journalists in the event of my death. They fear that scrutiny. If it weren't for that, the kids would be dead by now."

"We were going to stop and create some files

before we met Fowler in Cambridge?"

"No point now. Fowler is Mjolnir, and Odin has obviously taken over the operation to take me out. There can be no meeting now. They could pull the trigger on my children as we speak."

"Can't we find Odin and Fowler and save your children?"

"It's me and you, Craven. All we have are the clothes on our backs. We are miles away from the northwest. Your car is compromised. We have no money and no weapons. I lost my gun in the lake. There's nothing we can do. It's over."

Kane's head dropped so that he stared at the ground. His shoulders sagged, and he shuddered from the cold. Craven shook his head. They had come too far to give up now.

"We won't abandon your children to this fucking Mjolnir crowd, not whilst there's strength in us yet. Where is their base? There must be somewhere the organisation runs from, where they have their offices?

"Their HQ is in the southwest, but we'd need an army to get in there."

"Never mind that. Would they take Danny and Kim there?"

"They might. Now that they know I'm not in the northwest anymore." Kane looked up.

"You said you wanted to bring Mjolnir down, right?"

"I did, but it's impossible."

"What would we need to get inside their headquarters and get your kids out?"

"If they are even there," Kane sighed. "We'd need money for supplies, new clothes, a vehicle, and weapons. A lot of weapons."

"You seemed like a dab hand at sourcing or, actually, fucking stealing cars up north, so what's stopping us from stealing one down here? And I know a gangster who escaped from police custody with plenty of money. An arsewipe whose operations have recently been decimated, but he's armed to the fucking teeth. This bastard has also taken a girl you tried to help and is putting the poor lass to work in one of his brothels. So let's kill two birds with one stone? Think about your kids. They need you. You can't just give up and abandon them to their fate. What's the point of all that training? All that ability you've got with guns and combat if you can't protect your own family?"

"So your suggested course of action is that we, a retired police detective who has seen better days, and a wounded, broken down former soldier, should travel back to Manchester, take on Aivar and what's left of the Deli Boys, steal their remaining cash and weapons, free Yelena, get to Mjolnir headquarters, evade Odin's army of operatives and hope that my children are alive so that we can free them before killing every single Mjolnir agent we can find?"

Craven scratched at the stubble on his chin. Now that Kane had summarised what he was suggesting, it sounded ridiculous, especially given that he was currently half naked in the Cambridgeshire fens. "Yes," he said. "Apart from the bit about me having seen better days. I'm in my fucking prime, son."

Kane stood and pushed his shoulders back. "We'd better get started then."

FIFTY-SEVEN

"This is the place," said Kane. The locater flashed green on the tracker app, indicating that Yelena, or at least her tracker, was in the building across the road. It was a lap dancing bar only a stone's throw from Diego's in Deansgate Locks. The building was a three-storey hulk of brickwork on a corner where three back streets came together. It was ten o'clock in the evening. Up and down the smaller streets between Oxford Road and Deansgate, late-night cafes, bars, and small nightclubs came alive. Shutters opened, and bright artificial lights shone onto the rain-soaked pavement. A film of light rain drizzled onto the narrow streets so that flashing signs reflected in puddles as young people marched hurriedly from bar to bar to keep out of the wet.

"I'll be here with the engine running in five minutes," replied Craven. He wore a new overcoat, trousers, and a shirt bought fresh that afternoon. The former detective's face was covered in stubble so grey it was almost white.

"Wait at the end of the street, but park facing this way. When you see me come out, bring the car up."

Craven nodded and strode away into the rain. Kane watched him go. In the late afternoon, they had trudged out of the fens and taken a car from a lane close to the park. Kane had broken the window of the Citroen, and they had made the drive up north, using the car's air conditioning to dry the cash notes in Craven's soaked wallet. Kane had turned into a serial criminal. He'd stolen several cars since escaping Warrington Police Station, besides the multiple assaults and deaths. They were all in self-defence, or so Kane told himself. Before all of this, Kane had never committed a crime in his life. Sports had dominated his childhood, and then he had entered the armed forces. So there had never been an opportunity to mix with the wrong crowd as teenagers often did.

During the journey from Cambridgeshire, Craven had pulled in at a Tesco supermarket off the motorway. The two men had shambled in, their clothes filthy and stinking with fen water and mud, and came out wearing new basic Tesco clothing. Kane wore chinos and a long-sleeved t-shirt over tan chukka boots. The clothes didn't fit well, but they were warm and dry and were as much as they could afford with the crispy notes from Craven's wallet. Now that Odin knew Craven and Kane were working together, Kane wanted to avoid using bank cards. They would track all of Craven's bank accounts to pinpoint his location. Kane bought a burner phone in the supermarket phone shop and logged into the tracker application downloaded from the Android store. Both trackers were still active. Yelena's took them to the inner city of Manchester whilst Fowler's signal travelled west from London to Wiltshire, indicating a move towards Mjolnir headquarters, and Kane prayed that Danny and Kim were alive and with him.

Kane put the phone in his pocket and crossed the cobbled road towards the lap dancing bar. A long, rectangular sign flashed above the doorway with the word *Bunnies* in pink, surrounded by neon drinks glasses and musical notes. The sign was positioned so that people leaving the bars and nightclubs nearby could see it.

A bouncer in a black coat and gloves waved Kane inside, and he paid ten pounds to a thin woman behind a plexiglass window. A camera glared at him from the black-painted wall behind her, and a red dot above the dome-shaped lens flashed every few seconds. Kane stared into it, wondering if someone actually monitored the feed within the building. The woman gave him a token and asked for his hand to stamp it. He took the token, which entitled him to a bottle of beer at the bar and walked up carpeted stairs towards thrumming dance music. Another bouncer opened the door, and Kane entered a long room bathed with red lighting. There was a stage surrounded by stools and a young woman with copper hair gyrated on a glass pole. One customer sat on the high stools, and another two lounged at the bar with two Eastern European-looking girls draped around their shoulders.

"Bottle of Becks, please," said Kane to the twenty-something man behind the bar. More girls sat in cubicles talking to one another, each tanned with immaculate make-up and long multi-coloured nails. They wore bikinis or lingerie; Kane wasn't sure which. A raven-haired girl peeled herself from a booth and approached Kane. She sipped water from a bottle through a straw and walked on heels with a cat's gracefulness.

"Would you like a private dance?" she purred in accented English and flicked her hair.

"Where do I go if I want more than a dance?" he said.

"We can go somewhere, but can you pay?"

"I can pay."

"Follow me." She took his hand and led him

away from the bar, passing the dancing pole and its surrounding chairs. The girl swayed her head in time with the thumping music until they came to a door set into the back wall. A large bouncer with fierce eyes and a long beard stood guard, his tattooed arms folded across his chest. The girl said something to him that Kane couldn't hear over the music, and the bouncer looked him up and down.

"It's two hundred pounds to go up there," he said with a curled lip. Kane nodded thoughtfully. He had little time. Craven waited outside, and Kane had gambled on the hope that Aivar or his goons would be upstairs with the girls. He was counting on them being armed and having some cash. If that wasn't the case, he'd have no way of attacking Mjolnir HQ with anything other than a sharp stick or a supermarket bread knife.

Kane beckoned the bouncer towards him as though he wanted to ask a question. The bouncer frowned and leaned in. As he cocked his head, Kane smashed the bottle of Becks across the back of his skull and drove two fingers into the man's eyes. The girl yelped and tottered away on her high heels, and the bouncer fell to his knees, screaming and clutching at his eyes. Kane opened the door and strode into a dark stairwell lit by beads of lights that curled around each stair. He heard shouting and the pounding of shoes on the stairs before he saw the force of Deli Boys charging through the darkness towards him. Someone had been monitoring the front desk camera, and they had recognised Kane. Snarling faces emerged from the gloom like creatures from a nightmare, and Kane didn't have time to brace himself before the leading man, a muscled-up brute with a top-knot of black hair that resembled a tiny bowler hat, smashed into him.

FIFTY-EIGHT

Kane tumbled backwards through the doorway and into the lap dancing bar. He tripped over the kneeling bouncer with the gouged eyes and came up just in time to block a vicious kick aimed at his head. Another foot volleyed Kane in his ribs, and he creased up in pain. Fists hammered onto the back of his head, and he instinctively curled into a ball to protect himself. A hard, dull object thudded into his back, and Kane collapsed to the carpet, which stank of stale beer and cheap perfume. The dancers screamed and ran away from the explosion of violence, and the bar emptied of everyone except Kane and his attackers. The cold, hard bottom of a long-necked beer bottle slammed into the hand Kane used to protect the back of his head, and if he didn't do something quickly, he would die there in the seedy bar, and Yelena and his children would be left to their fates.

Despite the vicious onslaught, Kane smiled to himself. His attackers shouted and snarled. They kicked and punched the man who had destroyed their deli and stolen vast sums of money from their off-shore accounts. Kane smiled because the man the Deli Boys faced was Jack Kane, codename Lothbrok, a highly skilled special forces operator and counterintelligence government agent. This was his world now, violence and brutality. Undeterred by the pain in his wounded arm and shoulder, he caught a foot and twisted it savagely. He grabbed an attacker's fist and drew the arm towards him, turning his body and spinning his legs around to catch the falling head between the shin of one leg and the thigh of his other. He squeezed, and a bearded face turned instantly purple. The spider web tattoo on the man's neck bulged with straining veins. Kane dragged the choking figure around in a half circle, using the weight of his body to drive his attacker's back. There were eight of them. A knife glinted in the glare of a disco ball, and Kane broke the choking man's neck between his legs.

Kane surged to his feet, dodged a wild punch and thundered his own fist into that man's solar plexus. The knife came for him in a slashing sweep that would rip his throat open, but Kane stepped into it and caught the swinging arm with his elbow before headbutting the knifeman in the nose. Gristle and flesh crunched against

Kane's forehead, and he yanked the knife free. The beer bottle came for him again, and Kane swayed backwards as it flashed before his face. He reversed the knife and slashed the man with the bottle across the eyes before burying the knife in his chest up to the hilt.

The horde of attackers fell back from the explosion of extreme violence. One ran towards the exit, and the rest stared in horror at their fallen fellow gang members.

"Bastard!" roared the man with the top knot who had first barged Kane back from the stairs. He charged again, hoping that his hugely muscled chest and shoulders would drive Kane backwards. Yet Kane simply used the man's momentum against him and deftly threw him over his back. The brute landed with a thud, twisting onto his belly, and without hesitation, Kane stamped the heel of his shoe into the back of the fallen man's head.

The remaining two Deli Boys were young, in their early twenties. They glanced at each other, then eyed the blood-spattered bar and their savagely injured comrades. They both looked Kane up and down. Horror drew their faces taut. They stared in disbelief that an average-looking, middle-aged man in Tesco clothes could do this to their gang. Kane roared at them, bellowing like a starved lion, and the two men ran so fast that they tripped each other up as they hurtled towards the exit. Kane brushed himself down and made for the stairway at the bar's rear wall.

He took the steps two at a time and reached the top to find a corridor of rooms, and, ahead of him, there was a desk behind which sat two men in tracksuits. Without breaking stride, Kane hopped over the desk, kicked the first man square in the face, and drove the knuckles of his right hand into the second man's throat. They fell against the wall, and Kane bludgeoned them with a flurry of punches and kicks until they sagged down onto the tangerine carpet. Kane checked under the desk and found a baseball bat and a steel flick knife.

"I'm looking for Yelena," Kane said, grabbing one of the men by the scruff of his tracksuit top. "Is she here?" The man shook his head as though he didn't understand. Blood trickled from his nose where Kane had beaten him. "Is Aivar here?" The man grinned, his teeth washed with bright blood, and he pointed upstairs. The second man shot his arm out, pressing a button beneath the desk, and Kane cracked him across the skull with the bat.

No alarm rang out. The only sound was the repetitive thud of dance music from the bar downstairs. Kane walked around the desk and went along the corridor room by room. There were eight small, grim rooms, each with just enough space for a bed and a sink. Most were empty. One was occupied by a sad-looking black woman who screamed when he entered, and another by a tall woman with short hair who just stared at him with vacant, drug-dimmed eyes. Kane reached the end of the floor and turned into another stairwell leading up to the third floor. Just as he turned the corner, a fist cracked him across the jaw, and meaty hands grabbed Kane's t-shirt, throwing him back down the corridor. Five men surged towards him from the stairs, big men with angry faces. Kane saw the glint of a knife blade and knew he had come to the right place.

FIFTY-NINE

An enormous man with a ponytail screamed in pain as Kane broke his arm with an audible crack. He was the last of the five and joined his colleagues to writhe in agony on the bright orange carpet. Kane picked a knife up from the floor and pulled an iron knuckle duster from the hand of a man whose head he had driven through a plasterboard wall. Kane ran up the stairs, heart pumping, exhilarated by the combat. Any last remnants of David Langley fell away from Kane like a snake shedding its skin. The factory-working family man had wholly died in the fens, and what remained was a killer reborn. Kane moved like his old self. The five men were just gangsters, not trained special forces operators. Even with their superior numbers, they stood no chance against his training and experience. This was his world. Violence was his profession and his skill. Some men were fast runners, gifted footballers, good with numbers, or wordsmiths. Kane's gift was combat and death.

He raced up the stairs and crashed through a feeble plywood door. Instinctively, he rolled as he smashed through the splintering entrance, and as he did, gunshots thundered across the room. The wall behind him erupted in a spray of plaster and dust. He ground his teeth at the burning pain in his arm and shoulder. He could feel wet blood oozing beneath the makeshift dressings. Kane stood and marched towards the gunshot. The report told him it was an automatic weapon in the hands of an inexperienced shooter. The burst of gunfire tore up the wall in climbing bullet strikes towards the ceiling as the recoil forced the shooter's hands to rise. A man in a white vest clutched an AK-103 machine gun and roared at Kane incoherently. Kane threw the knife at him, and its blade sliced into his belly faster than the gangster could react.

More shouting erupted to Kane's right, drawing his attention to where four men stood around a seating area. Kane noticed a group of three girls lying there, floppy and utterly unfazed by the deafening sound of machine gun fire. Kane realised they were drugged. The Deli Boys were employing one of the cruellest tactics of the human trafficking playbook, making the girls dependent on heroin or some other opiate before putting them to work in the brothel as docile addicts.

A hulking man in a suit strode forwards, and Kane instantly recognised Aivar by his gorilla-like frame and the dark circles around his deep-set eyes. Aivar brandished a pistol and fired a shot at Kane, but the bullet missed by a wide margin. Kane charged straight at him without bothering to dive or duck out of the way of the gunfire. Shooting accurately at a moving target with a handgun was hard, especially under pressure, requiring experience and focus. Seizing the opportunity, Kane hurled the baseball bat at Aivar, and as the big man instinctively flinched away, Kane set about him. He stabbed Aivar in the thigh and chest before throwing the gang leader to the ground. Kane twisted the pistol from his thick fingers and shot Aivar in the knee. Then, as Aivar wailed in pain, Kane swiftly turned the gun on another gangster, who ran at him with a wild look on his face, machete held high, aiming to cleave Kane's head open, so Kane shot him in the chest before he had the chance.

The remaining Deli Boys ran for the stairs, and Kane hurried to where the three girls lay on a leather sofa. He breathed a sigh of relief when he recognised Yelena. Her eyelids fluttered, and she was in her underwear with fresh needle-track scabs on her left forearm. One of the three girls stared at Kane with bright blue eyes, lucidity beginning to clear the fog in her brain. Kane set his jaw and strode back to where Aivar rolled and moaned in pain. He crunched the heel of his shoe into Aivar's shattered kneecap, and the gangster roared in agony.

"I want your money, weapons, and ammunition. Tell me where to find them, and I won't kill you."

Aivar pointed a shaking finger to the back wall where a bar stocked with optics and beer pumps stood next to a wide-screen television. Kane walked across the room and found long cardboard boxes full of gun magazines and hundreds of copper-cased bullets. Beside the boxes were two sports bags filled with money but no more weapons. Kane stuffed as many magazines and bullets into the sports bags as he could, along with the AK-103 and the pistol.

"That man would have whored you out and drugged you until you died," Kane said to the blue-eyed girl. "Make him pay for that, and you can begin to heal." He handed her the flick knife. With shaking hands, she took the weapon and grimaced. The girl tottered cautiously toward Aivar in her drug-addled fog before flinging herself at him where he lay. Fuelled by her fury, the blue-eyed girl let out a piercing scream and attacked the ruthless gang leader with wild, blood-soaked savagery. Kane lifted Yelena over his shoulder, picked up the two sports bags, and left Aivar to be butchered by his victim.

I said I wouldn't kill him.

SIXTY

The wipers squeaked as they passed back and forth across the stolen Citroen's windscreen. The rain came down harder, peppering the window with relentless splashes. Craven checked the time on the dashboard clock. It had been eight minutes. He narrowed his eyes to stare through the lashing rain, but the window bloomed with steam, and he couldn't see the bar entrance clearly.

"Bloody thing," Craven whispered as he fumbled with the air conditioning unit, eventually locating the windscreen heater. The steam cleared, and Craven wound down his window to get a better look at the bar. Everything seemed calm. Maybe Kane had used his special agent training to slip inside undetected and find the girl, the cash, and some weapons to help them free his children.

Craven imagined Kane sliding along walls in the shadows, creeping past unsuspecting henchmen and then scaling the outside wall with the girl and the gear and no bloodshed. Rain came in through the open window, droplets of it hitting Craven's face. He licked his lips and shook his head.

What the fuck am I doing? If I get caught here with Kane like this, I'm fucked. Barb will be alone, and I'll be carted off to a prison full of the bastards I've sent down.

Before Craven had time to answer his own question, a figure in a white tracksuit burst out of the bar's front door and frantically ran up the street. His flashy trainers splashed in puddles as he hurried away from whatever horror unfolded inside. Craven's heart sank.

So much for being a 'secret' agent.

The door bouncer stepped out onto the pavement and stared after the running man, scratching his head. Then two more tracksuited thugs emerged from the doors as though a bungee rocket had fired them. One sprinted away down the street, while the other grabbed the bouncer's shoulders, urgently pointing into the bar, shaking him wildly, before both men took off into the distance.

The entrance to *Bunnies* opened again, and Craven leaned over to unlock the back door.

Kane exited the bar with a girl draped over one shoulder in a fireman's lift and carried a heavy-looking sports bag in each hand.

"Drive around the back," said Kane as he placed the young girl in the backseat of the stolen car, tossing the two black sports bags in beside her.

"Around the back?" asked Craven.

Kane held up a set of keys and hopped into the passenger seat. Craven hit the accelerator, and the Citroen took off. Its wheels slid on the wet cobblestones as he turned right into a narrow alleyway.

"Driving in stolen cars won't work forever. The police might catch up to us sooner or later," said Kane.

Craven glanced at him and then back to the road. A Deliveroo rider hollered obscenities as he was forced to jump off his bike to get out of the way. Kane showed more signs of trouble, bruising on his face and bloodied knuckles. He winced as he gingerly touched his injured arm and shoulder.

"I think that's the least of our worries," said Craven. "Any trouble inside?" He raised an eyebrow and turned the car into a small car park behind the lap dancing bar, only large enough for four cars and two long plastic bins on wheels.

"A little," replied Kane laconically. "No gangster is going to report his missing car to the police." Kane clicked the keys in his hand, and the lights on a black Range Rover flashed through the pounding raindrops.

"Did you kill anyone?" asked Craven, and the quizzical look on Kane's face underscored the vastly different worlds they operated in.

"Yes. Does that bother you?"

Craven thought about that for a moment. He had seen more of the Deli Boys' ruthless crimes than most during his lengthy investigation of their activities. They were the worst of the worst, men who brought vulnerable women from distant countries to use as slaves. The Deli Boys were drug importers and dealers. They ruined lives and cared nothing for the grief and desolation left in their wake. "Nah. Fuck them," said Craven.

Craven stepped out into the rain and grabbed the sports bags from the backseat. He ran the short distance to the Range Rover and put the bags in the boot. Kane carried Yelena from the Citroen and laid her down gently on the Range Rover's comfortable backseat. Police sirens tore through the rain-soaked Manchester night, and Craven took off his overcoat and covered Yelena's pale body.

"What did they do to her?" he gasped, noting the track of needle marks on her arm.

"You don't want to know," said Kane. He jumped into the driving seat, and Craven got into the passenger side.

"Was Aivar there?" he asked, and Kane nodded. "What happened to him?"

"You don't want to know about that either."

The Range Rover sped out of the car park and raced into the snarl of Manchester's streets and lanes. Craven stared at Kane as he wove the SUV between slower-moving vehicles and sped towards the M60 ring road. Craven had long since accepted that he was in this thing way over his head. Kane had provided the funds Craven needed to take proper care of Barb and get her out of the UK, and that made him a godsend in Craven's book. Kane was from a different world, where death and pain were as much a part of his everyday life as the daily commute was to an ordinary British citizen. He was a cold, brutal man, but Craven had to admit that Kane had brought more justice to the Deli Boys than they ever would have experienced in the judicial system. They were gone now, their leaders deceased, and their business ruined. Innocent women were safer now that Aivar and Rasmus were dead, and even though Craven knew that some other gang would fill the drug dealing void,

Kane's vigilante justice was satisfying. Would the police have saved Yelena from her terrible fate? He doubted it. So, he would continue to help Kane, even if he was out of his depth. Kane's children needed rescuing, and he would do what he could to make that happen.

SIXTY-ONE

Gilbertson House, an imposing stately home, was surrounded by lush fields and sprawling farmland. Fowler stared out of a bay window, watching a murder of crows swoop from a copse of silver birch trees. The classical Palladian villa had once belonged to an eighteenth-century earl or duke, Fowler wasn't sure which or who, and he didn't care. An imposing central block housed the principal living rooms and sleeping quarters. Two wings that were once occupied by servants now functioned as an armoury and bedrooms for agents when required. A tactical room butted onto the west wing. That room contained state-of-the-art digital equipment enabling Mjolnir to monitor satellite imagery and watch the world via inter-governmental data searching. Fowler didn't understand the tech involved with

Mjolnir's work, but the intel was usually good, and he trusted it.

He stared down at the gravel pathway winding in from the guarded front gate. The doors to the house were modern, reinforced and bomb-proof. However, the stairs leading up to the doors were as ancient as the house itself. Granite steps led down the pathway, and two heraldic lions greeted any visitors with majestic growls. Fowler stood at the window of one of the building's old drawing rooms, which still served the same purpose. Barnes, Nketiah and the others sat on armchairs or sofas of antique provenance. They drank decanted whiskey and port from crystal glasses, and a fire blazed in an ornate hearth. McCann was in an adjacent room with Kane's children, her injured arm in a sling, and the children watching YouTube on an iPad sourced from the technology room. The children had finally stopped crying for their mother and now just did as they were told in sullen silence. McCann made sure they were fed and given water and watched the children carefully.

The grounds around the HQ building were once arable farmland but were now part of the Mjolnir training compound. There was a firing range, which mirrored a SAS training setup, and there were driving tracks where agents learned to push various types of vehicles to their limits, ride motorcycles at high speeds, and drive cars, jeeps, vans, trucks and anything else that the Mjolnir quartermasters thought might come in useful in the field. Clutches of forests broke the grounds up, ranging from small copses to dense woodland. These were also useful for keeping agents up to scratch with outdoor survival techniques. Fowler himself had gone out into the forest there a year ago and spent a week with only his survival tin for company. He enjoyed the solitude, being at one with the land. Fowler contemplated whether he'd retreat into the woods once he retired from Mjolnir. He imagined himself living off the land in some distant forest of Canada or Australia, off the grid and out of the world's chaos.

Fowler turned his eye to his team as they quaffed expensive drinks and wondered if any of them kept themselves as sharp as he did. How honed and ready for battle were they? Times had changed, and there were fewer combat missions these days, less high-value targets to kill. Most missions now involved securing or destroying forms of technology, servers, or gadgets. Kane had always kept himself sharp. He and Fowler carried the same items in their survival tins, a remnant of their time in the Regiment. Both men could live for weeks out in the wild once they had their palm-sized tin and its strange contents. Amongst other things, Fowler's tin contained a wire saw which looked like a piece of string with two rings on each end, a flint and striker, alcohol wipes, a sewing kit, and a tampon to use as tinder.

"I don't know why we're hanging on to those brats," muttered Barnes, waking Fowler from his daze.

"In case Kane will exchange himself for his children," said Fowler, unable to hide the contempt in his voice. He disliked Barnes, but the contempt wasn't for him. It was for himself. "I don't enjoy being a child kidnapper any more than you do."

"Has he been in touch since the fens?"

"Not with me."

"What a cluster fuck that was. I thought Odin was supposed to be some sort of super-soldier. The best of us, a man to fear like the devil himself?"

"That was the rumour. Turns out he's just as unable to pin Kane down as the rest of us."

"We could have taken Kane down at the train station. Odin should have left it to us."

"You put paid to that when you shot up that pet shop like it was Afghanistan."

Barnes put his drink down sharply on an antique mahogany table so frail that it wobbled on its thin legs.

"He's got to be put down," Barnes snapped. "He's like a rabid dog, a traitor, grass, whatever you want to call it. What kind of man who has served and fought alongside his brothers and bled for the flag would turn on his own comrades?"

"It wasn't your call. You shouldn't have pulled the trigger until I gave the order."

Barnes took a step closer so that his nose was barely a hand's width away from Fowler's face. "He's your pal, and you've been too soft on him. You'd have buried him within five minutes if this were any other target. Files or no files."

"Back off." Fowler fixed Barnes with a flat stare.

The scar across Barnes' lips curled upwards. He eyeballed Fowler for a further ten seconds, then laughed and stepped away to pick up his drink. "Did you talk to Odin for me about getting out?" Barnes sipped his whiskey, the ice cubes chinking as he lifted the glass.

"The right moment hasn't presented itself yet."

"Maybe I'll just ask him myself. I'm tired of all this bullshit. I could make a fortune in private security work. Dubai, Qatar, somewhere cushy."

"Be my guest."

Barnes shot Fowler a withering look and stalked off to sit on a chaise lounge before which a chess set perched on a marble table top. Fowler sighed and stared out at a long field stacked with rows of hay bales and tracks that served as a live round training ground. Memories flooded back of moving through that same field with Kane years ago. Then, an unwanted memory revisited him in that moment – Kane flicking through pictures of his family during a layup in the desert. Kane's wife was dead now, and Fowler had stolen his children. This operation lessened him. The job to bring down Kane had diminished Fowler's career and reputation, in his own mind if not others. Who would remember him, and how would he be remembered? The CIA put a star on a wall for every fallen agent. What did Mjolnir agents like him receive? All they had were their wages, the ever-present danger, and a pension. If he died, they would leave his rotting corpse in an unmarked grave, abandoned and forgotten.

Fowler's phone vibrated in his shirt pocket, and he checked it. A text message.

No more meetings. Let my children go, or everyone dies.

"Get a check on the last text message on this phone," said Fowler, and he tossed his phone to Nketiah. "It's Kane."

SIXTY-TWO

Kane dropped the key card into a box at reception. The Premier Inn was basic but comfortable, and it had afforded him the chance to get a few hours sleep. He held the self-locking door open for Craven, who tottered through it carrying a large plastic box.

"Don't drop that," said Kane.

"Piss off," replied Craven, his forehead frowned and creased like the sea in a wild storm. Kane followed him outside and opened the boot of the Range Rover. Craven carefully placed the box inside, next to an identical container and the rest of the equipment they had spent most of the night preparing. "You can carry the next one."

"That's the last one." Kane closed the boot and locked the car.

"What are we going to do with the girl? She's going to struggle like hell, coming off whatever shit they were pumping into her veins."

Kane nodded at that truth and followed Craven back into the reception and up the stairs to the room they had booked with Craven's credit card. Craven pushed the key card into the door, and it creaked open on heavy hinges. The room reeked of the detergent and chemicals Kane had bought from a local hardware store. Now, they were less than an hour from Mjolnir's headquarters at a service area which contained the Premier Inn hotel.

Yelena lay curled up in a foetal position on a single bed. She rocked slightly, hugging herself and sweating beneath a white sheet.

"She can stay here today and tonight, then we take her home tomorrow," said Kane. "The Deli Boys don't exist anymore, so she can return to Warrington and bury her brother in peace. We'll give her enough money to make a new start. She's free now."

"What's all this we business? We aren't a team now. Unless this is like fucking Rain Man, and you're Dustin Hoffman."

"So, you're Tom Cruise then?" Kane smiled, which was perhaps the first time Craven had ever seen anything but a serious look on his face.

"Just don't start counting toothpicks on the way out of the hotel. Why are you so bloody happy?"

"Because today I'm going to see my kids." Kane missed them so much that his very being ached to be close to them. To hear Kim laugh at a silly joke or listen to Danny talking about Premier League football. He hadn't been able to hold or comfort them since Sally's death, and they needed him. Fowler's tracking device showed he was at Mjolnir HQ, and it made sense that the kids would also be there.

"Are you sure they'll be there?"

Kane shrugged. "Where else would they take them?"

Craven nodded slowly, but his eyes stayed locked on Kane's for a fraction too long. Kane understood the terrible thought in the back of Craven's mind. What if the children were already dead? But Kane couldn't contemplate that. He had to attack Mjolnir as though his children were alive and in the building. Their lives depended on his ability to get in and rescue them before Odin decided what to do with them, for no man, not even men as ruthless as Odin and Fowler, would kill or harm children unless they faced no other option. Kane was banking on that basic premise of humanity. That was how he was going to get his children back, by trusting that he knew

Fowler better than any man alive. They had bled together, lost friends together, and killed together. And there was no way the Fowler he knew would hurt a child.

"I suppose you know more about them than me," said Craven. "Those chemicals are still burning my throat. Will they work?"

"They should." Kane had picked up most of the items he needed to make some rudimentary explosives from a hardware chain store ten minutes from the hotel. Volatile household chemicals, some plumbing pipes, and three jerry cans filled with petrol wouldn't bring Mjolnir to their knees. The concoctions, however, would get their attention and distract them. "Listen, Craven. Once you've done your bit, get out of there. Don't wait for me. Get back to this hotel, take Yelena and go home."

"I thought you and I were a *team* now?"

"I mean it. It's going to get heavy in there. I'm not going in to talk. I'm going up against skilled government operatives intending to kill as many as possible. Don't put yourself in danger. Barb needs you."

"Enough of that bollocks. Let's get going."

Kane shook his head. He left a bottle of water on the bedside table next to Yelena, alongside some sandwiches and crisps he had bought earlier. She had enough there to keep her going until they returned. If they returned. Kane had the weapons taken from the Deli Boys, a Sig Sauer pistol and the AK-103. He had as much ammunition as he could carry, taken from the cardboard boxes at the lap dancing bar. Kane had already loaded four magazines of fifteen rounds for the Sig and four of thirty rounds for the machine gun. He was as ready as he would ever be to go up against Odin's small army. He just hoped he could get to Danny and Kim in time.

SIXTY-THREE

Fowler sat in the passenger seat of a black SUV, grinding his teeth and fingering the grip of his Glock pistol. Barnes hastened the vehicle along at breakneck speed, veering in and out of traffic. Fowler bit his tongue to stop himself from shouting at Barnes to drive more carefully because the last thing he needed was a road traffic accident and police attention. Magazines clicked into weapons behind him as Nketiah and Anderson checked their gear. Fowler hoped it wouldn't come to a gunfight, not in broad daylight.

The hotel was close to Mjolnir HQ and a long way away from the Cambridge Fens or the North West of England, where Kane had made his home. Kane was coming closer, like a predator stalking its prey. Fowler knew Kane better than most, and there was no way he would allow Mjolnir to threaten his children's lives nor let the death of his wife go unavenged. Fowler should have thought of it sooner. Just take the children somewhere Kane would find them. Let him come for them and then take him. The longer this operation went on, the more frustrated Fowler became, and the whole unpleasant affair left him with a sour curdle in his stomach. As Barnes accelerated through the tight gap between a lorry and a white delivery van, Fowler promised himself a holiday. Alone. Italy or the Caribbean. By a lake or a turquoise sea. Lots of alcohol and nobody to talk to.

The SUV swerved into a Premier Inn car park, and Barnes skidded the vehicle into a disabled parking spot by the entrance. Fowler sighed and again fought back the urge to swear at the man. There were a dozen other spots he could have parked in. It didn't really matter. They were going into the hotel to kill a man, so the parking spot was irrelevant. Still, it ground Fowler's gears. Fowler opened the door and met Odin striding up the cobble-locked pathway. The Commander of Mjolnir was stern-faced and ignored Fowler. He walked with one hand on the pistol holstered at his belt and wore a black cap to hide his face from any CCTV cameras. Fowler pulled his own cap down and followed Odin into the foyer.

Nketiah jogged into the hotel behind them, and they paid no attention to the acne-scarred young man on the reception desk who stared slack-jawed at their black tactical clothing and weapons.

"This way," said Nketiah, turning left towards a stairwell behind the elevators. Fowler followed her, just behind Odin and with six armed Mjolnir agents trailing him. Their boots echoed around the stairwell until Nketiah pulled open a heavy wooden door on the second floor. She marched along the brown, densely-patterned carpet, following a signal on her tracking device. The device was locked onto the signal emitted by Kane's phone, which he'd used to send the last text message to Fowler. As Fowler followed Odin and Nketiah, part of him wanted a fight there in the stale hallway of a backcountry Premier Inn. He wanted bullets to fly and blood to spill and for this whole sorry exercise to end. The other part of him knew that Kane would not be there. After all, Kane had been the best of the best; he was no amateur.

Nketiah stopped at a corner where the hotel hallway split off in two directions. She checked her device and raised her hand, pointing it outwards with her fingers extended. She gestured twice towards a closed pine door without a number on it.

Barnes charged ahead, the snarl on his face making it clear that he was about to kick the door in.

"Don't bother," Fowler uttered, shaking his head. "It's the cleaners' storeroom. Kane dumped the phone."

"But he was here," said Odin, casting his eyes along each of the two long corridors and the room doors stretching away ahead of them.

"Still could be," Barnes gruffed, and he punched the wall in frustration. He roared angrily, throwing his head back before kicking the door. The frame splintered, and the door swung back on its hinges. Barnes stormed inside and dragged a cleaners handcart out of the small room. As Barnes tore the storeroom apart, ripping shelves from the wall and kicking bottles of detergent, Nketiah bent and picked up a black mobile phone from the middle section of the cart, where it nestled on top of a neatly folded pile of white towels.

"Well, we can't go room to room," said Fowler. Kane had been there, and he'd known full well that Mjolnir would track the phone down the moment that his text message was received. "Keep a watch on the place and return to base."

Odin nodded and curled his lip. They marched out of the hotel at double time, and just as Fowler was about to jump into the passenger seat of the black SUV, a voice called to him.

"Thor, you ride with me," said Odin.

"Yes, sir," Fowler replied flatly.

He and Odin sat in the rear of the second vehicle as it sped out of the car park and onto the road towards Mjolnir HQ.

"What's he doing here?" asked Odin. His eyes searched Fowler's. There was a savage cunning in the planes of his angled face and in the depths of his dark eyes.

"Coming for his family," said Fowler.

"You think he'll attack HQ?"

"I've seen him go in and out of worse places, sir. He's likely drawn us out here to remove us from the building so he can make his play. We fell for it."

"Why didn't you say so earlier?"

"I wasn't sure. I wanted him to be at the hotel so that we could finish this once and for all."

"Well, if he is at HQ, we'll bury him there. Him and his whining children. Tidy this up with a neat little bow on it."

Fowler stared at the aloof commander, noting the calmness of his demeanour. "Doesn't it bother you, sir? Killing children? Fighting on home soil against one of our own?"

"Bother me how?" Odin raised an eyebrow.

"Like we are fighting the wrong enemy. Have

we turned from the right path, sir?"

"The right path, you say?"

Fowler shifted in his seat. The engine roared around them as the SUV raced back towards HQ.

"Of protecting the country, of fighting our real enemies."

"Your enemies are who I say they are. Don't forget that. We do what the police and other above-the-line agencies can't. We work in the shadows and do the hard things which must be done to protect this country. Mjolnir is the sword at the throats of our enemies. Are some of those things unpalatable? Yes, certainly. But is the United Kingdom a safer place because of what we do? Most certainly. Kane was a means to an end, a pawn in a larger game. We needed his evidence to remove some red tape, to give us more freedom to act how we see fit. And it worked, so Kane gave his life for the greater good."

"He's not dead yet. And who says it is the greater good? You?"

"Yes, me." Odin leant towards Fowler and stared deep into his eyes. "Are you losing your nerve, old boy? Do you need reassigning?" he drawled out the last word, emphasising its connotations.

"I haven't lost my nerve. You don't need to worry about me. Have I ever let you down?"

"No, so don't start now. Kane must die, and we must see it done."

Fowler stared out of the window, longing for simpler times – when the enemy fired first, and he fought under the rules of war. Days of honour, back when he and Kane were soldiers together. It felt like a distant memory, and as the blacked-out SUV sped along, Fowler couldn't shake the feeling that he'd changed, and not necessarily for the better.

SIXTY-FOUR

"They've gone in," Craven's voice resounded over the phone.

"Have you left?" Kane said into his own handset. The text message had worked, or it could have been Craven's credit card. Either way, Mjolnir had taken the bait.

"Yes. I'm on my way to you now."

"Don't let them get too close, or they'll make you."

"Bugger off, Kane. I know what I'm doing."

"OK. Stick to the plan. I'm going in."

"Wait!" Craven shouted down the phone just as Kane was about to hang up.

"Yes?"

"Be careful."

Kane hung up the phone and placed it in

the leg pocket of his black combat trousers. He reached down and dug his hands deep into the damp leaf mulch at his feet. They came up covered in the forest floor's filth, and Kane smeared it over his face and the backs of his hands. He slung the AK-103 over his shoulder and checked that the Sig pistol sat securely in his waistband. The evening drew in, and the sounds of the woodland grew louder. Animals out of sight shifted twigs and undergrowth. The fearful cry of a fox sang across the rolling meadows and fields of Gilbertson House. Kane knew the stately home well. He had trained there, stayed there and planned missions there.

Beyond the forest's edge, a line of wire fencing encircled a large field of wild grass. In the past, that field might have been a grazing pasture for horses or a riding field. But now it was a gun range for target practice. The gun range included obstructions such as piles of hay bales and human-shaped cutouts on pulleys, which were used as targets to be avoided or fired upon.

Away to the north was a set of two-storey concrete buildings. Mjolnir had constructed them for use as entrance, room control, and exit drills. Beyond the forest was an old 1980s passenger aeroplane for training agents in plane assault techniques and management. The main building was well-lit, with ground lighting that illuminated its walls and windows, and the whole place was well-monitored by CCTV cameras. Despite this, Mjolnir didn't expect that their facility would be attacked. Only a handful of people in the world even knew that the Mjolnir agency existed, never mind where its HQ was located.

Odin and Fowler had taken the bait, which thinned the number of agents inside the building. But Danny and Kim would still be well guarded. There could be as many as a dozen highly trained agents using the facility to brush up on the latest weapons and gadgets or simply hone their shooting or hand-to-hand combat skills.

Ideally, Kane would have thoroughly scouted the house for twenty-four hours or more, carefully observing the guards' positions, patrol patterns and the frequency of people coming and going both day and night. But there hadn't been time for that. His children were in there, and it was time to strike whilst Odin and Fowler were away. He took off running through the forest, his black combat boots crunching on fallen twigs and leaves. The forest itself reeked of dampness and rot, and Kane came to a stop by the trunk of a sprawling oak tree and pulled the cutting tool from his backpack.

Kane had purchased some necessary items for the assault at the hardware store, and the wire cutters he'd chosen bit through the green wire fencing with ease. Kane had also bought black workman's trousers with leg pockets, a black jumper, rope, a knife, and a few other things he thought might come in useful for the attack. Kane clipped at the wire until there was a hole large enough for him to squeeze through. He slipped inside and powered into an all-out sprint across the gun range. The sun came down behind the forest of oak, hazel, birch, and elm, and Kane ran to a stack of hay bales and stopped in a crouch. He waited for ten heartbeats, ears alert for any sound of alarm, but there were none. Kane set off again, weaving between a handful of static human cut-outs in the gun range, and came to the three-hundred-yard line. Kane crouched once more beside another bale of hay, and this time he heard voices.

Two guards patrolled the building's perimeter, each likely assigned a different stretch of the building's encircling pathway. However, such was their confidence in the secrecy of Mjolnir's base of operations that the two men walked casually together as though there were out for an evening stroll. Each man wore a pistol at his hip, and Kane saw no sign of semi-automatic weapons. He noticed a dome-type camera on the apex of the gun range hut. It was little more than a locked shed where agents could find ammunition and paper targets. Another camera blinked on a timber pole to the west of the building at the corner of the driveway. With the lights and power on, there was no way Kane could approach the building and remain completely hidden. Cutting the power would instantly raise the alarm that the place was under attack, so Kane's best hope lay in their confidence in the secrecy and security of the HQ complex.

Kane sprinted away from the gun range and followed the two guards. He ran through the light, unable to get close to the building without avoiding its glare. In contrast to the approaching pathway, the walls had some shadowed entry points, nooks and places where the network of lighting failed to illuminate the building's perimeter. Kane hoped the cameras were not monitored. But if they were, he prayed they were overseen by an operator who had watched the feed screens for days, weeks, months and even years without incident. Such a person would not be an eagle-eyed screen watcher. Instead, they'd read a newspaper or scroll through their phone rather than watch the same screens for days and months on end without activity.

Kane ran along the pathway kerbstones, careful not to tread upon the tiny shingle-like gravel which covered the space between his encircling path and the building itself. He reached the walls and stood with his back against the cold stone, controlling his breath, quiet and still. He peered around the corner. The two guards were ten paces away. He could easily burst into a run and eliminate them both in a heartbeat, leaving his entry to Mjolnir's HQ unguarded. But the best plans in war often go awry, and just as Kane thought the pathway to rescuing his children was clear, everything went wrong.

SIXTY-FIVE

A guard's radio crackled, and the man reached over to his right shoulder to click the receiver.

"He's here? Are you sure?" said the guard in a broad Birmingham accent.

Heat kindled in Kane's belly, rising to his chest. He had expected the warning call to come in from Odin or Fowler, but he'd planned to be inside the building before it did.

"Yes, sir." The guard's hand fell away from his receiver, and he turned to his colleague. "Lothbrok's coming, and he could be here already. I'll stay here. You fetch the MP5s and call everybody out."

"What about…" the second guard began, but he didn't get to finish. Kane came at them with all the speed and strength he could summon. He didn't want to fire his weapons until absolutely necessary because that would instantly give his position away. So instead, he charged them with his knife drawn, a small weapon whose blade was no longer than Kane's fingers. But it was enough.

The second guard half turned as he sensed Kane approaching from behind. Kane sank the knife into his liver and ripped the blade sideways, slicing through woollen jumper, t-shirt, and flesh. The man gasped under the impact and fell to his knees, clutching at the terrible wound. Kane kept moving and stabbed the blade towards the first guard's throat, but he blocked the blow with his forearm and tried to knee Kane in the ribs. The guard knew what he was doing. He moved with deliberate and effective force. They trained every Mjolnir agent in hand-to-hand combat, and the guard was no exception. But Kane was a different animal. Kane swept away the guard's standing leg, and as he toppled backwards, Kane went with him and drove the knife point into the softness of the man's gullet before he had even hit the ground.

Kane turned and quickly clasped his hand over the second guard's mouth to prevent him from crying out at his injured liver once the initial shock wore off. Kane broke the man's neck with brutal efficiency. He let the man fall. Two dead. Yet more enemies were coming. He had to move quickly and act without pity or remorse. These men held his children prisoner and would have killed him in an instant, so he felt no guilt for their deaths. He dragged a tactical, bulletproof vest from the first guard and slipped it over his head.

Boots crunched on shale at the building's southern wall, and Kane took the radio and a lanyard from the neck of a dead guard and moved towards the building. He switched the radio off, hurriedly moved away from the sound of approaching boots, and followed the grey stone to a small side door. Above its lintel was another dome-shaped CCTV camera, but Kane ignored it. The door appeared to be made of wood but was, in fact, a heavy metal alloy. Beside it was a silver swipe card unit, and Kane used the card inside the plastic lanyard to enter. The door clicked, and Kane slipped inside the building. The floor was old slate, clean lines and dark beneath a ceiling lit by fluorescent strip lighting. Kane pulled the AK-103 from his shoulder, checked the magazine, and moved forward. He walked with his legs crouched and weapon in front, poised and ready to fire at any enemy who came towards him. The door behind him closed on its own hinges, and Kane turned a corner to find a corridor with one door on the left and one on the right. Up ahead was a set of steel-reinforced stairs. Kane opened the first door, taking a long step to position his foot parallel to the doorframe. With his weapon raised, he stepped confidently inside, scanning each sector of the room, staring down the barrel of his gun. It was a training room padded with blue mats designed for unarmed combat training.

The room was empty, prompting Kane to move on and secure the second room on that level. He opened the door and stepped inside, noticing an array of knives and bladed weapons mounted on the wall, and the room was equipped with the same blue mats. Kane recalled they used the room for knife practice, and the blades mounted on the wall were blunted or rubber. He moved his weapon around each sector, and his finger twitched on the trigger as the gun barrel came to rest on a Mjolnir operator. She wore the same combat gear as the guards outside, though she was unarmed.

"On your knees," said Kane. "Hands on your head. Move slowly."

She dropped to one knee. Then, with a sudden movement, she flung her right arm out towards Kane, and a shining object flashed through the air too fast for him to respond. The knife blade clattered off his chest and spun away harmlessly. Luckily, she had been practising with a blunted training knife. The woman used the split second of distraction to charge at Kane. She shrieked like a demon, knocking the barrel of his AK-103 aside and aiming a punch at his face. Kane ducked under the blow and tried to crack her head with the stock of his rifle. The woman blocked with her elbow and kicked him in the stomach. She grabbed Kane's arm and launched herself onto his back. She was small and light, but she wrapped her legs around his throat like a vice and tried to drag him down to the mats. Kane gasped for breath and drove her backwards, smashing her into the cinderblock wall. Her grip loosened, and Kane threw her over his head. As she hit the mats, the woman spun on her back and tried to kick Kane's leg. He fell upon her, his elbow cracking into the meat of her face, with all his body weight behind it. The woman fell unconscious, and Kane moved on, his throat bruised from the death choke she had almost fastened around his neck. He rolled his wounded arm and shoulder to keep them loose and winced at the pain.

As Kane left the knife room, a beeping sound came from the opposite end of the corridor. Kane ran, taking the stairway two steps at a time. He reached the top just as the door at the end of the corridor swung open. It was the same door leading outside, where Kane had left the two dead guards. He knelt to watch from the top of the stairs. Four guards eased through the doorway, moving with precision and forming a compact line, hands on each other's shoulders.

The lead guard cautiously swept the corridor with his MP5 held firmly in both hands.

The guards would sweep the rooms downstairs, and Kane left them to it. He had to keep moving. He found himself in the kitchens of the stately home. A larder opened up to his left, a walk-in fridge to his right, and the kitchen's silver worktops and cooking surfaces shone before him. A red fire extinguisher hung from the wall, and above it was a fastened coloured map of the building. Kane examined it. The children would most likely be on the first or second floor, and he was on the basement level. With his rifle poised and ready, Kane swept each sector of the kitchen before following its length towards a set of swinging doors. He waited.

Footsteps rang out on the steel staircase which led up to the kitchen area. The four guards were approaching fast. Kane set his feet and crouched with his weapon raised. The four men came into the kitchen, closely behind one another, moving in a rhythmic flow like a serpent. Once all four guards were inside, Kane opened fire, and the noise of the AK-103 inside the kitchen was deafening. Each crack of gunfire was like an explosion of sound reverberating off worktops and ovens. The first guard fell with a bullet in his throat, and his blood splashed brightly onto the polished silver surfaces. The second turned and fell with a bullet in his shoulder, and the third guard returned fire. All hell had broken loose in Mjolnir HQ, and Kane was at the storm's furious epicentre.

SIXTY-SIX

The silenced MP5's muzzle flashed, and the weapon spat three bullets that slapped into the white-painted wall behind Kane. He dived onto the sanitised floor, the smell of bleach eye-watering amongst the grey and blue flecks of the laminate flooring. Kane opened fire from his prone position, and the bullets from his weapon tore open the ankles of the third guard and ripped into the thighs of the fourth. They went down howling in pain, and Kane dug a hand into the thigh pockets of his trousers to pull out a new magazine. He clicked the magazine release panel on his weapon, removed the old mag, and clicked the fresh one into place. Despite rounds still remaining in the old magazine, he wanted to meet his next enemies fully loaded.

Kane left the kitchen and clicked on the stolen radio. He was in the house itself. Dark wood-panelled walls stretched upwards along a high stairway carpeted in deep red. He knew where he was. The place had changed little since Kane had last been there.

"He's on level one, repeat, Lothbrok is on level one," came the crackling voice over the radio. Kane clicked it off again. The floor above rumbled with the sound of boots moving across the centuries-old timbers, and Kane made his way up the stairway towards them. A white face peered over the balcony, and Kane squeezed the trigger of his rifle. The old wood splintered and shattered, sending shivers of timber down the stairs. Voices above him barked orders at one another amid the chaos, and a flash-bang grenade came flying over the polished wood bannister. It bounced on the stairway to roll towards the kitchen before it exploded. It was too far away to disable Kane, and he leapt up the remaining stairs. The Mjolnir operators would wait for the grenade to go off and then proceed cautiously towards him. But Kane had other plans. He was not immobilised or stunned, so Kane came over the lip of the stairs and fired bursts from his AK-103. The space opening up before him was the grand entrance hall, all polished tile and marble, with another double stairway curving up to the first floor.

Kane moved towards the entrance hall, killing any Mjolnir operators who showed themselves. He left rooms and pillars unsecured behind him, not wanting to waste any more time before getting to Danny and Kim. The call had come in from Odin or Fowler to warn the operators inside the building that Kane was there, and they could just as easily order the deaths of his children. So Kane pressed ahead, ignoring the bullets darting past his head to thrum into the walls around him. He killed a sandy-haired Mjolnir agent with a bullet to the forehead and dropped another with a shot to the guts. An agent threw another flash-bang in Kane's direction. The small, black cylinder bounced on the floor tiles, and Kane kicked it back the way it had come. He thrust himself into an alcove beneath the stairs and shielded his eyes. The flash-bang grenade detonated with its one-hundred-and-sixty-decibel explosion, engulfing the entranceway with a blinding light from its mercury and magnesium contents.

The hall filled with smoke, and Kane used that confusion to run towards the stairs. A figure moved, and Kane shot at it. Reaching the base of the stairs, he hurriedly ran up the right-hand side of the two curving arcs, which led to a vast second floor where the bedrooms were located. Kane's only priority was to find Danny and Kim, and he knew his best chance was on that floor. He made it halfway up the stairs when a bullet slammed into his chest, sending Kane sprawling on the shiny wooden steps. He gasped for breath, thankful that he had taken the vest from a fallen guard earlier. But just as he tried to get to his feet, a monstrous figure cannoned into him, sending Kane flying down into the entrance hall.

Kane lost his grip on the AK-103 and rolled into his fall. He came up on one knee and grabbed for his pistol, but a fist smashed into the right side of his face, knocking him from his feet, lights exploding in his eyes. His attacker was an enormous man with a neck bigger than Kane's thighs and a broad face framed by a crow-black beard. The big man swung his fist at Kane again, but Kane swerved aside from it and drew his pistol from his trouser waistband. The big man's face dropped in surprise. He had so wanted to use his strength and training to fight Kane that he hadn't considered Kane might be carrying an unholstered weapon. Kane shot him once in the leg, dropping the monster, and then once in the skull to finish him.

The stairs stretched away, and Kane laboured up them this time. Smoke from the grenade and the attack by the big man had drained his energy. But he had to continue. Danny and Kim were close. He could feel it. They could be in a bedroom on the next floor, so Kane forced himself to climb, one foot after the other. His head ached from the punch he had taken, and his breath came ragged from the bullet caught by his vest. The phone in his pocket vibrated, and Kane answered.

"Kane?" came Craven's voice.

"Yes," he wheezed.

"Odin, Fowler, and the others are back."

SIXTY-SEVEN

Craven reversed into a pine forest just before the right turn into Mjolnir headquarters. He did exactly as Kane had ordered. He drove far ahead of their vehicles so that they wouldn't spot him and then hid from view with his headlights off. Their two black SUVs sped around the bend and up the road towards the stately home, racing past Craven's hiding place. Craven called Kane to let him know they were coming, and he put the Range Rover into drive, following them without his lights on.

He knew this was dangerous. These men were armed and intent on killing Kane and his family, but Craven steeled himself to the risk. The bottles and cylinders Kane had fashioned from the items bought at the hardware store jiggled and sloshed in the backseats and the car boot, and Craven hoped he would be back with Barb when this was over. She would kill him herself if she knew the risk he took with his life.

Kane was doing his bit, entering the house, going in as quietly as possible to find his children and get out in one piece. But Kane expected trouble. He had told Craven as much – that he should prepare for carnage, for all-out war. So, even though he could be travelling to his death, he drove up that winding road in the dusk of a spring evening, surrounded on both sides by dense forests.

The pines opened up into a sweeping, shallow valley. Fields and clutches of trees sprawled away in the twilight to where a huge stately home stood bathed in golden light. Inside that house, bright lights flashed, and Craven swallowed. They were the flashes of a gun battle, where Kane fought for his family.

So much for entering the mansion quietly, then.

The place was vast, the type of grand construction built by heroes of the British Empire, men who had made fortunes off the backs of labour in India, Africa, and the Americas, back when Britain ruled the seas.

Craven followed the SUVs as they raced through a security post, and the guard at the barrier followed them on foot, drawing a weapon from a holster at his hip. The guard left the gate unmanned, so Craven drove through the open barrier and parked his car in a section of the approaching pathway that remained bathed in darkness. It was too far away from the building itself to be caught in its array of dazzling lighting. Bodies leapt out of the SUVs and ran to the rear of the vehicles to pull machine guns from the boot of each car. Craven recognised Fowler and Jacobs in the bright lights. He killed the engine of the Range Rover, and then his jaw dropped in horror as a black minibus came hurtling across a field behind the building. It bounced and rocked on the grass as though driven by a madman before coming to a screeching halt beside the two SUVs. Six armed men in dark army fatigues popped out of the sliding side door, each carrying a machine gun like Fowler and Jacobs.

Craven swallowed hard. Kane faced a small army of ruthless soldiers armed to the teeth, and he undoubtedly needed Craven's help. Of course, Craven didn't really know what he was doing and was likely to get himself killed, but he had to try. He stepped out of the Range Rover as quietly as possible, clenching his teeth at the sound of the door opening. He worried that the noise would carry across the driveway to be met by a hurricane of bullets flying in his direction. Craven waited, his back against the car's shining paintwork, but no bullets came. So, he shifted quietly to the car's rear, opened the back door, and popped the boot. There, in tidy plastic boxes, were the makeshift explosives Kane had made from the supplies bought at the hardware store.

"You aren't going to kill anyone with this stuff," Kane had said at the hotel. "Hopefully, you can wound a few of them, but your job is to distract them. Keep as many of them away from me as you can."

That had sounded fine at the time. But as Craven stared at the Molotov cocktails, pipe bombs and nail bombs, he realised that Kane had actually meant that it was Craven's job to keep the machine gun-toting psychos away from Kane by attracting them towards him with homemade explosions. It was a fucking death wish, but Craven had never been a man to err on the side of caution. He pulled a long, flexible lighter from his pocket, the sort used to light barbecues or stoves, and without hesitation, he grabbed an armful of bottles and pipes and ran into the darkness, praying that he didn't blow himself up with the unpredictable incendiaries.

SIXTY-EIGHT

Kane coughed and steadied himself on the top bannister. The first floor comprised a lounge area and a balcony which ran around the perimeter and led to the various bedrooms. Kane hoped Danny and Kim were in one of those rooms, so he steeled himself, forced the pain and dizziness of the fighting out of his body, and moved ahead. He walked carefully, his pistol out in front, moving in sweeping motions in case an enemy should burst from a closed door or come up the stairs behind him.

Each door was dark, shining wood in the Regency style with gold handles. Kane opened the first one and swept each section of the room. It was empty. He opened the second door and did the same. As he cleared the rear of the room, a sound like an exploding firework rattled the window, and Kane risked a look outside. It was

Craven. It had to be. Another explosion came from further away, followed by shouting and the thrum of semi-automatic weapon fire. They were after Craven, and Kane hoped the hulking detective had the wits to keep moving and use the falling darkness to stay alive.

Kane came out of the second room and gasped as he walked into two figures clad in black. One was a black woman with her hair gathered under a beanie hat, and the other was a stocky man with a twisted, scarred lip. Kane stared at them, frozen for a heartbeat as their silenced MP5s swept around from where they pointed across the balcony, coming in his direction. He saw surprise in their widening eyes, and Kane charged at them. He drove his elbow into the woman's chest and front-kicked the scarred man into the balcony's bannister. They reeled backwards, and Kane fired a shot from his pistol, but the scarred man twisted away just in time and fired a burst from his MP5. The bullets thumped into the wall where Kane had stood a fraction of a second earlier. He was already moving, engaging the woman to stop her automatic weapon from pointing at him. She bared her teeth and punched him in the stomach. She tried to throw him over her hip, but he moved to her back. The scarred man roared in anger, his aim blocked by the woman's body.

The woman jerked and stamped her foot,

trying to rake Kane's instep, yet Kane kept her body between him and the scarred man. Kane fired his pistol again, but the scarred man had moved to the side to get a clear shot.

"I killed your wife, Kane," the man hissed from his scarred mouth. "She died on her knees, begging for mercy."

The shock of those words was like a punch to Kane's face. Here was the man who had killed Sally, the only woman he had ever loved and the mother of his children. The surprise caused him to loosen his grip around the woman's neck, and she drove her head backwards to butt Kane in the nose. He jerked away from the pain, but anger swamped his senses. A white-hot thing of revenge and hate. He brought the pistol close and shot the woman in the side of the head and then pushed her dying body towards the scarred man. Warm blood flecked Kane's face as it splashed on the wallpaper. Her falling corpse ripped the MP5 from the scarred man's hand, and he kicked her body aside so that she tumbled over the bannister and down into the entrance hall. Kane fired two quick shots, both of which caught the man in the chest. His body armour absorbed the bullets, and he charged, roaring and barrelling Kane backwards.

The two men crashed through the third door in a welter of splintered wood, spat curses and snarling hatred. Kane rolled and blocked a punch from the scarred man before unleashing a strike of his own. They wrestled, snatching and twisting to grab a wrist or leg to find a hold they could exploit in a dominant position. But both men were skilled fighters, and each could counter the moves of the other. It was a deadly game of chess-like combat as they sprawled on the polished wood floor.

"Daddy!" cried a small girl. Kane's heart leapt in his chest because it was Kim.

SIXTY-NINE

Kane twisted his head around and glimpsed Kim and Danny in the grip of a dark-haired woman with one arm in a sling. Kane recognised her as the woman he had shot in the pet store. Pain sliced across Kane's jaw, and he grunted. His distraction at the sound of Kim's cry had allowed the scarred man to whip a knife from his belt and slash Kane's face. The blood seeped down onto his neck, and the knife came again, this time cutting his shoulder. The scarred man flashed a grim smile, sensing that he was getting the better of Kane. But Kane wasn't just fighting for his own life, and the sound of his weeping children gorged his body with strength. He caught the scarred man's knife hand in a vice-like grip and twisted it aside. Kane struggled to his knees and forced the man away from him. He took a punch to the ribs and ignored the pain.

Kane stood and swiftly drove the flat of his

hand into the scarred man's nose. He released his grip on the man so that he could grab his knife hand with both of his own. Kane snatched the knife, reversed the blade in his right hand, and stabbed it into the scarred man's eye so hard that the tip of its blade scraped on the back of his skull.

Kane turned to the woman who held his children.

"Let them go. No need to die here today. It's over," he said slowly and deliberately.

She let go of the children, pushing them to the floor and grabbed for a gun holstered at her hip. Another explosion thundered outside, and the window smashed as nails came flying through the glass to pepper the papered walls and antique furniture. The woman shrieked and brought her uninjured hand to her face where a nail had ripped a bloody wound across her forehead. Kane ran at her, punching her wounded arm and grabbing the pistol from her holster. He dragged her around in a wide circle and threw the woman out of the window.

"Danny, Kim!" he gasped, gathering his children up into a bear hug. They trembled with fear, their tears wet against Kane's face. A lump grew in Kane's throat, and he held them both tighter. The two most precious things in the world, which Mjolnir had almost taken from him.

"Drop the gun, Jack," a familiar voice uttered, and Kane looked up to see Fowler pointing the muzzle of an MP5 at him from the broken doorway.

"You don't need to do this, Simon," said Kane. He dropped the pistol and pushed Danny and Kim behind him. "We can all just walk away. I know you. You don't want this."

"Want has got nothing to do with it. I have orders."

"They used me; they used all of us. That ambush in the tunnels, that was a setup, too. Mjolnir engineered it solely to gain more control and power in their grubby fists. We lost mates that day. Just so Odin and his cronies could act with impunity and above governmental scrutiny. Sally's gone, Simon."

"You shouldn't have turned on us. None of this needed to happen. It's your fault, Jack, not mine." Fowler shook his head, and his bottom lip turned in on his teeth.

"It's their fault. We are just pawns. We mean nothing to them."

"Shoot him, Thor," barked Odin, the man Kane had known as Jacobs. He came into the bedroom with a pistol held at his side. Gunfire thundered outside, and again Kane hoped that Craven could keep himself alive.

"You ruined my life, Jacobs," said Kane.

"Jacobs doesn't exist, you fool. Now, Thor, kill this traitor and his whining children. That's an order."

"Is it true?" asked Fowler, the muzzle of his weapon shaking. "Did you set up our team in the tunnels?"

"You do not ask questions, Thor. Kill them all!" Odin shouted.

"Did you send our team to die in those fucking tunnels?" Fowler turned and aimed his weapon at Odin. "Tell me the truth."

"The truth is beyond your understanding. The world is a terrifying place filled with cruelty and savagery. We cannot combat those enemies under the restrictions and supervision of government bodies. So, I did what I had to do to change that. Now, thanks to that sacrifice, we can act with autonomy. We can meet our enemies with an unfettered brutality of our own."

Fowler shook his head. Kane saw the crushing weight of Odin's betrayal on his drawn features. Odin sneered, sensing Fowler's reluctance to kill his old friend. He raised his pistol, yet before Kane could react, Fowler shot Odin twice. The Commander of Mjolnir fell away from the doorway and disappeared over the balcony.

SEVENTY

The gunshots shook Fowler awake as though he had been in a daze. He watched Odin fall over the balcony and turned to Kane. His old friend crouched, bloodied from the fight of his life and smeared with mud and the blood of his enemies. The two children huddled against the wall, holding each other in terror. In that moment, Fowler realised how far he had fallen, how distant he was from the man he had once been. Shooting Odin had come as a reflex. He simply couldn't stand by and watch Kane and his children die. It felt like the first righteous thing he had done in years.

"Let's get out of here, Jack," he said, lowering his gun and holding out a hand to Kane.

"If this is a trick, I'll put a bullet in your face," Kane snapped, keeping the pistol trained on Fowler's head.

"No tricks. Let's go, for old times' sake. For the friends we've lost, let's get your family out of this place." Fowler gestured to the children, and Kane nodded. Fowler turned to the door and raised his MP5. "Follow me."

He moved along the balcony, Kane's hand on his shoulder. They had done this countless times together, but in those days, it was in enemy territory. The explosions outside had stopped, and Fowler wondered how Kane had wreaked so much havoc for one man without access to weapons or explosives. But then, Kane had always been a clever bastard.

Fowler swept his weapon around his field of vision, and four Mjolnir operators came up the stairs. They saw him and hesitated, recognising one of their own. Fowler opened up on them, firing his weapon in short, accurate bursts. They died on the stairs, and Fowler kept moving. Kane was still behind him, and he could hear the children whimpering. Fowler felt strangely alive again, lightened like a weight had been lifted from him. One of the four figures twitched as they passed, and Fowler fired a bullet into the man's face.

They came out of the front door into the smoke-swirling evening. The explosions had left strange chemical smells in the air, and two

Mjolnir agents crouched beside the stone lions who guarded the entrance to the stately home. Fowler shot one in the back of the head, but the other agent turned. She was short, with a blonde ponytail falling from a black cap to cascade over her back. She turned with astonishing speed, and her weapon flashed before Fowler could squeeze off another round. Something hit him hard in the throat, and he fell backwards. His head banged on the concrete, and he couldn't breathe.

Adrenaline masked the pain, and it took a few seconds for Fowler to realise that she had shot him. Blood gurgled in his throat, choking him like he was drowning. For a moment, Fowler panicked, and then a sense of calm descended over him. Another gunshot thundered nearby, and then Kane's face appeared above him, staring him deep in the eyes.

"Thank you, Simon," said Kane. Fowler grabbed his hand. Holding it tight. There was no fear, even though he knew he was dying. Fowler's vision blurred. Darkness came for him, and although he had never been a religious man, he felt something warm waiting for him. Fowler hoped that in the end, by helping Kane and the children escape, he had wiped his slate clean. He had done terrible things in his life, but perhaps this last action somehow helped balance it all out.

SEVENTY-ONE

Craven ran towards the grand entrance, emerging from the shadows for the first time. His fingers were singed and sore from the fuses, cloth, and other things he had set alight before launching them at the house as he skirted around its perimeter. Gunfire had crackled around him but never directly where he was positioned. Instead, they had fired at where the explosions erupted.

He saw Kane bending over a dead man whose throat was torn to bloody ruin. One hand clutched that of the man, and the other placed tenderly on the dead man's face. Two children clung to Kane's leg, a boy and a girl, their faces stained with tears.

"Bloody hell," sighed Craven as Kane looked up at him. "I can't believe you did it. That was like a war zone."

"Thank you," murmured Kane. He spoke to the dead man, who Craven recognised as Fowler. Kane stood and gathered the children close to him. "Kids, this is Mr Craven. He's our friend. We can trust him."

"Come on," said Craven, and he led them across the shale driveway to where the Range Rover waited in the shadows. He glanced back at the house, windows smashed and smoke billowing in blue and white patterns amongst the perimeter lights. Many gunmen had entered that place, and only Kane had come out. But the children were safe. Craven would never have guessed Kane was capable of such violence when he had first met him at Warrington Police Station. That had only been a few days ago, but it felt like much longer.

Craven drove the car out of the open gate and towards the country road. The road was uneven, and the children's heads bobbled and rocked in his rearview mirror. They stared straight ahead with wide eyes and pale faces.

"You did well," said Kane as the country road merged with a dual carriageway, and Craven headed north. "I couldn't have done it without you."

"Well, I have the money you took from the Deli Boys. So, I reckon we're all square now."

Kane smiled and nodded. The road zipped past, and the weight of all he had been through hit Kane like a freight train. Everything he had known had somehow been turned upside down. He couldn't fathom Odin, the subterfuge, the ultimate betrayal. Of course, Kane's evidence had given Odin the additional power he'd sought, but surely, he still had to answer to someone. He recalled their conversation at the Cambridgeshire Fens – of how Odin had said Kane had made things inconvenient for him. Still, Odin was dead and gone. And so was Sally. It was time to mourn her. Memories of their lives together played out in his mind. Kane let himself remember Sally, her eyes, her smile, and the times they had laughed. The world was a darker place without her. Craven drove in silence, carrying them away from the ruin of Mjolnir's HQ. The car was starkly silent compared to the explosions and gunfire, and the minutes rolled by as Kane walked amongst memories of happier times.

Craven turned the car onto the M6 motorway, and Kane looked into the backseat. The children had nodded off, their heads leaning back against the plush seats, mouths agape and fast asleep.

"I have one more thing to ask," Kane said, and he kept his eyes fixed on his children as he spoke. "It's about Danny and Kim."

"What?" Craven replied, raising his eyebrows, struggling to keep his eye on the road.

"They won't stop coming for me. And I need my kids to be safe, out of harm's way. I hope we are free now, but if others come, I can't have my children put in danger again."

"Who can come after you now that you have taken down your old agency?"

"There are more of them, and there always will be. If they come for me again, will you take my children, Craven? You and Barb are good people. I love the kids with all my heart, but sometimes love requires the greatest of sacrifices. I'll send you more money, and I'll keep in touch. Can I come to you in Spain if Danny and Kim are in danger?"

Craven and Barb had never had children of their own, and he knew Kane was right. They would always hunt him. They couldn't allow a rogue agent who had all those secrets in his head to roam around freely. He could expose governments and bring down powerful people. So Craven would take Danny and Kim if necessary. He wasn't sure how he'd explain any of this to Barb. But if it came to it, she would love them with all her heart.

"Of course, you can come to us. But where will you go?" Craven asked.

"Out of the country, somewhere quiet. Best if you don't know."

"I hope you find peace, Kane." That hope was genuine, but Craven wondered if there could ever be peace for a man like Kane. The world was a cruel and dangerous place, and it needed dogs like Kane to protect the sheep from the wolves. He pondered that as the car raced north. What if there was a way to find and punish the evil men and help people who needed it most?

AUTHOR NEWSLETTER

Sign up to the Dan Stone author newsletter and receive a FREE novella of short stories featuring characters from Lethal Target.

The newsletter is a monthly email containing news on upcoming book releases from Dan Stone. No spam, just great info on Jack Kane books.

Sign up here for your FREE book of short stories

Or visit the website at https://danstoneauthor.com/

BOOKS BY THIS AUTHOR

Ultimate Deceit

The second book in the Jack Kane Thriller series.

Jack Kane returns in an unputdownable follow up to Lethal Target.

A former Special Forces soldier and Government Agent is pursued by ruthless and violent operatives.

Jack Kane is a man on the run... a secret agency wants him dead... and he is a family's only hope of finding their kidnapped daughter. .

Kane is pursued by savage gangland members and vicious assassins. Can he survive and save a kidnap victim in his fast paced adventure packed with action, twists, and unforgettable characters?

ABOUT THE AUTHOR

Dan Stone

Dan Stone is the pen name of award winning author Peter Gibbons.

Born and raised in Warrington in the North West of England, Peter/Dan wanted to be an author from the age of ten when he first began to write stories.

Since then, Peter/Dan has written many books, including the bestselling Viking Blood and Blade Saga, and the Saxon Warrior Series.

Peter now lives in Kildare, Ireland with his wife and three children.

Printed in Great Britain
by Amazon